his own Heaven

THE BENNETT'S BASTARDS SERIES

JENNIE KEW

HIS OWN HEAVEN

Copyright © 2020 by Jennie Kew
Published by Wooden Key Press
Edited by Hot Tree Editing
Cover design by Mayhem Cover Creations

ISBN: 9780648209478

www.jenniekew.com

For Max, my gentle ginger giant,
who kept me company as I wrote this
book and all the ones before it.

Aug. 2003 – Dec. 2019

"This sexy story is not for the weak of heart but those that enjoy a story with heart and grit and passion."
Review for *His Own Heaven*

"...there is a doozy of insecurity, emotional growth, vulnerability, trust, strength, and many more emotions swirling underneath, ready to suck you in."
Review for *His Own Heaven*

"The characters will pull on your heart strings and leave you breathless."
Review for *Revenge and Redemption*

"...enough steam to have you needing a cold shower..."
Review for *Dirty*

Chapter One

"Charlie, what the fuck are we doing here?"

Tobias Bennett's twin didn't spare him a glance as he continued filling out the form on the clipboard in his hands. "Speed dating," he said, as if the answer were obvious.

With so many bodies crammed inside, the heat in the pub was stifling. Toby popped another button open at his throat and drew in a steadying breath. He hated crowds with a passion. "I thought speed dating went the way of the dinosaurs. Isn't everything online now?"

"It's making a comeback," said the kid behind the bar with the overly coiffed hair and excessively groomed beard. Making a show of whatever strange concoction he was pouring into a martini glass, he added, "People have finally figured out they're less likely to get catfished in person."

Toby stared blankly at the hipster. "Catfished?"

"Fake online profiles luring people into fake online relationships for the purpose of defrauding them," Charlie said matter-of-factly, handing him the pen.

"How do you know?"

"I know things," his brother said, defensively. "Sign here."

Toby frowned at the clipboard. "What am I signing?"

Charlie, always the more dramatic of the pair, groaned like he was the most put-upon man in human existence. "Just sign it."

With a raised brow and a resigned sigh, Toby scribbled his name on the bottom of the form and handed the clipboard to the kid behind the bar.

"Okay, since you're first-timers, I'll give you a quick rundown of the rules. One, there is a two-drink limit. If you drink more than two drinks, you will not be allowed to continue. Two, men stay in one place and the ladies come to you. Each 'date'," the kid said, using honest-to-God air quotes, "lasts five minutes. At the end of five minutes, a bell will chime, and the ladies move on to the next 'date'. If you hit it off with someone and wish to continue talking, you can either exchange numbers and hook up later, or you can leave the dating pool. If you choose to leave the dating pool, you will not be allowed back in for the rest of the night. Three, harassment of any kind will not be tolerated. Got it?"

Toby and Charlie exchanged a look. "I think we got it," Charlie replied, grinning like an idiot.

"Excellent. Can I get you guys a drink?"

"We don't drink," they said together, then walked towards the back of the pub.

"Check out the honeys," Charlie whispered, a noticeable bounce in his step.

Toby cocked one brow, his gaze sliding sideways to stare at his brother. "What is with you tonight?"

"Besides the fact I can't remember the last time I had

sex?" At Toby's continuing stare, he said, "What? I've been busy."

"And I haven't? I've been working seven days a week since Rebecca quit."

"Yeah, but you don't take it home with you, do you? I feel like all I do these days is work," he said, noticeably irritated. "And when I'm not working, I have the girls. So excuse me for being a responsible parent by not having sex with random women when I'm looking after my impressionable teenage daughters."

Sighing quietly, Toby said, "Fine. I'll endure an evening of torture so you can get laid."

Charlie flashed him one of his signature grins, the one that made women trip over their panties and fall at his feet. "You never know, little bro. You might get lucky too. It's not like you couldn't use a good fuck. You've been twitchy all week."

Toby snorted. *Twitchy.* That was an understatement if ever he'd heard one. He'd jerked off so many times in the past week he was amazed his dick hadn't fallen off. And since the woman he was lusting after was off limits, maybe finding a partner for the night wasn't such a bad idea. *Fuck.*

At the very least, he could use a distraction from the fantasies that had played on an endless loop in his mind's eye since Monday afternoon.

But then he scanned the group of women milling about at the rear of the pub and nixed the idea immediately. Some of them looked like contenders—tall women with shapely backsides—until he glanced at their fancy footwear and calculated their actual heights. Without their shoes, he guessed most of them would be lucky if they were anything more than five feet and maybe five inches tall.

In other words, they were small.

And he knew from experience that even if these women found him attractive enough to go home with, he still wasn't getting laid. Standing at six feet and eight inches in height and weighing in at 125 kilograms, most smaller women were too afraid to even flirt with him, let alone take their clothes off and let him fuck them.

Especially the way Toby liked to fuck.

Charlie reckoned it had more to do with his attitude than his altitude, but Toby had seen the fear in too many women's eyes not to recognise it now.

The fear he'd tear them in half, break them somehow.

His twin was a different matter. A different man. Standing only two inches shorter, Charlie was still a big bastard, but he had charm on his side. He knew how to talk to women, how to engage them in conversation and put them at ease with his size. He knew how to make women want him. Try as he might, Toby just couldn't do it. He didn't know how to flatter and cajole, and the Dominant in him didn't want to.

His Dominant side wanted to cut through the bullshit and get on with it, longed to hear the sound of tearing fabric as he ripped a woman's clothes off. Craved the sight of a soft body bound to his bed and spread open for his pleasure. The cracking of his palm as it connected with a pliant arse, the feel of supple lips wrapped around his hard cock as he thrust deep down a throat. A woman's screams as her orgasm took hold, the soft panting breaths that tickled his side and chest as he lay beside a lover and held her close after a good, hard fuck.

But another quick scan of the dating pool left Toby with no illusions.

He'd be going home alone tonight.

Charlie leaned over, whispered, "Hey, if one of us does get lucky tonight, you wanna share?"

Lips twitching into a grin at his brother's eagerness, Toby said, "Sure. As long as she's into it."

"We're twins," Charlie said, shrugging. "They're always into it."

He was right. Toby had never understood why, but the twin thing was a definite draw card for certain women, and he and Charlie were usually more than happy to oblige them. But at the age of forty, they were both getting pretty sick and tired of the single life, of nothing but work, work, the occasional one-night stand, more work....

The thought of sharing a woman relieved Toby's tension though, took away the mild panic he always felt when he was forced to participate in small talk with random strangers. If Charlie hooked up with someone first, then they could all leave together and the torture would end.

Toby didn't even care if the woman didn't go for the sharing idea. Not that he'd knock back sex if it was on offer —Charlie wasn't the only one suffering a chronic case of blue balls—but he was just as happy to go home, read a book, and rub one out if it meant not talking to people.

"How long does this go for?" he said.

"One to two hours, depending on how many people show up."

Here's hoping it's one, he thought as a tall, slender woman with dirty-blonde hair brushed past him. The brief contact sent a jolt of electricity through every nerve in his body, every muscle, every bone. Toby couldn't move, could only stare, transfixed by the sway of her hips as she sashayed to the rear of the pub.

"Fuck. Me," Charlie breathed. "Could those jeans get any tighter?"

"Shit." Toby knew those shapely hips. That colour hair. Those long legs and elegant gait.

That *fan-fucking-tastic* arse....

"What?" Charlie said, still staring at the woman's backside.

"I think...." Toby narrowed his gaze and studied the woman again. "I think that's Lucy Barton."

"Who's Lucy Barton?"

"My new office manager." He swallowed hard. "I hired her this week. She starts work on Monday."

Charlie threw back his head and laughed, the full-bodied sound drawing the attention of pretty much everyone as they walked through the pub. Then he stopped and squeezed Toby's shoulder. "Wait," he said, dropping his voice to a near whisper. "Is this chick the reason you've been so twitchy? I'm thinking she has to be, judging by your reaction." Then, grinning like the pain in the arse he was, he added, "Is she cute?"

Toby shrugged Charlie off and took a step back. Lucy Barton was an employee and was therefore *off limits*.

The fact she was temptation incarnate was irrelevant.

Gaze glued to Lucy's arse, he took another step back and shook his head. He needed to remove himself from the situation before he did something stupid, like proposition his new hire and get himself slapped with a sexual harassment lawsuit.

But what if she says yes? a little voice whispered in his head.

Toby ground his teeth together. *No. Not going to happen. Safer to leave.* "I'm outta here."

But before he could retreat any farther, Charlie caught his wrist. Pulling him close, his brother hissed, "Tobias Ulysses Bennett, if you don't take a chance on this woman, I swear to God I will go out of my way to pick her up and fuck her every which way come Sunday."

Toby's eyes narrowed on his twin as a sudden possessive need gripped his spine and held on tight. He peeled Charlie's fingers away from where they encircled his wrist. "You even look at her funny and I'll tell Abby what really happened to Mr Poochie."

Charlie went very still, undoubtedly calculating the pleasure he'd find between Lucy's thighs and weighing it against the hell his life would become if their little sister discovered the truth about the day her beloved childhood teddy bear disappeared.

"I really hate you right now."

Toby grinned. "No you don't." Then he flicked his gaze towards Lucy again and said, "Mine."

He didn't even have to wonder at the unmistakable desire he felt as he sought her out in the crowd. It was the same emotion he'd felt when she'd strode into his office Monday afternoon to interview for the office manager position at Bennett's Gardens and Landscaping. The same emotion he'd been fighting all week.

The one to which he longed to surrender.

In the name of due diligence, he'd done a quick internet search on Sunday afternoon and found nothing outwardly concerning about Miss Barton. No criminal record, no nude selfies, and oddly, only a very small social media footprint, certainly nothing with photos. According to her résumé, she was forty years old, same as him, and her hobbies included reading, rock climbing, pancake art—whatever the fuck that was—and volunteering at her local animal shelter.

He'd liked her before she'd even set foot in his office.

The fact Lucy had also worked as the office manager for a private security firm for the better part of a decade was just the icing on the cake. She had more experience than the other five candidates combined and was a shoo-in for the job. Interviewing her was more of a formality than anything else.

But when she'd entered his office and shot out her hand to shake his like she was executing a military manoeuvre, he'd almost swallowed his tongue. Then he'd almost hired the second most qualified candidate because... *holy fuck!*

Toby had never met a woman more in need of a good spanking than Lucy Barton. Never met one he'd wanted to spank so desperately full stop. And not because she deserved to be punished, though if push came to shove, he was certain he could find something to punish her for—there had to be at least one spelling error on her résumé—but because he'd never met a woman so tightly wound and in need of release.

Her whole demeanour had called to him and his hands had itched to pull her into his lap and bend her over his knee, to feel the softness of her arse against the callused skin of his palm.

To mark her flesh and make her his.

Dressed in a dark blue suit and high-necked blouse, her hair pulled up in a tight knot on the back of her head, the woman had given off a prim schoolmarm vibe, completely at odds with the quiet, quirky yet kinda cool woman he'd envisioned when he'd read her résumé. Adding to her overall air of stick-up-her-arse-edness was the fact she'd sat ramrod straight in the chair opposite him with her hands folded neatly in her lap and a challenging expression on her face.

His carefully controlled Dominant side had come to life at that challenge, sliding through him like liquid heat, making his cock jerk to life. He'd had to swallow down a moan at the thought of forgoing the job interview in favour of bending her over his desk, hiking her skirt up her gloriously long legs, and fucking her senseless.

Her direct stare, the stubborn jut of her chin, and the way she'd tilted her face towards him, prominently displaying the wealth of scars covering the right side of her face and neck.... She'd practically dared him to insult her, as though she was used to people making a fuss about them, used to people judging her based on something as arbitrary as her looks, and she was feeling him out. Testing him.

He'd smiled at that. At her... not courage exactly, but ballsy-ness. It had felt like she was saying "This is me. Take it or leave it", and dear God, had he wanted to take it.

She was chaotically beautiful.

And Toby had thanked his inappropriately timed erection, certain it was the only thing stopping him from vaulting over his desk, fisting his hand in Lucy's hair, and shoving his tongue down her throat.

To distract them both, he'd said, "So, tell me about pancake art. What's that all about?"

For a second her eyes had widened, but then her whole body had relaxed and an almost-smile had danced at the corners of her very kissable mouth, never lifting her lips too far, never giving him what he'd quickly come to believe would be a prize of uncalculatable value. Never giving him a true smile, but definitely showing signs of the woman he'd believed her to be before she'd entered the room.

By the time she'd walked out of his office—giving him a delicious view of the nicely rounded arse she'd generously poured into her pencil skirt—he'd made up his mind to win that smile.

And as much as he'd fantasised about all the wicked ways he'd like to make her smile, in reality he'd envisioned leaving her a surprise welcome gift on her desk on Monday morning—a dwarf cactus in a pretty pot, or a flowering bonsai, perhaps.

He hadn't figured on running into her at the Redland Bay pub on speed dating night less than a week after meeting her.

But when he remembered his body's visceral reaction to her presence—both in the office and the pub—he realised Charlie was right. Besides his very own stick-up-his-arse-edness, there really was no reason why he couldn't fuck Lucy Barton *and* give her miniature plants.

Challenge accepted.

Charlie grinned at him. "So much for enduring an evening of torture, eh?" he said, pulling Toby from his wandering thoughts.

"Shut up, Charlie." He craned his neck, trying to see the woman from a different angle, making sure it was actually Lucy he was perving on, but her hair fell down around her in waves that hid her identity from him. He blew out a frustrated breath.

Please be her.

"And you never answered my question," his brother whispered as they listened to the woman in charge give another rundown of the rules. "Is she cute?"

Toby sighed, knowing his brother wouldn't let it go until he got an answer. "Remember what Dad always says about beauty?"

"The most beautiful things in life are often the most useless?"

Toby smacked Charlie up the backside of his head. "No, you twat. A woman's beauty isn't seen, it's discovered."

"So that's a no on the cute. Got it."

Glancing sideways, he caught sight of his brother's

broad grin. Charlie never could resist teasing him, and Toby took the bait every time.

"You're an arse," he said, chuckling quietly.

"You love it," Charlie replied, then leaned closer and whispered, "I guess this means sharing is off the table."

Lips twitching into a lazy smile, Toby said, "We'll see."

Chapter Two

D*on't freak out.*
     Don't freak out.
     Do not. Freak. Out.

Lucy repeated the words over and over in her head as she tried—and failed—to ignore the enormous man standing at the rear of the local Friday night meat market.

Her new boss.

Her new so-fucking-fuckable-it-should-be-illegal boss.

Oh how she wished the floor would open up and swallow her whole, because *mortified* didn't even begin to describe how she was feeling at that particular moment in time.

Dressed in her tightest jeans, her favourite blouse, and the sluttiest shoes she owned, she'd gone out with only one purpose in mind.

Get laid.

It'd been ages since she'd been to a speed dating night, and the only reason she was even there was because of *him*. He of the ridiculously tall and insanely hot.

Tobias Bennett.

She hadn't stopped fantasising about the man since she'd walked out of his office Monday afternoon, and masturbating just wasn't getting the job done.

She needed dick.

Preferably one attached to a man who knew how to use it, was willing to overlook her own physical shortcomings, and whom she'd never have to see again after a night of wham, bam, thank you, ma'am.

That had been the goal.

And that goal was quickly circling the drain.

She couldn't possibly go ahead with it now Tobias had seen her. What would happen if they ended up at the same table together? On a "date". Hell, it would be just her luck he'd turn out to be some kind of antiquated prude who thought only "loose women" turned up at these events, and while it was perfectly fine for him, a man, to be there, good little girls like her should be at home, tucked up in bed with a book or knitting or something.

She almost laughed out loud. *A good little girl.* Firstly, she was forty years old, so hardly a girl. And secondly, no one had ever accused her of being either good or little. Nope. When it came to describing Lucy Barton, those terms were right up there with subtle, meek and whatever the fuck the opposite of sarcastic was.

She'd been told more than once her mouth would get her in trouble one day. And when one day had come, it had seen her out of a job. Okay, so it wasn't the only thing, but it hadn't helped. Then again, you'd think a decade spent working for the one company, weathering all sorts of changes in that time from operating systems to managing directors, would earn her a modicum of loyalty. But no. Because when it came down to gaining a new client worth a squillion dollars or retaining an employee worth considerably less than that, her mouth had tipped the scales in the client's favour.

Even if he'd been the one in the wrong.

She clenched her jaw and shoved the thoughts away. Now was not the time to dwell on the past.

Pretending to casually glance around the pub, Lucy tried simultaneously judging the distance to the nearest exit, calculating the fastest escape route to said exit, and getting in one more peek at the deliciousness that was Tobias Bennett. If she timed it right, she could slip out through the crowd before the speed dating actually began and avoid any further embarrassment in front of her new boss.

"Should have worn my cherry Docs," she muttered, staring down at her hot rod–red patent leather stilettos. Ironically, the most impractical of all her shoes for making a fast getaway.

"All right, gentlemen," the lady running the speed dating said. "If you could move to a table and take a seat. And ladies, good luck!"

Everyone moved at once, and instead of sneaking out as intended, Lucy somehow got dragged farther in, carried away on the sea of hormonally driven singles as they sought their next conquest.

And that's when it happened.

As Lucy attempted to escape her fate, she was shoved from behind and stumbled into a kid in his twenties, who instantly recoiled from her. "Whoa there, ugly," he said, exaggerating his show of horror. "A little early for Halloween, isn't it? What are you supposed to be anyway? A zombie hooker?"

The guy standing next to him pretended to cough to hide his laughter. He wore a T-shirt that read "bearded for her pleasure", the words fashioned in the shape of a thick mountain-man style beard. She assumed he wore it as a joke, as he had no beard to speak of. Two girls who looked barely old enough to drink stood behind them, giggling into their vodka cruisers.

Instead of telling them off, Lucy bit her tongue and offered the little shits her very best resting bitch face, because the last thing she wanted when she was trying to make a run for it was to draw even more attention to her situation by causing a scene. But before she could turn and walk away, a large hand rested on her shoulder.

"Apologise to the lady." Tobias Bennett's deep voice vibrated through her, setting every one of her nerve endings on fire and making her body tingle with awareness in all the best places. *Oh holy crap.*

So much for the quick getaway.

"Now." Another hand, accompanied by an equally deep voice, landed on her other shoulder.

Glancing up at her boss, she watched the muscles tick in his jaw as he glared at the arsehole who'd made fun of her. A quick look at his friend and she came face-to-face with a pair of crystalline blue eyes almost identical to Tobias's and an easy smile stretched across his impossibly handsome face.

"Evening, beautiful," he said with a wink.

Beautiful? Lucy did a double take, and the jerk-off twenty-something snorted. She bristled at the dismissive sound and gritted her teeth, tamping down the urge to say something and make the situation worse. But it seemed Tobias had no such reluctance. He stepped forwards and folded his thick arms across his impressive chest, causing the dark blue cotton of his button-up shirt to pull tight around his biceps.

The big man's less-than-subtle power move made her insides clench with need, and Lucy suppressed a whimper as she wondered what it would feel like to be held in those strong arms.

"I said apologise to the lady," Tobias growled again, glaring down at them like they were shit on the sole of his shoe. "Now."

The jerk's friend paled, as if he'd only just realised exactly how huge her rescuer was. To be fair, the man made Lucy feel small, and she stood at just a smidge under six feet tall, even when she wasn't wearing five-inch-high follow-me-home-and-fuck-me shoes.

The jerk scoffed again, as if the whole situation was so beneath him, then rolled his eyes. "I'm sorry, okay? It was a joke. Jesus." Then he shook his head and muttered under his breath, "Bitch."

Lucy sighed. "Wow, okay. You know what, I was prepared to let it slide, but you just couldn't help yourself, could you?" She leaned closer, invaded the ignorant little twat's personal space and turned her scars towards him. "Take a good look, junior," she said quietly, smiling grimly as the jerk visibly stiffened. "A long time ago in a galaxy far, far away, I was a firefighter. I'm *ugly*, as you put it, because I put my life on the line to save a four-year-old kid from a burning house. But I'm guessing from your expensive-looking haircut and clothes and, what, the Mercedes in the car park"—the jerk nodded and swallowed hard—"that you've never sacrificed anything for anyone in your life. But sure, you go ahead and call me names if it makes you feel like a big man." She let her gaze travel deliberately, disdainfully up and down the arrogant brat. "You in your skinny jeans and ironic T-shirts, playing at grown-ups in Daddy's car as you bang impressionable schoolgirls you have zero intention of calling after you shove them in the back of the taxi you so very predictably have on speed dial, you sad little boy. So yeah, I just may be the ugliest bitch you'll ever meet, but at least I'm only ugly on the outside."

Face flushed with what she hoped was embarrassment —and maybe a little fear—and eyes darting to the side, the jerk stammered, "I'm... I'm sorry." Only this time it was said with a modicum of contrition.

"Get out of my face," Lucy growled, then sighed softly as the jerk and his friends scurried away to join the dating pool. The lady in charge caught her eye, pressed her lips into a thin line, and shook her head. Lucy had been there often enough to know what that meant. Good ol' rule number three: "harassment of any kind will not be tolerated." Except what they really meant was "harassment of any kind towards people we deem socially acceptable will not be tolerated. Freak show rejects need not apply." Which explained why Skinny Jeans McGee wasn't receiving the same glare of disapproval currently pointed at her. He may have been an arsehole, but at least he was a good-looking arsehole.

Lucy nodded towards the door. "I'll just go."

"Do. Please. And take your friends with you."

Lucy frowned. "Friends?"

Behind her, someone cleared their throat, a hint of amusement enriching the deep timbre.

She stiffened. Somehow, while she was ranting at the jerk, she'd forgotten Tobias and his friend were still standing there like two enormous sentinels, watching over her even as she made a fool of herself in front of her new employer.

Hands clenched into fists to hide her anxiety, she pasted on a smile and slowly turned to face them. "So, am I fired?" she asked, only half joking.

Perfectly carved eyebrows arched over fathomless blue eyes, and the sexiest grin she'd ever seen on a man tugged at the corners of his full lips. "No."

He turned to his friend, and they seemed to talk to each other without actually saying anything at all, just a few raised brows and nods in her direction. Then they bumped their fists together and the whole world turned upside down as Lucy found herself being tossed over Tobias Bennett's shoulder and carried out of the pub.

"What the hell?"

One strong arm banded around her legs, holding her in place so she couldn't kick—or perhaps fall from an extreme height—while his other hand landed on her arse. *Smack!*

Lucy gasped at the sharp sting, then rubbed her thighs together and moaned as a glorious ache began to throb between her legs. *Fuck.*

She could use some more of that.

A moment later she was standing upright again, Tobias gripping her hips like a vice, preventing her from toppling over when her high heels wobbled on the gravel surface of the car park. She grabbed his arms to steady herself.

Oh, wow....

His biceps were even thicker than she'd thought. Harder too. She gently squeezed them, but it was like fingering steel.

"Are you all right?" he said, keeping his voice low.

The single lamp in the car park shone with a dull yellow light, illuminating him from behind and casting his face in shadow. It made the already fearsome man look downright terrifying, like a huge spectre looming over her. But Lucy found she wasn't afraid. She was intrigued.

And more than a little turned on.

She licked her lips and nodded as she got her bearings.

"It's nothing I haven't heard before," she said, shrugging. Then, because she'd rather not kill the mood by throwing a pity party for one, she added, "Where's your friend?"

"Right here, beautiful." A shuffling of gravel drew her attention to the man rounding the back of the black truck parked beside them. "And may I just say, that was fucking awesome! A true pleasure to watch. Entitled little shit didn't know what hit him."

Tobias reached into his pocket, then tossed a set of car keys at his friend. "Lucy Barton, meet my brother, Charlie Bennett."

Charlie bowed slightly, then looked up at her from under dark lashes as that same grin from earlier played across his face. "His older, wiser, better-looking *twin* brother," he said, winking. Taking her hand in his, he pressed his lips to the backs of her fingers, right between her index and middle digits. The gesture wasn't lost on her, and her pussy clenched in response. "It's a pleasure to meet you, Lucy Barton." His voice was a rich purr of masculine confidence.

Wide-eyed but amused by his audacity, Lucy rolled her lips between her teeth as she repressed the laughter clawing its way up her throat. Turning to Tobias, she said, "Is he always like this?"

Casting a long-suffering look at his brother, he sighed. "Sadly, yes."

When she laughed out loud, he looked down at her, a half smile curving his delectable mouth. He lifted his hand and stroked the blade of one big finger over her scarred cheek. Lucy shivered, and it had nothing to do with the cool sea breeze blowing in from the bay.

He stepped closer and backed her up against the cab of the truck. "I've wondered all week what your smile would look like."

"Have you?" she said, another shiver skittering through her. Lucy couldn't remember the last time someone said they'd been thinking about her. Most people tried *not* thinking about her. In fact, she was fairly certain her parents had tried so hard to not think about her, they'd completely forgotten she existed at all. But before she could let that little joy-thief of a memory steal her mojo, she did what she'd dreamed of doing all week long and slid her hands over his chest, felt the ridges of hard muscle under his shirt twitch and flex. *Jesus, is he this hard everywhere?* Suddenly breathless, she whispered, "Tell me, Tobias, what else have you wondered about?"

"Call me Toby," he said, the other half of his mouth curling upwards, completing his sensual smile. "And I'd rather show than tell."

"Show me, then."

"Come home with us and I will."

Chapter Three

"Us?" Lucy gasped. "Both of you?" Her fingers curled in his shirtfront as her eyes widened to a comical degree.

Toby chuckled. Charlie too. Even in the dim light of the car park, it was easy to see the intensity of her interest—and her uncertainty—in her lovely whisky-coloured eyes. "Yes, both of us. If that's what you want."

Her pretty pink tongue darted out to moisten her lips, drawing Toby's attention to the way her scars pulled slightly at the top right corner of her mouth, giving her a tiny permanent sneer he hadn't noticed before. He had a sudden and powerful urge to lean down and kiss that little imperfection, to explore and taste and discover if it was as soft and luscious as the rest of her mouth looked.

"And if I don't want?" she said, interrupting his wayward thoughts. A slight frown pulled at her brow, and she dropped her hands to his forearms and gripped them tightly, as though readying to shove him away and make a break for it should she not like their answer.

"Then you choose one of us," Charlie said, leaning

against the truck. His hungry gaze slid over Lucy's slender figure in a predatory way, but she either didn't notice or didn't mind because her grip relaxed.

"Or neither of us," Toby added.

Aiming a pointed stare in his brother's direction, he restrained an urge to block Charlie's view. *Strange.* He'd never been jealous of his twin before, but the thought of Lucy choosing to go home with Charlie instead of him made something inside him snap. Unleashed something primal deep within him. He'd felt something like it once before, a long time ago, but never this strongly. Never this completely. It made him want to wrap her up in his arms and not let go. He wanted to protect her. Cherish her. Keep her all to himself.

Possess her.

But another part of him longed to fulfil her desires, to taste her, tease her, pleasure her, even share her if that was what she wanted. He just wasn't sure he could sit idly by and watch if she chose his brother over him. His jaw clenched and he felt the muscle in his cheek tick. If that happened, it'd be better for everyone if she went home alone. Otherwise, Charlie might end up with a black eye.

And a broken jaw.

And dickless.

The last thing Toby wanted was to frighten Lucy and push her in his brother's direction, so he took a calming breath and slowly let it out. "We're happy to drive you home and walk you to your door if that's what you'd prefer, but whether we give you a ride home—"

"Or give you the ride of your life," Charlie interrupted, winking at him. *Arse.*

"It's your choice."

Lucy nodded slowly. "So, one of you, neither of you, or

the two of you together, huh? You boys are spoiling me for choice." Her tongue darted out again to wet her lips, and then she sucked her bottom lip between her teeth and slowly released it. Toby tracked the movement like a hawk tracked its prey, watched the plump little pillow darken with blood, and licked his own lips in response. His cock twitched in anticipation.

"I've had threesomes before," Lucy said, "and I freely admit the idea of a threesome with you pair is *very* attractive, but you're both so... *not* the type of guy I usually go home with. I'd be lying if I said I wasn't a little over-whelmed right now."

"I'd be worried if you weren't," Toby admitted, pleased by her caution in what was a potentially dangerous situation. Not that either he or Charlie would hurt her, but she didn't know that. Yet.

It also made him wonder what type of men she usually slept with and just how many times she'd put herself in harm's way in the pursuit of getting laid. She hadn't seemed like the type of woman to live recklessly, but maybe he'd misjudged her. On the other hand, if she were opposed to taking risks, she wouldn't be going home with him.

And he really, really wanted her to go home with him.

Slipping one arm free of her grip, he reached out and caught a lock of her long wavy hair. He rubbed the silky strands between his thumb and fingers, then lifted it to his nose and inhaled her scent. *Gardenias.* Sultry, exotic. He let his gaze travel the length of her lithe body once more. *Intoxicating.* The fragrance suited her. When she didn't shy away from the possessive gesture, contentment rumbled through his chest. He didn't miss the slight parting of her lips either, or how her body swayed closer to his. Hope bloomed inside him and cooled his anxiety. "What can we do to put your mind at ease?"

"Maybe," she said, her tone breathless as she watched him play with her hair, "if I had more information to go on?"

Toby let the strands of blonde hair sift through his fingers and fall away from him. "And what more information would you be needing, baby?" Lucy's gaze flicked deliberately to Toby's crotch, lingered for a moment, then moved back again. "Naughty girl," he said, grinning. "But you don't get to see my dick unless you come home with me."

"Fuck, she can see my dick anytime she wants," Charlie said, his hands dropping to his belt.

"Stop showing off," Toby growled. Gripping Lucy's hips once more, he turned her slightly, angled her body away from his brother.

"Just giving the lady what she wants," Charlie returned, shrugging. But at Toby's continuing glare, he resumed his position leaning against the truck and shoved his hands in his pockets.

A wicked grin overtook Lucy's face. "If Charlie showing me his dick makes him a show-off," she said, lifting her hands to toy with the buttons of his shirt, "are you a *bigger* show-off or smaller?"

Now it was Toby's turn to gawk as his own natural shyness came to the fore. Did she really just ask him if his dick was bigger than Charlie's?

Thankfully his twin stepped in. "Unfortunately, beautiful, that is one area where my little brother has me beat."

"Unfortunate for you maybe," she tossed at Charlie. Then she pressed her palms flat against Toby's chest again and returned his stare, her uncertainty replaced with humour. "Sounds like a win-win situation over here."

He liked having her hands on him, even if it was

through the cotton of his shirt. But with any luck, that would soon be remedied. With any luck, he'd soon have her stripped bare and riding his cock for the rest of the night. "Have you made your decision, then?"

She bit her lip again. "Not quite."

Fingers flexing against her rounded hips, Toby said quietly, "What else do you need from us?" He wanted her to be as sure about this as he was and was willing to do just about anything to put her concerns to rest.

"Well, it occurs to me that many men talk a good game, but when it really comes down to it, talk is the *only* thing they're good at."

"What's wrong, Lucy?" Charlie said, folding his arms over his chest as his impatience reared its head. He cocked a brow. "Don't believe me when I say I have a big dick?"

Lucy smiled sweetly and held her hands up defensively. "No, no. That I believe. It takes a big man to admit his dick is smaller than his brother's." Toby snorted. Charlie flipped him off. Lucy continued, "I was thinking more along the lines of... kissing."

Toby smiled down at her. "Kissing?"

"Kissing," Lucy repeated, her smile playful yet tentative. "You can tell a lot about a man by the way he kisses."

"Me first," Charlie said, moving closer.

But Lucy's gaze didn't shift from Toby's, and his breath caught in his lungs. Did she want him to go first? Or was she waiting for his permission? His cock swelled against his leg at the thought, at that small hint of submission. It was all he needed for any lingering tension, any residual jealousy to ease out of him.

Mine.

Gently, Toby stroked his fingertips over her scarred cheek and nodded. "Him first."

"Yes, Sir," she whispered, then turned to face his brother.

Charlie was an expert at seduction, at deducing a woman's secret desires and making them a reality, but if Toby was right and Lucy was submissive, his charms wouldn't go far. She'd no doubt find his kiss pleasurable, but he doubted she'd wilt in his arms as so many women had before. Charlie adored women, worshipped them, and he went to great pains to ensure he never hurt them, only ever leaving them in a puddle of pleasure. But if Toby's hunch was correct, leaving Lucy in a puddle of pleasure would require at least a little hurt. Possibly more than a little.

He watched, openly and unashamed, as his brother slid his hands into Lucy's hair and held her steady, as his mouth descended on hers.

The usual sounds followed—moaning, heavy breathing—but their body language told Toby more. While Charlie's hands had travelled down Lucy's back, one resting at her waist while the other cupped the softness of her arse and pulled her closer, her hands had barely moved, going only from his chest to his shoulders and not in any way that would indicate any urgency or sense of possession. She didn't cling to him like a drowning man would a life raft, or as though she needed him to carry her out of the darkness and into the light. No, her hold on Charlie looked almost... polite in nature.

The kissing equivalent of a handshake.

Toby wanted to punch the air in victory but restrained himself. Barely. He reminded himself that her lack of reaction towards his brother was no guarantee he'd fare any better. Hell, for all he knew, that *was* how she showed passion, in which case his first impression of the woman was the right one, and the sooner she went over his knee and got a damn good spanking, the better.

His cock hardened further at the thought of laying her over his lap, one hand in the small of her back, holding her in place, the other delivering a series of stinging slaps designed to make her quiver and squeal, to make her bones melt, her mind relax, to let go. Let her know he would take all her worries away and look after her. That he would carry the weight of her world on his shoulders. That he would free her from whatever it was that held her back and show her the true meaning of passion.

Without warning, Charlie lifted the hand cupping Lucy's arse and spanked her. It was nothing more than one firm whack on one half of her backside, but a muffled whimper escaped her and her fingers curled into his shoulders, pulled him closer. Toby's gut tightened, the action confirming his hunch, and he shot a glance at Charlie's face. His brother was staring at him as he continued playing tonsil hockey with the luscious woman in his arms—*bastard* —and Toby's jealousy reared its ugly head once more.

"My turn," he growled.

Immediately, Lucy disentangled herself from Charlie. "Wow," she said, her voice little more than a throaty exhalation of breath. "You are *really* good at that."

Charlie smiled down at her, his expression warm, his gaze sensual. "Thanks. You're pretty great yourself."

Toby noticed her hand lingering on his brother's chest and his emotions swelled again. "My turn," he repeated, snatching Lucy's hand in his and spinning her towards the truck.

Using his big body, he caged her against the passenger door, pressed his chest to her back, and nestled the thick evidence of his arousal against her arse. With slow and deliberate purpose, he gathered her hair together near her scalp and held it tight in his fist. Then he wrapped his other hand around her throat and gently squeezed. Not to harm her but to let her know what she was getting herself into. To let her see him for what he was.

A sick, twisted bastard who would control her body, her mind, her spirit.

If she let him.

Chapter Four

Lucy leaned into the security of the palm around her neck, let its warmth, its strength permeate her flesh and fill her with a sense of calm she hadn't known in far too long. Combined with the sharp sting of her hair pulled taut in his other hand, Toby had her wriggling with desire in less time than it took for his brother to wink.

The man hadn't even kissed her yet and Lucy wanted to climb him like a freaking tree.

This was what she needed. What she wanted. Not that Charlie's attention had been unwanted, but he'd failed to excite any real hunger for him. His kisses had been enjoyable, certainly, and she hadn't lied when she'd said he was very good at it—the man's technique was flawless—but it wasn't until he'd added that little bite of pain at the end that she'd seen a faint glimmer of hope that he wouldn't be just like every other man she went home with after one of her speed dating sprees.

Nice enough—if somewhat desperate—but ultimately disappointing.

Charlie was handsome—gorgeous, really—with his

neatly trimmed brown hair, pale blue eyes, strong jawline, and lean, muscled physique. Not to mention her own personal kryptonite—dude was tall. *So very tall.* And Lucy really did love nothing half as much as a man who made her feel short, but all the good looks and aerial postcodes in the world couldn't make up for his lack of dominance.

Toby's brother was without a doubt a strong and disciplined man—a body like his didn't happen by chance—but it was the wrong sort of strong for her liking. The wrong sort of discipline. *Annnd* she was pretty sure he'd only slapped her arse because he had also noticed a lack of any real interest on her part, and he'd thought to change things up a bit.

It had worked too.

The instant his hand had landed on her arse, her pussy grew wet and throbbed with wanting. But before she could press him for more, Toby had demanded his turn, and that rich baritone had pulled her away from Charlie as easily as if he'd reached out and grabbed her with both hands.

There'd been no way in hell she could have resisted his command.

Immediately, she'd complied with his wishes, but she'd also left one hand on Charlie's chest, letting him know he wasn't totally forgotten, just not her main point of focus in that moment. Then Toby had snatched her hand away from his brother like a child who was tired of sharing his toys.

Lucy had half a mind to be mad at him—*so rude*—but the instant his hand had wrapped around her throat and she'd felt his impressive erection pressed against her arse, her brain had tapped out and let her sadly neglected nether regions take the win.

He gave her hair a tug, and her mouth fell open to expel a harsh breath. Then she felt his lips, soft and hot, where they brushed against the shell of her ear. His heated breath tickled, and her whole body shivered at the ethereal caress. "Mine," he growled, and then his mouth fell upon her skin.

Breath after breath shuddered in and out of her lungs as he kissed and licked her scars. Up the side of her throat and across to her earlobe, along the edge of her jaw and then back down to nuzzle in the crook of her neck. The damaged flesh was so sensitive to touch it felt as though every erogenous zone in her body had relocated to wherever Toby's mouth was, pushing the line between pleasure and pain.

The sensation was exquisite.

And she wanted more.

Curling one hand around his thick wrist, she gripped him tightly in a silent plea. Toby didn't disappoint, his fingers tightening around her throat until the only breath she drew was the one he allowed her.

Lucy was usually pretty good at keeping her needs in check. Adult toys and internet porn did most of the heavy lifting, with the occasional one-night stand thrown in for good measure when she needed a little something extra. Like a nice pair of callused hands or a talented tongue or the weight of a warm body—or sometimes two—pressing down on top of her. Sometimes it just came down to wanting someone she could hold a conversation with.

Conversation consisting of more than talking to herself as she put fresh batteries in her vibrator.

But as good as she was at sexual self-reliance, she couldn't deny the adrenaline rush coursing through her at the feel of the dominant man behind her. The way his fingers pressed against her skin, controlling her breathing, her life, made her mind slip sideways. *Such a rush.*

Her eyelids fluttered, and her knees grew weak. She trembled in his hold.

So close....

Toby chuckled quietly by her ear. "Oh, Lucy. You're submissive as fuck, aren't you, baby? But don't you float away on me. Not yet. I intend to play with you a lot more than this before I let you fly."

Eyes springing open, she caught his piercing gaze in the reflection of the driver-side window and swallowed hard against the hand still locked around her throat. She sank her teeth into her bottom lip, but nothing could stop her whimpering moan. Just as squeezing her thighs together was useless against the pulsing sensation Toby's words had caused between her thighs.

"We should get out of here," Charlie said, moving closer, and Lucy heard the jingle of car keys. "Maybe take this somewhere more private than a car park?"

Lucy held Toby's reflected gaze and lifted her chin slightly, challenging the big man at her back. "But Toby hasn't kissed me yet," she said, hoping her tone sounded more confident out loud than it did in her head. She licked her suddenly dry lips. "How do I know I even want to go home with you? How do I know you're not wasting my time? That you're not just all talk?"

Toby chuckled again, an ominous rumble of sound that vibrated through her body and lit up her lady parts like a Christmas tree. "Oh, you're coming home with us. I have no doubts about that."

"Why?" she said, brow furrowed. She was genuinely curious to know how he saw their encounter unfolding.

His grin was feral, his eyes narrowed. "Because I only talk when I have something worth saying," he growled, tightening his fist in her hair. "I can give you what you want. I can give you what you *need*. And you need it, don't you, baby? You need to be dominated, held down. Fucked. Used. You want to be my little fuck toy, don't you, Lucy?"

Her whole body quivered as her pussy clenched around nothing, aching to be filled by the hard cock still pressed against her arse. "Yes," she hissed. The sting in her scalp had her tilting her head back, hoping to rest it on his broad shoulder, but he shoved her forwards against the cold metal of the truck door. Away from him and the warmth of his big body.

"Yes what?" he snarled.

Lucy swallowed down an excited moan. "Yes, Sir." Her pussy flooded with warmth.

Then Charlie spoke up, his deep voice thick with concern. "Tobes, ease up. You're hurting her."

"Am I hurting you, Lucy?" he asked, his tone amused. She shook her head. "Say the words. Put Charlie's mind at ease."

She slid her gaze towards his brother and barely held back an excited shiver at seeing him watch her, seeing that concern mingled with lust. "He's not hurting me."

And he wasn't. He was, however, driving her wild. She pushed her arse out and thrilled at the contact as she brushed against his thick erection.

Toby chuckled again and thrust forwards, pinned her between the bulk of the truck and his own solid mass. "And are you wet for me, baby?"

"Yes, Sir." Her voice trembled with desire. She dared to lift her gaze and meet his in the reflective surface. "So wet."

When he growled in response, Lucy instinctively went to drop her chin and lower her gaze, to submit, but he wouldn't let her. His grip shifted from her throat to her chin, and he held her head high. Testing his grip, Lucy tried to wrench free, but she wasn't going anywhere. It was an amazing sensation, hot, dirty, exciting... and dangerous.

She couldn't afford to forget herself. Or him. Tobias Bennett wasn't just some random bloke, and this wasn't just some no-strings hook-up. This night, these actions—*her* actions—had real-life consequences. And the weight of those consequences began pushing down on her, choking her more efficiently than Toby ever could.

But it seemed the man was as perceptive as he was dominant, discerning her anxiety with ease. He held her reflected gaze, his eyes narrowed but curious. "What's wrong, Lucy? What aren't you telling me?"

"I want this," she whispered, unable to conceal the desperate edge in her voice. "I really do want this."

The constant pull on her scalp ceased, replaced by the gentle throb of release before he let go of her chin and turned her to face him. Gentle fingers stroked her cheek and brushed her hair from her face, and his deep voice was soft when he spoke. "But?"

Lucy bit her lip to hold back her cry of utter frustration. There she stood, on the brink of experiencing the absolute best sexual fantasy she could've ever imagined, knowing she'd probably never get this opportunity again, and she was stalling. She'd been stalling from the beginning. Because as sexy as Toby was, and as hot as she knew the sex would be....

Consequences.

"You're my boss," she said quietly, hoping he was intelligent enough to read between the lines.

She'd already had to leave one job and wasn't looking to go through that again. She needed to work—not for the money, although that was nice. She needed the comfort and the reassurance that came with the routine of an office. She needed that little bit of control in her life to stop her mind from spinning out of bounds and taking her to the dark places, to the recesses of her psyche she'd rather forget.

Toby slid his hands through her hair and gripped the back of her skull, then tilted her head and lowered his lips to hers. It wasn't as aggressive a kiss as she'd expected from him but rather a gentle exploration, soft but sure, and by no means less erotic. And when he forced her lips apart and flicked his tongue between them, he groaned, the sensual sound urging her to fist her hands in his shirt and haul herself closer. To feel the warmth emanating from his rock-hard body as she rubbed herself against him like a bitch in heat.

But then it was over. He pulled back and ended it, and Lucy mewled at the all too brief, blink-and-you-miss-it move. It hadn't been a kiss so much as a tease, a temptation, and she wanted more.

He gave her more. But not in the way she'd expected.

"I'm not your boss, Lucy," he said, smiling down at her. "And you're not my employee. Not tonight."

"Not tonight," she echoed, letting the underlying meaning in his words filter through her brain. But she'd been burned before. Needing clarification, she added, "Then what are we?"

"We're just two people—"

"Three people," Charlie interjected.

Lucy shook with supressed laughter, the sudden burst of emotion easing her tension.

Toby glared at his brother. "Three people," he continued, "looking for a little fun and maybe a little comfort in the arms of another."

She stroked her hands over his shoulders and down to his thick biceps. "I have admit, I do like your arms."

Toby grinned, and her knees threatened to buckle again. *So damn sexy.* "So, what do you say, Lucy? Am I taking you to bed, or am I taking you home?"

Staring up at him as her brain chased itself in circles trying to second-guess the decision she'd already made, she said, "What happens in the bedroom stays in the bedroom?"

He nodded slowly. "Of course."

Lucy swallowed hard, then said what she'd been wanting to say from the moment Toby had tossed her over his shoulder and smacked her arse. Her mind was more than made up, and she was done stalling. "Then I guess you're taking me to bed."

"I'll drive," Charlie said, nudging them out of the way of the driver door and climbing into the truck.

Toby took her hand and led her around to the passenger door, but before he opened it, he pinned her against it and slashed his mouth over hers. The kiss was hard and fast and over all too quickly.

"Are you sure about this, baby?" he said, his face suddenly serious, his eyes searching hers. If he was looking for doubt, he wouldn't find any. Not now. "I won't be offended if you change your mind. I don't want you to feel like you have to do this."

Lucy smiled at his concern. He didn't want her to feel coerced or obligated. Used. Not in some sleazy way, at least. She let her gaze drift over his broad shoulders and chest, traced small circles around his nipple and sucked down an excited breath when he groaned.

"I want this. I want to be your fuck toy. One night only, no strings, no repercussions."

His gaze darkened and he pressed himself closer, ground his hard cock against the junction of her thighs and hissed out a breath. He opened his mouth as if to say something, but the window rolled down and his brother spoke before he could.

"Are we gunna have some fun or what?"

Toby's gaze never left hers, but his face softened slightly. "Lucy?"

Lucy grinned. "Let's fuck."

Chapter Five

I t was usually a twenty-minute drive from the pub in Redland Bay to their acreage in Sheldon, but with minimal traffic, Charlie's lead foot, and the god of green lights on their side, they managed to do it in twelve.

"Do you two do this often?" Lucy said, her voice breathy.

Charlie turned off the main road and onto their driveway. "Do what?" He tapped his fingers against the steering wheel, impatient as they waited for the enormous wrought-iron gate to slowly trundle sideways, allowing them access to their property.

"Pick up random women and share them."

"You're not random," Toby growled in her ear. No. Taking Lucy home with him had been a very deliberate choice. And as much as he applauded her stance on no-strings-attached sex, he was more than a bit concerned about her declaration of their tryst being for one night only. He'd hoped for a little more. Maybe even a lot more. But he guessed they'd cross that bridge when they came to it and wouldn't let it spoil their evening.

Sitting almost sideways on the bench seat, he held Lucy against him, nestled between his thighs. He liked her there, her weight against his body comfortable, natural, and with her back pressed to his chest, her head resting on his shoulder, and her legs spread, he had access to all of her. They'd not been on the road more than two minutes before Toby had wrenched her jeans open and slid his hand between her legs.

Currently his middle finger was deep inside her wet cunt, stroking the rough flesh of her G-spot and delighting in all the little noises she made, the way her back arched when he stroked her harder and faster, then softer and slower again. Loving the way her fingers dug into his thighs, the way she bit her lip to stifle her sultry moans.

And failed.

"We're home," Charlie announced as he pulled up in front of Toby's house and cut the engine.

Sliding his hand out of Lucy's jeans, Toby grinned as she whimpered. "Open," he said, holding his finger in front of her mouth. And then it was his turn to whimper—only his was more masculine and grunt-like—as she obeyed him without question, taking his finger between her lips and sucking it clean. "Good girl," he murmured, his cock painfully hard in his jeans. Especially now that he was imagining her sucking his cock the way she was sucking his finger. The way she used her tongue was inspiring, and the little nip of her teeth when she released him... *sublime*.

Helping her out of the truck proved too tempting to resist, and he ended up carrying her all the way to his front door before he put her back on her feet.

"You going to carry me over the threshold too?" she said, the teasing tone of her voice matching the mischievous glint in her eyes.

"Careful what you wish for," he shot back with a wink. Her quick intake of breath sent a jolt of lust straight to his dick.

"Hey, Toby?" Charlie said, following them into the house.

"Yes, Charlie?" Toby replied, flicking on the lights and adjusting the dimmer switch. He wanted to seduce the woman, not make her blind.

"How do you feel about a game?"

Lucy's eyes narrowed with caution, and her gaze darted between the two of them. "Game?"

"Catch?" Toby said, ignoring her query.

"Catch," Charlie replied with a single nod, rubbing his hands together and grinning like a lunatic.

"Uh, guys?" Lucy said, taking a step back as they both stepped towards her. "What's 'catch'?"

"You run," Toby said.

"And we try to catch you."

"The first one to catch you wins."

Folding her arms over her chest, she lifted one brow, her expression one of cautious curiosity. "Wins what?"

"You," they said in unison.

"First man to catch you is the first man to have you. The first to fuck your hot pussy."

"Or your sexy arse."

"Taste your sweet mouth."

"Suck your spectacular—"

"Okay, okay, I get it," she said, laughing. "What are the rules?"

"You run, we catch. It ain't rocket science, beautiful."

Toby chuckled as Lucy threw his brother a sour look. "Bite me," she said.

"Only if you ask nicely."

Shifting her weight from one foot to the other, she tightened her arms across her pert breasts and flashed them a tight smile. "Well, what happens if you fail to catch me?"

"We don't fail," Toby said, enjoying the banter. In all the time he and his twin had done this—not that they'd done it a lot—he'd never had this much fun. Talking was never high on the agenda with other women. Probably because he'd never met a woman who fascinated him as much as Lucy Barton did.

"Oh?"

Charlie smirked. "We *never* fail."

"We'll see," Lucy said. Then she burst into a run across the lounge room, hurdled the coffee table, vaulted over the couch, and disappeared into the kitchen.

"Fuck me," Charlie said, gaping after her. "What just happened?"

Glancing down at where she'd been standing, Toby saw a pair of bright red stilettos sitting on the polished hardwood floor. He'd been so distracted by her tits he hadn't even noticed she'd kicked them off. "We just got owned," he said, a slow grin stretching across his face. "That's what happened."

"Come on, slowpokes!" Lucy called out from the kitchen. "It ain't rocket science."

Charlie shook his head and grinned. "She's mine."

"Not if I catch her first," Toby said, shoving Charlie out of his way.

"Cheaters never prosper, little brother."

It took only seconds to reach the kitchen and realise Lucy was gone. Yanking open the door to the walk-in pantry revealed she wasn't hiding in there. Opening the laundry door yielded similar results.

"Come out, come out, wherever you are," Charlie sang

softly as he lifted the tablecloth covering the dining table and looked underneath.

"Kinda defeats the purpose, doesn't it?" Lucy said, smacking Toby's arse as she bolted past him and into his conservatory.

He turned to see where she'd been hiding—behind the floor-length curtains in the dining room—and realised she must have been standing on tippy-toe with her slim figure plastered to the glass. It was the only way she could have prevented the voluminous fabric from bulging out around her. The only way for him not to have noticed her. "Clever girl." He shook his head and laughed softly, not worried about not catching her. Not now. There was no way out of the conservatory unless she came back out the way she went in.

She was trapped.

Not so clever now, are you, baby?

He nodded at Charlie, and they entered the plant-filled room, flicking on the lights. Toby spotted her immediately crouching behind a clump of potted ferns, her hiding spot given away by her reflection in the glass walls. Lucy seemed to realise this as well and tried to run again, heading for the door at the far end of the room. She cursed when she found it locked.

"There's no escape through there, beautiful," Charlie said. "That's the door to my house."

Lucy sucked her bottom lip between her teeth and looked around, seeking another means of escape. When her gaze landed on Toby, then flicked between him, Charlie, and the door back inside, he knew she knew she'd lost. But still, she made a valiant attempt at getting away again, and if it wasn't for the fact that she seemed to make a concerted effort to not damage his collection of native Australian orchids, she might have succeeded.

Arms pumping as she ran straight for the gap between them, she squealed as they reached out for her, then laughed as she struggled ineffectually in Toby's arms when he lifted her off her feet.

"I win," he pronounced triumphantly, grinning as he set her down again. Locking one arm around her waist, he grabbed her arse in his other hand and hauled her closer. Now she was barefoot, their difference in height was more pronounced, and Toby towered over Lucy, making her tilt her head all the way back to look up at him. His grin broadened when she slid her arms around his waist and cupped his arse in both hands, giving him a squeeze. An appreciative moan rose from his throat, and she squeezed him again.

Staring up at him with an amused expression on her pretty face, she cocked one brow, drawing attention to the fact it was slightly shorter than the other. On closer inspection, Toby realised her eyebrow had been truncated by the edge of the burn scar that carved through her face. It was more faded there and not as noticeable. He couldn't stop himself from tracing the mottled flesh with his fingertip, or from noticing her amusement slipping into desire.

"Maybe I let you win," she said, her voice huskier than before.

Toby licked his lips. "And maybe I should put you over my knee for telling such blatant lies."

Lucy's eyes darkened as she pressed herself closer. Toby's gut clenched with need, and he almost forgot they weren't alone.

"I told you, beautiful," Charlie said from behind her, breaking her spell over Toby and drawing both their gazes.

His brother patted her cheek and threw her a pitying look. "We never fail."

Lucy pretended to glare at Charlie—*smug bastard*—until Toby laughed, the sound vibrating through her until any real annoyance she felt simply melted away. It was such a wonderful sound, deep and rich and honest.

"You are so fucking cute," he said, nuzzling against her cheek—her scarred cheek—causing her to shiver with awareness. Then his voice roughened as the Dominant side of him took over. "And I'm going to fuck you so goddamn hard." He shoved her towards his brother, but his gaze never left hers. "Strip her," he said. "And don't be gentle."

His gruff words made Lucy's eyes flare wide and pure desire shoot through her body, leaving her hot and needy. Breathless. "Don't you want to strip me yourself?"

Slowly, he shook his head. "I don't trust myself not to rip your clothes."

Lucy shrugged. "I'd be okay with that." And she would. Toby ripping her clothes off in his need to get her naked sounded hot as fuck and would definitely be a new experience.

Toby looked amused by her statement, his mouth edging into a smile once again. "Sadly, you will have to go home at some point, and I'd rather not embarrass you by sending you home naked."

She smiled up at him, the thought of walking across her front yard without a stitch of clothing on filling her imagination. What would her neighbours think? Mr Davis from across the road would be scandalised and give her a lecture on decency. On the other hand, Mrs Miller, who lived next door, would probably applaud, yell, "Rock on," at the top of her lungs, and invite her over for a cuppa.

"I'm willing to risk it," she said.

"I'm not," Toby replied, nodding at his brother. The finality in his voice told her the conversation was done.

Charlie's arms came around her then, and he yanked her back against his chest. His very naked chest. He'd already slipped off his shirt and discarded it on the floor, and the feel of his heated skin at her back made her turn to look at him. He was a very appealing man, visually speaking. His torso was smooth of hair and rigid with muscle, his biceps were thick and strong, and his hips were narrow and defined by those glorious ridges of muscle she'd taken great delight in perving on at the fire station so many years ago.

His grin was cocky. "Like what you see?"

Lucy snorted. As if he needed an answer. The man knew he looked good. He didn't need her opinion adding to his ego. So instead she smirked and said, "You'll do."

As handsome as Charlie was, as built and—*God help her* —as tall as he was, Lucy still preferred his brother. His equally handsome, just as exquisitely built, and even *taller* brother.

"Look at me," Toby growled.

Wetness flooded her pussy, and she clamped her legs together. His voice was so commanding, so deep and rough, and had a melodic quality to it that appealed to her on a baser level. Again, she obeyed him without question, lifting her gaze to his, eager to know what would happen next. "Yes, Sir."

His gaze softened when she said "Sir", and her heart fluttered in her chest. She suspected Toby Bennett was truly dominant. Oh, she'd met her fair share of men who thought they were all that, insisting she beg and crawl and call them "master" within five seconds of meeting them, but not a single one of them had succeeded. Not for a lack of trying, of course. And their failures had caused them to sneer at her, to belittle and degrade her. And, most tellingly, to blame her for their inadequacies. None of them had understood.

It took more than a big ego, a domineering attitude, and a copy of *BDSM for Dummies* to make a man... *more*.

Powerful.

Sensual.

Dominant.

And Toby Bennett had those qualities in spades.

It was in the richness of his voice, the smooth baritone that vibrated with command. The sternness of his diamond-bright eyes and the way they darkened, softened when she obeyed. And the raw power that emanated from him didn't come from his physical strength or his size but from the way he arrested the attention of everyone in the room without even trying. In fact, Lucy wouldn't have been surprised if Toby wasn't even aware he had that ability. He'd seemed completely oblivious to it in the pub, the way every woman in the room had ogled him and Charlie like a beefcake buffet.

The Bennett brothers stuck out like a sore thumb. Everyone had noticed them as they'd walked through the crowded rooms, men and women alike. How could they not?

The twins were huge!

Okay, so *she'd* missed them when she'd first entered the place, but that was because she'd been too busy hiding her scars behind her hair to see them. Her brain had quickly caught up though, registering who'd she'd run into only *after* she'd brushed past him, when it was too late to turn around and rush out again without looking weird. The best she'd been able to manage was praying her new boss didn't notice her as she'd stood amongst the other singles in the dating pool.

But notice her he did.

And now they were here, in his house, surrounded by a veritable jungle.

About to get naked.

"Look at my brother, beautiful," Charlie murmured by her ear. "Do you see how much he wants you?"

Lucy looked. She couldn't not look. And she saw. The ice blue of his eyes as he stared down at her was mesmerising. Anticipation skittered over her flesh, leaving a trail of goosebumps in its wake. Or maybe she was just cold. They were inside a room made of glass, after all, exposed for all to see. Anticipation morphed into apprehension. She sucked in a sharp breath and stilled.

Exposed.

"The lights," she blurted. When Toby and Charlie just stared at her, she added, "Shouldn't we turn off the lights?"

Toby silently watched her, his icy gaze fixed on hers for what felt like an eternity. Then he tilted his head slightly and frowned, but when he spoke, his voice was gentle, his tone curious. "Are you ashamed of your body, Lucy?"

What? "No, I'm not ashamed," she said, straightening her back as a frown of her own tugged at her brow. Being raised in a family of firefighters—*male* firefighters—had taught her many lessons, the first of which was "healthy body, healthy mind, healthy heart." Charlie wasn't the only one in the room who knew they looked damn good, and Lucy had worked fucking hard to do so, despite her scars.

"Then why do you want the lights off?" he said. "No one can see us from the road, if that's what you're afraid of."

She hadn't even thought of that. But now she did. *Shit.* Could people see them? She peered around his big body and squinted as she tried to see past their reflections to the dark expanse beyond. She could barely tell the difference between the night sky and the shadows of the trees, but it would be much easier for someone to see in than it was for her to see out.

"Lucy?"

The sound of her name spilling from Toby's lips drew her attention again, his rich baritone caressing each syllable the way she wanted his hands to caress her skin. Firm yet affectionate. She shivered. She wanted to wrap his voice around herself like a sexy, sinful blanket.

"What?" What were they talking about?

Toby sighed softly. "Why don't you want us to see your body?"

Oh, yeah. That. She dropped her gaze. "It's not that I don't want you to see me. I do. I *really* do. It's just...."

"Just what, beautiful?" Charlie asked quietly, resting his hands on her shoulders. The gesture was comforting, as was the endearment, but she'd done this often enough to be cautious. Often enough she'd regret not addressing the elephant in the room sooner rather than later.

"It's just that other people are usually more bothered by my scars than I am." She took a breath and lifted her face, saw the intense curiosity shining in Toby's eyes. "It's not just my face that's scarred," she said. "Most people can't handle it." She looked away again. "Many people are cruel and I... I don't want you to be disappointed if I turn out to *not* be what you're expecting."

Toby cupped her cheek in his big hand and lifted her sombre face to his smiling one. There was so much kindness in his expression, so much warmth, that Lucy had to bite the inside of her cheek to stop her emotions from overwhelming her. No one had smiled at her like that in a very long time. Not since her brother, Michael, died.

Seventeen years.

Seventeen very long and lonely years.

He leaned down and pressed his lips to hers, soft and quick, but when he pulled back, a languid heat had replaced the gentle warmth in his gaze. A heat that simmered with promise.

"Baby, you couldn't disappoint me if you tried."

Chapter Six

T oby smoothed his hands over Lucy's hair and pushed it back from her face. He didn't want her hiding behind her long silky locks any more than he wanted her thinking he couldn't bear to look at her. He wanted to see every inch of this woman.

Scars and all.

The real kicker came when he realised she was staring up at him with something akin to *gratitude* shining in her eyes.

Gratitude. *Fuck.* What sort of treatment was she used to if a few simple words of encouragement made her feel grateful? This was a woman who exuded confidence and carried herself with grace. An educated, well-spoken woman. A woman he wanted to know better.

Much, much better.

So where did this uncertainty come from?

Or was this her submissive side asserting itself again?

It wasn't uncommon for strong women to seek out Dominant men. And contrary to popular belief, submissive women were strong. It took an incredible amount of self-awareness and fortitude to trust someone the way a sub trusted her Dom. Although, Toby's interactions with Lucy so far had led him to believe her trust wouldn't be given easily. She may be willing to fuck him, even let him share her with his brother and make her scream in ecstasy, but people were always more reckless with their bodies than they were with their minds and hearts. And it was in the taking care of a sub's mind and heart where a Dominant's true colours shone.

Any man could make a woman beg. Few could make them surrender.

One night only. That was what she'd said to him. For Lucy, this was all about the sex. But for him this night had become about so much more than that. He would find out her secrets. He would earn her trust. And he would have her for more than one fucking night.

But to make that happen, he had to show her he was worth taking a chance on, which meant it was time to put his money where his mouth was.

It was time to take what he wanted.

Tightening his hand in her hair, he pulled her head to one side and leaned down to murmur in her ear. "Do you know how to sew?"

A choking noise came from the back of her throat. "I beg your pardon?"

"It's a simple question, Lucy," Toby said, straightening so he could stare down at her guarded expression. He ignored Charlie, smirking at him over the top of Lucy's head. "Yes or no?"

Lucy swallowed hard. "Uh, yes, Sir. I can sew a little, stitch on buttons, mend small tears, that sort of thing." She licked her lips nervously. "May I ask why?"

Releasing her hair, he slid his hands to the front of her

blouse and fingered the thin, silky fabric, teased a fingertip under the edge of the plunging neckline and tugged it away from her warm body. "Because I've changed my mind," he said. "I do want to undress you myself."

Then he ripped her top clean in half, the sound of tearing fabric an exclamation mark punctuating the mood in the room.

Any wariness that lingered in Lucy's gaze was completely obliterated by the lust he saw there now, the emotion darkening her whisky-coloured eyes to a deep amber that shone with need.

Toby tipped his chin at his brother. "Strip her. I want her naked and on her knees."

Charlie got to work and tugged the remains of Lucy's shirt off, then worked her skinny jeans down her legs—and not in any way that could be construed as sexy. Lucy rolled her lips between her teeth and laughed silently as Charlie struggled to remove the skintight denim.

"How the bloody hell did you even get these things on?" he grumbled, practically turning the jeans inside out to pull them off her legs.

"Trade secret," she said, snickering, her hands on Charlie's shoulders for balance as he yanked the clothing free of her feet.

Toby lifted his hands to his own shirt and began slipping the buttons loose, but when his brother finished stripping off Lucy's outer layers, leaving her standing there in nothing but bits of creamy lace pretending to be panties and a bra, he gave his shirt the same consideration he'd given hers and ripped it open. Lucy laughed freely whilst shielding herself from flying buttons. The sound was the perfect blend of sultry and joyous. It was a sound he could definitely get used to hearing more often.

After dropping his ruined shirt to the ground, Toby grabbed a wide cushion from the daybed behind him and tossed it on the floor by his feet. Then he looked at Lucy... and did a double take.

A flash of metal winked at him from where she stood under the soft conservatory lighting.

Charlie had removed her bra and was crouched behind her, helping her step out of her panties, which explained why he hadn't said anything.

His brother obviously hadn't seen what Toby was staring at, with his mouth hanging open and his heart pounding in his chest and his breath sawing in and out of his lungs like a fifteen-year-old kid getting his first real glimpse at actual boobs.

Lucy's nipples were pierced, each rosy bud transected by a shiny silver bar.

Toby hadn't thought his cock could get much harder.

He was wrong.

And sure, he'd seen piercings before, but he'd never seen them attached to breasts as gorgeous as Lucy's. She was an ancient goddess come to life, her breasts so pretty and perfect they deserved to be worshipped. He reached out to touch her, to pluck at those hardened peaks and feel them against his fingertips, but pulled his hand back before he made contact. Any words of praise his brain could conjure dried on the tip of his tongue, because if he touched her now, he could kiss foreplay goodbye. If he felt the softness of her breasts, felt the heat of her body warm his touch, he knew he'd lose control. *Him.* Tobias 'The Control Freak' Bennett. He would take her hard, fast, and unprepared. He would hurt her.

Mustn't hurt her.

Lucy shifted nervously as he continued staring at her, then lifted her arms to cover her chest.

"Don't!" he said sharply, then breathed a small sigh of relief when she lowered her arms to her sides once more. "I'm a man of few words, Lucy," he continued, reining in his emotions as he continued staring at her nipples, "but no one has ever rendered me speechless before."

Charlie stood up then and frowned at the pair of them. "What are you talking a... bout," he said, finally seeing what Toby did. His eyebrows shot up into his hairline. "Fuck me," he breathed. "That's hot."

Lucy sucked her bottom lip between her teeth and ducked her head, a pale blush staining her cheeks. Toby immediately reached out and hooked a knuckle under her chin, lifted her face back to his.

"Don't ever hide from me," he said gently. "No matter what, okay?"

She smiled, and the blush on her cheeks darkened. "Yes, Sir," she replied, standing taller again, her confidence shining through.

Toby traced his fingertips along her collarbone, enjoyed her little shiver and quick intake of breath when they glanced over the scarred flesh near her shoulder. "I enjoy hearing that word on your lips."

"Which word?" she said, her lips twitching into a secretive smile. "Sir?"

"The other one. I hope to hear it a lot tonight. Starting now," he said, folding his arms across his chest. "Get on your knees."

"Yes, Sir," she said quietly, then sank onto the cushion by his feet.

So fucking submissive.

"Good girl," he murmured, and again her eyes lit with

need. His cock twitched impatiently. "Before we begin, I want to ask you some questions about your limits and experience. Is that all right?"

Resting her hands on her knees, Lucy stared up at him. "Yes."

"Good. Firstly, you said earlier that you've had threesomes before, correct?"

"Yes."

"With two men?"

"Yes. And two women."

Charlie had taken a seat on the daybed behind them, but Lucy's answer made his ears prick up. "When you say 'two women', do you mean you were one of two women with one man, or do you mean you with two other women?"

Her grin was fast and smug, but her gaze never left Toby's. "Both."

Charlie groaned. "So fucking hot."

Toby shook his head and chuckled to himself. He shouldn't really be surprised by his brother's reaction. When it came to sex, Charlie was definitely the tamer of the pair. On the other occasions they'd shared a woman, Toby had let Charlie set the pace. They'd fucked them hard and fast and in all manner of positions, sometimes separately while the other watched, sometimes together, stuffing their playmate to overflowing with their cocks. But they'd never ventured into the heavier territories of kink. Well, except that time one brave soul had begged Toby to spank her, claiming she was an experienced submissive. He'd barely uttered the words "grab your ankles" and gotten in one good swat before she'd screamed her safeword at him and admitted her *experience* was mostly academic.

That had been a disappointing night, having his true nature inflamed only to be doused just as quickly. And while he doubted he'd have the same problem with Lucy, he needed to be sure. Hence the questions.

"Have you had anal sex?"

Chin lifting, her grin broadened. "Yes."

"Did you enjoy it."

"Very much, yes."

"When was the last time you did it?"

"With another person or by myself?"

Toby fought to hide his excitement but couldn't stop a grin from lifting one corner of his mouth. "Both."

"With another person," she said, her brow furrowed as she remembered. "About… two years, give or take."

Two years was a long time. They'd need to be careful with her, take their time preparing her. "And by yourself?"

Heat infused her cheeks once more, but she held his gaze and didn't hide her face from him. *Such a good girl.* "Yesterday."

Behind them, Charlie groaned, and Toby could hear the sound of flesh on flesh as his brother worked his cock in his hand.

As he stared down at Lucy, a wicked thought crossed his mind: Had she been thinking about him in the same way he'd been thinking about—who was he kidding, obsessing over—her?

"And yesterday, when you were fucking your own arse, were you thinking about me?"

Sinking her teeth into her bottom lip, she nodded slowly. "Yes."

Yes was fast becoming Toby's favourite word. Especially when it fell from Lucy's soft mouth.

He reached down and ran the pad of his thumb over her plush lips, grinned when she nipped at him and caught the digit between her teeth. "Lucy, are you here of your own free will?"

He already knew her answer, but it never hurt to get ongoing consent when you were about to defile a woman in all the best ways imaginable.

Her smile was broad and genuine. "Yes."

Toby let go of the breath he hadn't realised he was holding and asked Lucy one more thing. "And while you're in my house, do you agree to do as you're told, like a good little fuck toy should?"

She squirmed on the cushion by his feet, and Toby could have sworn he heard her whimper. She nodded eagerly. "Yes, Sir."

Reaching down, he cupped her scarred cheek, smiled when she leaned into his palm and rubbed against him, already drawing comfort from his touch. "I'm going to take such good care of you, baby. Now, tell me your safeword, and then we'll move on to your hard limits."

"Foxgloves," she said, and his knees trembled. *Foxgloves*. His favourite flower.

So fucking perfect.

She could have been imagining it—and probably was— but Lucy could have sworn Toby wobbled on his feet when she said her safeword. *Ridiculous*. She shoved the thought away and focused on more important things, like listing off her hard limits and hoping like hell she wasn't making a huge mistake.

Not that she was worried about Toby and Charlie hurting her, just that she really hoped her earlier hunch about Toby was correct and that he was in fact a true Dominant, a man who could satisfy all her physical wants and needs as well as her psychological ones. Because one, what was the point in being there if she wasn't going to get what she came for, and two, she genuinely liked the man and didn't want to have to look for another job purely because he'd turned out to be all show and no go and she could no longer hold any respect for him.

"I can give you what you want. I can give you what you need. And you need it, don't you, baby?"

Yes. Yes she did.

Charlie wasn't dominant. That was obvious. But he was sexy and sweet and a total voyeur if the noises coming from the daybed were any indication. And really, it was probably for the best that only one of the brothers was dominant. If Toby turned out to be as intense as she hoped he was, she wasn't sure she could handle that intensity times two.

Just then, Toby reached out and stroked the blade of his finger along the edge of her jaw. His touch was gentle, even though his hands were rough. She liked the feel of his skin on hers. It was warm and inviting, and she wanted more. Much more.

"What are your hard limits, Lucy?" Toby's voice was as gentle as his touch and just as rough.

Lucy listed off everything she'd never do, which pretty much amounted to anything illegal, anything that drew blood, and anything involving bodily fluids that weren't semen.

"And facials," she added, unable to keep the hint of venom from her voice. "They're degrading, and I won't do it."

"I thought women loved getting facials," Charlie said.

Toby chuckled. "I believe she means the porno kind, not the cosmetic kind," he said over his shoulder.

"To be honest, I'm not overly keen on the cosmetic kind either," Lucy said, drawing the big man's attention back to her. When he gave her a quizzical look, she pointed to her scars. "They don't react well to foreign substances."

His frown deepened. "Do those foreign substances include wax?"

Wax? She swallowed hard and clenched her thighs together to quash the sudden throbbing in her clit. It didn't work. "Wax is okay," she blurted, the words tripping over each other in her haste to get them out.

"I think she likes the wax idea," Charlie teased, getting to his feet. "I wonder what else she'd like."

What would she like? At this point she'd like to scream in frustration. She hadn't had sex with an actual human being in what felt like forever, and these guys were driving her crazy, dragging it out like they weren't certain she was a sure thing and they were going the extra mile to be sure she wasn't going to bolt out the door the first chance she got.

Okay, so she did, in fact, appreciate that they were taking her safety seriously and getting to know her preferences instead of simply charging into the unknown like some of the fumbling bumblers she'd come across over the years. It showed they knew what they were doing, which was gratifying, and it showed they cared about her pleasure as much as their own, which, in her experience, was rare.

But they also had to know the anticipation was killing her.

Seriously. She was naked, wet, and willing and—besides Toby's magic finger ride in the truck—neither one of them had even tried to cop a feel yet. Which, again, made for a refreshing change, but *come on!* She was crawling out of her skin with need, and they were just standing there looking like every woman's sexual fantasy come to life and...

Not. Touching. Her!

She curled her hands into fists where they rested on her knees, let her fingernails bite into the soft flesh of her palms until it hurt. Then she let the pain redirect her focus.

She could do this. No problem. If the Bennett brothers wanted to draw this out and make an evening of it, who was she to complain?

She was the woman whose last sexual encounter had been with a bloke so uninspiring she'd actually dozed off during his insipid attempt to go down on her. He'd been so insulted by her lack of enthusiasm that he'd stormed out of her house. She'd been so insulted by his lack of talent that she'd finished herself off with her bullet vibe and some internet porn.

She hadn't been back to speed dating since—not until tonight. And only because Toby Bennett had made her desperate. And now he was making her desperate and crazy.

"I think maybe she'd like us to fuck her now," Toby said, and she didn't miss the undertone of humour in his rich baritone. "What do you say, baby?"

Lucy closed her eyes and unfurled her fingers so they lay flat against her thighs. *Finally*. "Yes, please."

"Then how about you take out my cock."

Eyes snapping open, Lucy shot a quick glance at Toby's face before levelling her gaze directly in front of her. At the cock in question.

She'd gotten a glimpse of Charlie's thick length when he kicked off his jeans and moved to stand behind her again and *damn!* The man wasn't kidding when he'd said he had a big dick. He was huge. Which—*holy shit*—meant Toby's was even bigger.

"...that is one area my little brother has me beat."

As she lifted her hands to his fly, she moistened her lips with a quick flick of her tongue, then swallowed hard. Why was she so damn nervous all of a sudden? It was just a dick. She'd seen plenty of them in her forty years of life. One more was certainly no big deal.

Right?

The zipper's metallic purr sounded loud in the quiet of the conservatory, and she rolled her lips between her teeth to stop a fit of giggles from escaping.

"Everything okay down there?"

Lucy huffed out a laugh. She was being stupid. Hadn't she just been complaining they were taking too long, and now here she was dragging it out even more. And for what? Because she'd had a momentary lapse in maturity, the sound of the zipper reminding her of a funny scene from one of her favourite movies—right before it was insinuated that the hero had an enormous cock.

"Everything's fine, Sir," she said, quickly glancing up at the man towering over her.

A knowing grin decorated his handsome face, causing his eyes to crinkle in the corners, and she couldn't help but smile back. But then he cocked one brow and thrust his hips at her face, a not-so-subtle reminder of what she was supposed to be doing.

With a flick of her wrist, Lucy popped the button at Toby's waist, parted the denim flaps, and pulled his jeans down his impossibly long legs. And it was then she realised that even if she'd seen a thousand dicks in her forty years of life, she'd never seen anything that would have prepared her for Toby's. Because it wasn't *just* a dick, and it most certainly *was* a big deal.

It was the biggest freaking deal she'd ever seen.

"Dear Lord!" she breathed, pressing her hand to her

chest as if it could stop her heart from thundering its way out through her ribcage.

"Is there a problem?"

"Um... no, Sir. Not a problem. Exactly. It's just that you're, uh...." She tilted her head to the side to look at it from a different angle, as if that would somehow make it more likely to fit inside her without an intensive warm-up session first. "Well, it's just...."

"What?"

Lucy blew out a shuddering breath. "Your body is very... proportionate, isn't it?"

Toby didn't bother hiding his amusement at her observation. "Is that your way of saying I have a big dick?"

Swallowing hard, she nodded, her gaze never leaving the flawless monster in front of her face. "Yes," she said. "Yes it is."

But it wasn't just that it was big. It was, objectively speaking, gorgeous. Which was really saying something considering male genitalia was not the most attractive thing on the face of the planet. Toby's dick was long and thick, the root of it as thick as her wrist. And it wasn't overly veiny or bent at an odd angle like some she'd seen but straight as an arrow and smooth like silk, tempting her to stroke her fingers along its steely length, to taste it. To take her time and savour it.

Put simply, Tobias Bennett had the most perfectly formed dick she'd ever seen. The gold standard of cocks. Hell, even his balls looked nice.

"Lucy, baby?"

She could hear the smile in his voice and didn't have to look at him to know he was grinning at her and the look of utter wonderment on her face. "Uh-huh?"

"My eyes are up here."

"Okay," she murmured, then licked her lips again. "But you know that thing you said before, about being rendered speechless?"

His perfectly manscaped cock bounced around in front of her face as his whole body shook with laughter. "Yes."

Giving in to temptation, Lucy took the object of her desire in her hands, leaned forwards, and licked away the pearl of pre-come that had gathered at the tip. Then she looked up at him with a wicked smile and said, "Ditto."

Chapter Seven

Toby kicked his jeans away, then fisted his hands in Lucy's hair, guided his cock between her soft lips, and *faaark*....

She wrapped her mouth around his throbbing shaft with all the confidence of a woman who knew exactly what she was doing, and for all his strength of will and self-control, Toby was powerless against her.

Head falling back, he closed his eyes and let out a long, low appreciative moan.

"Tobes?"

Charlie's quiet voice pulled at him, and as much as he wanted to ignore his brother, he couldn't. They were in this together. But when he lifted his head and opened his eyes, all he saw was his twin with a kind yet knowing expression on his face.

He nodded towards the door at the far end of the conservatory, the one leading into his own house. "Maybe I should go...?"

Toby wasn't surprised by the offer. He'd made it himself often enough and always to a resounding "no". But they'd never done this before with someone they knew, someone they—*he*—was interested in on a more personal level.

Glancing down at Lucy, he watched for a moment as she bobbed back and forth, pulling his thick cock deeper with every suck. She had one hand wrapped around the root of him, the other gripped his hip, and her gaze was glued to his navel in a look of fierce concentration. Though if Toby had to guess, he'd say she was actually concentrating more on pretending not to overhear their conversation than she was on giving him a blow job.

Did he want Charlie to leave?

The whole reason they'd gone out in the first place was so Charlie could get laid, and honestly, could he really deny his brother the sheer bliss of this woman's expertise?

Yes, he realised. *Easily*. He could very easily deny his brother the ecstasy of Lucy's mouth—and the rest of her—and keep her all for himself, but as he looked down at her and caught her guarded gaze, he knew who should make the decision, and it wasn't him.

If Lucy wanted him alone, he wouldn't complain, and he knew Charlie would bow out gracefully and let them have their fun. And if she wanted them both as originally planned, that was fine too. But if she did want them both, Toby knew—as he had from the beginning—he'd have to rein in his darker impulses.

Charlie was an adventurous man but by no means a particularly kinky one. It also meant finding a way to keep Lucy in his bed long after Charlie retired for the night so he could let those darker impulses out to play.

He'd promised her, after all, that he could give her want she needed, and if he were being completely honest with himself, he needed it too.

He wouldn't be satisfied with anything less than total dominion over her.

Not when it came to Lucy Barton.

And yes, even if it could only be for one night.

"Lucy, baby," Toby said, gathering her hair in one hand and easing himself out of her mouth. He suppressed a groan when she sucked hard on the head of his cock, then let it go with a wet *pop*.

Before either Toby or Charlie could speak further, she dropped her gaze to the floor and spoke quietly. "Is it my scars?" she said. "Is that why you don't want to stay?" Her hands rested on her knees, balled into fists, and she refused to lift her head and look at them.

Charlie's jaw dropped, and the brothers shared a look of panic as they realised their misstep.

"Oh no, no, no, beautiful," his brother murmured as he crouched down beside her. "That's not it at all."

Toby joined them on the floor and cupped Lucy's cheek in his hand. "Charlie only meant...." He looked at his brother, silently imploring him for help. He'd never been very good at this type of conversation, at soothing someone's hurts.

Talking in general had never been very high on his list of priorities. He preferred action over words, a sure yet gentle caress over an indulgent platitude. And if he had to talk, he kept it brief. Or abrupt, as he'd been told on more than one occasion. Many more.

Thankfully, this was not a problem for Charlie. "I only meant that you and Toby are more suited to each other, sexually speaking, and maybe you would enjoy yourselves more without me here."

Lucy lifted her gaze to Charlie's, her expression wary,

her hands still clenched into fists. "And if I want you to stay?"

Charlie smiled kindly, then pressed a soft kiss to her lips. "Then I'll stay," he said, then grinned and added, "As long as you realise that if this"—he indicated the three of them with a wave of his hand—"was a tub of Neapolitan ice cream, I'd be the strip of vanilla."

A burst of laughter escaped Lucy, and her expression softened with the effort. "There's nothing wrong with vanilla," she said, then kissed him again.

Toby relaxed as he watched the tension ease from Lucy's posture, watched her lean into his brother's embrace and deepen their kiss.

When she pulled away, she turned to Toby, her expression hopeful. "Is it okay if Charlie stays with us?"

The fact she'd asked his permission made his blood sing through his veins, and he knew in that moment he would do whatever it took to make this woman happy. "Of course it is," he said. "Tonight is all about you, about giving *you* what you want, what you need. Okay?"

Lucy nodded, then gifted him with another full smile. "Okay." Then her smile faltered and she rested her hand over the scar that trailed down from her right shoulder, both drawing attention to and trying to conceal the damaged flesh. "And I'm sorry I jumped to conclusions. It's just that, well, you know...."

"People are dicks?" Charlie said, tugging her hand away and kissing her shoulder.

"Yeah."

"You don't have to apologise," Toby said. "We know what it's like to be the outcasts for reasons beyond your control." Cupping her face in both hands, he pulled her closer until her lips were barely a hair's breadth from his own. "I promised I'd take care of you, Lucy, and I intend to do just that. Can you—*will you*—trust me to see to your needs, with or without my brother?"

He heard her swallow hard, saw her eyes dance back and forth as she processed his words, felt her breath slip over his lips. "Yes," she whispered.

Closing the minuscule distance between them, he took her mouth in a slow-burning kiss, deep and passionate. When he pulled away, the air was filled once more with lust and wanting, an electricity that zinged between them, connecting them on a cellular level.

His heart raced with renewed anticipation as he stared into her pretty eyes. It was time to really get this show started. "Charlie, give Lucy a ride."

His brother groaned. "Fuck yeah." Then he lightly slapped Lucy's arse and urged her up on her feet so he could lie beneath her with his head on the cushion. Tilting his head back a bit so he was looking at Toby, he said, "You sure you don't want first taste? You won the game, after all."

Toby climbed to his feet, then took Lucy's hands and steadied her as she straddled Charlie's face.

"You can taste her pussy first," he said, stroking her hair like a beloved pet before twisting the long blonde strands around his fist and yanking her head backwards. Lucy's eyes rolled back and her mouth fell open on a soft moan. She liked the pain. Needed it. And he wanted to give it to her. He wanted to satisfy that dark, primal part of her, make her crave more of it, more of him. "I've found a better prize."

The instant Lucy settled in place over Charlie's mouth,

he went to town, licking and sucking and nibbling in a way that screamed "I love pussy!"

Strong hands banded around her thighs, spreading her wide and keeping her open for him to feast on. His fingers dug into her soft flesh, his fingernails leaving little weals in her skin, adding a small bite of pain and ratcheting up the pleasure he was eliciting from deep inside her.

Up one side and down the other, he licked along the creases of her legs where they joined her body, working his way closer and closer to her centre before reversing direction and moving outwards again. Over and over he did that, getting closer and closer to her clit, circling the tiny nerve-filled nub with the tip of his tongue but never actually touching it.

He was driving her crazy.

And then there was Toby.

With one hand still fisted in her hair, he bent and kissed her hard, licked inside her mouth and tangled his tongue with hers. She was breathless when he pulled away again, breathless and so fucking turned on her skin felt like it was on fire. And she would know.

Then Toby straightened to his full height and drew his cock over the seam of her mouth. "Open up, baby," he said, his voice like gravel.

Lucy obeyed, then moaned as he slowly fed the broad head of his cock between her lips once more. Gripping his hip to steady herself, she cupped his balls with the other hand. *Oh my God*—they were heavy. Toby moaned as she massaged and gently tugged on them, and she swallowed down cry after cry as Charlie's tongue finally found its mark and flicked mercilessly against her clit.

Oh God.

On the one hand, she wanted to throw her head back

like a wild thing, grind herself down on Charlie's face, and scream and curse as her orgasm took hold, but on the other hand, she was really getting off on the deep, guttural moans she was wringing from Toby as she sucked his dick and tasted his pre-come.

The man was fucking delicious.

Just then, Charlie lifted his chin and rubbed his stubble over her clit, and she almost came on the spot. Her body jerked, and she had to grab both of Toby's hips to stop herself from toppling over. Another pass of stubble over the sensitive nub had her lurching backwards, and Toby's cock slipped free from her mouth.

"Where do you think you're going, baby?" he said, tightening his hands in her hair.

"I need to come," she moaned, rocking her hips back and forth as Charlie thrashed his head from side to side. The friction, the sensation was amazing. *So close....* "Sir. Please."

One big hand wrapped around her neck, and Toby half lifted her off her knees, dragging her up by her hair and her throat, lifting her off his brother's face. She gasped and grabbed his wrists, using them to take her weight and ease the sting in her scalp. "You want to come?" he growled, bending to bring his face close to hers.

She was so wet, so turned on by his display of strength and control. "Yes, Sir. Please."

"So do I," he said, his lip lifting in a snarl as he lowered her back to her knees. "Open up and take me deep."

Warmth pooled in the pit of her stomach and her clit throbbed with urgent need, his command taking her to the edge of her control.

Mustn't come. Not... yet....

Not without permission.

Tilting her head back a little, she opened her mouth wide and took Toby's cock as deeply as she could, which was more than she'd thought she'd be able to, considering his size. His groan of pleasure as he slid deep was gratifying. His masculine growl of approval as she wove her tongue around the steel of his shaft was simply music to her ears.

Behind her, she could hear the unmistakable sound of Charlie taking his cock in hand again, the slapping of flesh on flesh adding another level of excited urgency to his muffled grunts as he continued eating her out.

Lucy closed her eyes and let the sounds of sex surround her, let the physical sensations she was feeling guide her. The nip of pain from Charlie's fingernails and the frenzied flicking of his tongue drove her to grind down on him, uncaring if he could breathe under there or not. And the sting of Toby pulling her hair and the measured thrusts of his hips made her grab his arse in both hands and pull him closer.

The pain in her scalp eased as he let go of her hair and started petting her again. Her responding moan was almost a purr and vibrated along Toby's shaft.

His breath shuddered out of him. "Eyes on me, baby," he groaned, and when she opened her eyes and looked up at him, he traced his fingertip around the jagged edge of her scars. Cutting across her forehead and over her too-short eyebrow, past the corner of her eye and then curving over the apple of her cheek, slashing across the corner of her mouth, then dipping under it to follow the swell of her lower lip before slipping down over her chin, her neck, her collarbone....

His touch made her shiver, his words even more so. "You are so goddamn beautiful."

Unlike his brother, who she suspected bandied the

word around as a means of maintaining distance from his sexual partners—*don't have to remember their names if you call them all the same thing*—when Toby said she was beautiful, Lucy actually almost believed him. The conviction in his voice as he'd growled the word had tears pricking behind her eyes, threatening to make a fool of her.

But Lucy was no one's fool. Not anymore.

She worked Toby's cock with her teeth and tongue until his breathing was as ragged as hers. Gentle scrapes with her teeth were followed by the long, slow glide of her tongue as she slipped it along the sensitive underside of his cock's bulbous head, then teased the tiny slit on the end. She tasted more pre-come. He was close.

She was closer.

Who knew where Charlie was at?

Lucy sped up her movements, bobbing back and forth like an emu on speed, and all the while she continued staring into Toby's ice blue eyes. He blinked slowly as he stared at her, as though it were taking all his concentration to control himself. She liked that, liked thinking she had that power over him, and it spurred her on even more, made her even more determined to make him come and earn his praise.

"Lucy," Toby panted. His chest rose and fell with exaggerated breaths, and his gaze bored into hers. "Come with me, baby. Come with me. Now."

And that was all the warning she got before the big man stiffened and shot his load down her throat, roaring at the glass ceiling of the conservatory like a wounded beast. But it was enough to trigger her own release, and her body clamped down hard, her thighs quivering against the side of Charlie's head as his talented tongue continued its mercenary pace against her clit.

A moment later Charlie came too, his big body shaking under hers for a few seconds before slumping against the floor.

The next thing she knew, big, warm hands were clamped around her waist and lifting her to her feet. Toby pulled her into his embrace and held her for a long moment, gently stroking his hands up and down her back while pressing kisses against her temple and hair.

"Charlie, you alive?" he murmured at the prone figure behind them.

An unintelligible grunt and a mumbled "fuck me" affirmed his brother's continued existence.

"And you, Lucy?" Toby cooed softly, petting her again. "How are you?"

Lucy snuggled against the giant man's chest and sighed contentedly. "That was quite possibly the sexiest thing I've ever done. Thank you, Sir." Then she pressed a kiss to his chest and slowly trailed her lips upwards until she was nuzzling the stubbled flesh of his jaw right below his ear, smiling all the way.

A rich chuckle rumbled through him and stretched her smile even wider, but movement behind them had her turning in his arms. She watched Charlie get to his feet. He moved quite gracefully for such a big man.

"I concur," he said, grinning at them. "That was the sexiest thing in the history of sexy things. And Tobes, just an FYI, your woman has thighs of steel. Squeezed my head so damn hard when she came I thought it was gunna pop off my shoulders."

Heat burned through Lucy's cheeks and she buried her head in Toby's chest, even as she laughed at the audacious statement. "Sorry."

"Don't be. It was hot as fuck."

Toby laughed, the rich sound almost washing away her embarrassment over Charlie's words, but it wasn't enough to stop her brain from snagging on something he'd said in particular.

"Your woman."

Did she imagine Toby's arms tighten around her when he'd said it? Surely that was just wishful thinking.

And when the fuck did she start wishing for anything more than a fun time?

One night. That was her rule. It had served its purpose for a long time, and there was no need to change things up now. No matter how sexy Tobias Bennett was, no matter how he made her feel, he was still her boss, and come Monday morning, every sexy thing in the history of sexy things would be just that.

History.

She would have catalogued her memories and filed them away in her spank bank, only to be called upon in the privacy of her own bedroom.

Because a memory was all she could afford.

"You ready to go upstairs?" Toby said, cupping her face and dragging her back from her melancholy.

"Depends," she said. "What's upstairs?" Cocking her head to one side, she stared up at him with cautious curiosity. "Do you have a secret sex room?"

Charlie shook his head, laughing. "Close enough."

Lucy sucked down a gasp of surprise. "I was kidding," she said, rubbing her thighs together as she stared up at them. "Do you actually have a sex room?"

Toby grinned wickedly, kissed her hard, then grabbed her wrist in his vice-like grip and dragged her back inside the house. "You'll see."

Chapter Eight

If Toby thought the sight of Lucy on her knees, her intoxicating gaze locked on his as they shared one hell of an orgasm, was spectacular, it paled in comparison to the look on her face as she took in his bedroom—or more accurately, one wall of his bedroom.

With her eyes wide and her fingertips pressed to her lips, she stared at his collection of whips, floggers, canes, and paddles like a starving man stared at a feast—with unabashed longing and hunger.

Toby watched with something akin to pride as Lucy took a tentative step closer to his array of accoutrements, and his cock twitched with renewed life as he watched her glide her slender fingers over his favourite riding crop. The aged brown leather was soft to the touch, the shaft supple and strong, and its leather keeper left one hell of a red welt on a shapely arse or thigh.

His cock thickened at the thought of decorating Lucy's body with such marks, of criss-crossing his way across her creamy flesh until she came, screaming her pleasure. Screaming his name.

Just then, Charlie entered the room and dumped everyone's clothes in a heap on the floor. Lucy spun away from the wall like a naughty child caught doing something, well, naughty, and Toby took the opportunity to really admire her. All of her this time, not just her face, tits and arse.

Her hair cascaded all the way down to her waist and shone under the muted bedroom lights with shades of dark blonde mixed with honey brown, reminding him of rich butterscotch. Soft to the touch, it felt good wrapped around his fist.

The unscarred half of her face was fresh and pink with no visible laugh lines until she smiled, and even then the lines softly feathering from the corners of her eye and mouth were barely noticeable. If he didn't already know she was the same age as him, he would have thought her to be much, much younger and believed himself to be a dirty old man for all the things he wanted to do to her.

Fuck, he was a dirty old man regardless.

Her body was long and lean and lightly muscled. Not surprising considering she'd once been a firefighter and listed rock climbing as a hobby. Her legs were slim and ended in feet he considered almost dainty for a woman of her height, but her arse was good and round and soft, and her hips flared out in a way that made him want to grab them hard as he drove himself into her from behind. Her waist was small, her breasts too, small and perfect, and... *fuck!* The sight of those nipple rings piercing those sweet peach-coloured nipples, the memory of them rubbing against his chest when he'd held her tightly, made his cock as hard as granite.

When he'd held her in his arms before, he'd felt the scars on her back, the ones she hid under that mass of butterscotch-coloured hair. He'd traced his hands over her skin and marvelled at the difference in texture. On the left side, her skin was unmarred and soft, smooth to the touch and supple against his palm. But the other side, like her face, neck, and shoulder, was raised slightly and uneven, but at the same time the skin there felt smoother somehow, almost silky under his fingertips.

And as he'd gently explored her scars, she'd gripped the muscles on his back, exhaled a shuddery breath, and shivered against him. She'd closed her eyes and bit her lip and pressed her body so close she'd practically moulded to his chest. But she'd neither protested nor cried out in pain.

Interesting.

A slight nod at Charlie was all he needed to get his brother moving across the room, and together they advanced on Lucy, surrounded her and touched her all over again.

Toby placed himself behind her, gathered her hair into a ponytail, and gripped it tightly in his fist. "I love your hair. It's so soft," he murmured, bending down to bury his nose in it. "Smells so good."

"Gardenias," she said with a sigh, confirming his earlier suspicion.

He tugged her head to one side, and she let loose a breathy moan that made his gut tighten and his cock twitch. Then she leaned in to him, giving him free rein as his lips met her skin and he began a leisurely exploration of her shoulder and neck.

"Toby," she gasped, his name a plea. But a plea for what? "Sir."

Keeping his voice low and calm, he said, "Your scars are very sensitive to touch, aren't they, baby?"

Lucy nodded quickly, as though she didn't want to

spare the brainpower required to provide an explanation. "Uh-huh."

Toby leaned down and kissed her, and she moaned into his mouth, but a moment later, she broke away with a gasp. A quick look over her shoulder confirmed his brother had two fingers deep in her pussy and was fingering her nice and slow. Good. Toby wanted her begging for release before they fucked her, and Charlie knew how to finger a pussy like a virtuoso knew how to finger a violin. Knew how to pluck and play and tease to make the sweetest music erupt from within her.

"Why?" Toby asked, keeping the conversation going for no other reason than to keep her off-kilter. To see in how many directions they could pull her concentration before she snapped.

"Why what?" she groaned, rocking her hips, no doubt grinding her clit against Charlie's palm. Toby landed a sharp slap on her arse, smiled when she yelped and then whimpered. "Why, Sir?"

He yanked her head back so he could watch her face, then growled in her ear. "Why are your scars more sensitive than the rest of your skin?"

Her eyelids fluttered, and her mouth hung open on a moan. "I don't... don't know," she stammered. "I read some-where that it might have something to do with the in... inconsistent way the collagen forms as the skin heals, that it traps the ne...nerve endings closer to the surface." Her voice went up an octave, the last word coming out as a squeak before she swallowed hard and her whole body shuddered.

"Don't let her come," he barked at his brother, and Lucy cried out in protest as Charlie took a step back.

His brother lifted his hand and Toby groaned when he saw how it glistened, then felt a stab of jealousy when

Charlie stuck his fingers in his mouth and sucked them clean. That was twice now Charlie had tasted her pussy, and Toby hadn't tasted her at all.

"She's so fucking wet," Charlie said, grinning even as he stared at Lucy with a look of wonder. "Gushed all over my hand when you spanked her."

Toby gripped her chin in his free hand and turned her face towards his. "Is that true?" When she nodded, he stole a hard, passionate kiss. "Good girl," he murmured against her lips. He was rewarded with a bashful smile and down-cast eyes.

So fucking sexy.

"Trapped nerved endings, huh?" Toby's grin turned wicked. "So if I were to do this...." He bent down and used the tip of his tongue to lick a slow path across her shoulder and down her back, all the way to where her scar ended at the top of her right buttock. Lucy's body shivered and shook, her hands fisted by her sides as her sultry moan filled the air. "It would make you feel... what?"

She laughed the way people did when they couldn't believe someone had asked something so dumb. "Horny."

"How horny?" Charlie asked eagerly, watching the pair of them with his lady-killer smile firmly in place and one hand wrapped around his dick. His brother wanted to get this show on the road. So did Toby.

"'If someone doesn't fuck me hard and fuck me soon, I will scream' horny," she growled through clenched teeth.

Toby moved to stand beside Charlie and folded his arms across his chest. "Hey, Charlie?"

Mimicking his stance, his brother replied, "Yes, Toby?"

"Did my little fuck toy just growl at us?"

"I believe she did."

Stepping towards her, his brow furrowed, Toby backed

Lucy up against the wall, reached behind her, and grabbed his riding crop. When he held it up in front of her face, her eyes momentarily widened with fear, then almost immediately shuttered with pleasure.

Bless her little masochistic heart.

She was probably going to enjoy this even more than he was.

"Get on the bed."

Toby barked the command, and Lucy obeyed.

"Yes, Sir," she said, moving quickly to sit on the end of the biggest freaking bed she'd ever seen in her life.

Honestly, it must have been custom-made, because it looked to be about eight feet square and sat nestled in a solid-looking timber frame with four thick posts rising up from the corners. There was no canopy stretched across the top of them, however, but large wrought-iron rings secured near the top and bottom of each post.

A sudden rush of arousal at the sight of those metal rings had Lucy squeezing her thighs together and wishing that someone would hurry up and fuck her.

She was so damn close to begging for it, the words perched on the tip of her tongue, ready to slip free at a moment's notice.

Take me. Use me. Fuck me. Please!

"On your hands and knees, baby," Toby directed. "Face the bottom end of the bed. That's it. That's my good girl."

Her insides lit up like fireworks every time he uttered those words, leaving her feeling warm and happy.

"Good girl."

If anyone else had said them to her, she'd have told them

to fuck off. But when Tobias Bennett told her she was a good girl, her objections to the condescending title melted faster than ice cream in January.

She was *not* a girl. And she was far from good.

But he was just so damn imposing, so bossy, and that deep voice of his resonated with restrained power making every command he issued sexy as fuck. *Get in the truck? Sure. Suck your cock? It would be my pleasure. Get on the bed while you stalk towards me with a riding crop in your hand and a devilish glint in your arctic eyes? Ahh, okay!*

Lucy was beginning to think she'd checked her brain at the door, because what she was doing was so far off script from her usual one-night stand behaviour it wasn't funny. She couldn't even remember the last time she'd had a three-some, let alone one with two of the hottest men she'd ever met, both intent on pleasuring her until she screamed in ecstasy.

Had that ever happened?

And what in the ever-loving hell was she doing in her boss's house, in her boss's bed, with her boss and his twin brother?

Although, you know... *twins*. So that was one more item ticked off the ol' fuck-et list.

Yep. She'd definitely left the smarter portion of her brain at home. It was either that or the more primal part of her brain had simply hijacked her good sense and taken advantage of the rare opportunity she'd been presented with, knowing she'd overthink it and chicken out at the last moment if it didn't.

"I'm not your boss, Lucy... Not tonight."

No, Tobias Bennett wasn't her boss. Not technically, anyway. Not until she signed the employee contract on Monday morning. Until then he was just a Dom. A Dom she'd found at a freaking speed dating event, of all places, the odds of which were like finding a million-dollar diamond ring at a flea market.

She knew if she hadn't grabbed what was probably her only chance to be with him in both hands, she'd have kicked her own arse all the way to Timbuktu while dragging the heavy weight of regret behind her.

Because, to be completely honest, her usual date night conquests tended to be vanilla through and through. There hadn't been a single kinkster amongst them, which was just another reason why she didn't bother going out all that much anymore.

And the local BDSM scene left much to be desired. Populated with gossips, bullies, and try-hards, it had reminded her of high school, only dressed in fishnets and black PVC corsets, like a budget production of the *Rocky Horror Picture Show*.

The few genuine Dominants she'd met over the years had been in high demand and had made it abundantly clear she was not high on their list of priorities. So Lucy had preferred to go without rather than sit around waiting for someone to give her whatever scraps of attention they had to spare.

She'd spent enough of her life doing that, waiting for her bipolar mother and her indifferent workaholic father to acknowledge her existence.

She didn't wait for anyone anymore.

At least that was what she liked to tell herself, and in most situations, it was true. But she was beginning to realise this was not one of those situations.

As soon as she was in position, the mattress dipped and bounced as Toby crawled into the centre of the bed and knelt behind her. Anticipation started as a tingle in the base of her spine, and she tried to guess what he'd do next.

Would he use the crop without warning and paint her arse with red stripes? Or would he spank her first, warm her flesh and give it a pink glow? How hard would he strike her? And when would he fuck her, finally filling her with that beast of a cock? All of these questions and more raced through Lucy's head as she waited.

And waited.

Annnd waited.

Lucy knew only a minute or two had actually passed, but when the sexiest man alive was kneeling behind her, naked as the day he was born, blessed with an erection that would make the gods weep, and still not touching her, it felt like a freaking eternity.

What the hell was Toby doing back there? Was he trying to make her crazy? Was this all part of her punishment for growling at him?

She worried at her bottom lip and fought the urge to fidget.

She failed and wriggled her hips, clenched her buttocks, unsure if she was dreading the fall of the riding crop or eagerly anticipating it.

Charlie stood at the foot of the bed, his hands anchored on his slim hips, watching her squirm. "What's wrong, beautiful? You want this?" He reached down with one hand and stroked himself. "Or something else?"

Rolling her lips between her teeth, Lucy stared at his gorgeous cock. It wasn't as big as Toby's, but it was still damn impressive. Bigger than average and pointed directly at her. Lucy slowly nodded, then licked her lips. Yes, she wanted it, but he stood too far back for her to have it.

Flicking her gaze upwards, she caught sight of Charlie's

grin, that sexy-as-fuck smile that made her feel pretty just because it was aimed at her. She wondered how a man with a smile like that wasn't drowning in pussy and needed something as pedestrian as speed dating, the last refuge of the lonely and desperate.

But when she opened her mouth to speak, she felt the first lick of fire against her arse and screamed instead.

"I think five should do the trick, don't you?" Toby said from behind her, followed by, "Charlie, put something in her mouth to keep her quiet."

His brother winked at her, then stepped closer. "Open up, Lucy. Show me how you made my brother come." Gripping her chin between his thumb and forefinger, he added, "No biting."

"No promises." She grinned, then opened her mouth wide.

Charlie smirked. "Cheeky."

As soon as the head of his cock hit her tongue, the second blow of the riding crop hit its mark, and the most delicious burn began to spread over her flesh.

Lucy's cries were muffled, but each thwack of the leather against her body made her jerk forwards, lodging more of Charlie's cock in her mouth. She whimpered, Charlie moaned, and Toby smoothed his big hand over the welts on her arse, making her shiver under his gentle caress. His calluses stood out more sharply against the overstimulated flesh, and she wondered what they'd feel like when he cupped her breasts and rubbed them against her piercings. Something else he had yet to do.

It was almost like he knew where she wanted him to touch her most and was deliberately avoiding those places. As if he knew denying her his touch would drive her nuts and make her crave him more. Which as an experienced

Dom—and Lucy no longer doubted that Toby was experienced—he would know.

Sneaky bastard.

He was *trying* to make her beg!

And he was bloody close to succeeding.

Normally she'd try to fight it, might even be a brat about it and push Toby's buttons, earn a little extra punishment, but it had taken her too long to figure out his plan, and she was beyond primed.

Lucy was ready to explode.

Chapter Nine

When the fourth blow landed, Lucy was so close to coming she wanted to cry. Her elbows buckled, and Charlie's cock slipped from her mouth as her upper half collapsed against the bed. Her nipples grazed the bedding and she moaned loudly, the friction a delicious buzz of sensation that made her breasts tingle and tighten.

"Up," Toby snapped. "Hold your position until I tell you otherwise."

Arms shaking under the strain of her own weight, Lucy groaned but did as she was told. "Yes, Sir."

As soon as she was in position again, the fifth and final blow scorched across her flesh. Lucy cried out even as her mind slipped sideways. That was the only way she knew how to describe the sensation.

Subspace.

It was an amazing state of consciousness where she felt so calm, so languid, yet so... blissful. And the fact she felt it here and now told her more than she could have hoped for.

Her mouth hung open and her eyelids shuttered. Her thighs clenched and her body quivered.

So close....

"Holy shit!" Charlie breathed.

"What?"

Cupping her chin, he lifted her face, but Lucy was too buzzed to notice him. "I think she's gunna come. You haven't even fucked her yet and I think she's gunna come."

Two big hands gripped her hips, a sizeable cock nestled against her arse, and a warm body pressed against her back. "Are you going to come for me, baby?" Toby murmured, his warm breath tickling the scar that curved around the shell of her ear. "If I touch you like this—"

He slid one hand between her legs, stroked his finger through her slick cunt and over her clit, and anything else he might have said was lost as Lucy's orgasm exploded into being, obliterating her high by taking her even higher.

Her whole body shook as she splintered apart. Her fingers curled into the bedding, and her limbs trembled with the effort of holding herself up as Toby had commanded. He touched her with such a sure, steady hand, rubbed her clit with an exacting motion that made her eyelids flutter and her mouth fall open to emit a sound she wasn't even certain was human.

It felt so fucking good, as though every nerve ending in her body had sprung to attention all at once to salute their new master. And she was helpless to stop them. Not that she wanted to because—

"Oh my God!" she screamed as another ripple of ecstasy spread through her, making her back bow and her thighs clench around Toby's hand, making him chuckle behind her.

Wet, open-mouthed kisses rained down on her,

following the length of her spine. Warm, strong hands grazed her sides and down her legs, latched onto her ankles and flipped her over, and then there he was, looming over her spent body.

Toby. Sir. His expression stoic, his gaze ever watchful as he glanced down her body and back again.

Lucy smiled at him, happy and content as her orgasm faded and a deep, languorous feeling stole over her.

But they weren't finished yet.

"Charlie, condoms, top drawer."

"No." The word was out of her mouth before she could think better of it. Then she said it again, more deliberately. "No."

Toby's eyebrows arched into his hairline, and he shared a long look with his brother. When he returned his questioning gaze to hers, he said, "You don't want to fuck?"

"Yes. I mean no. I mean... I want to fuck, Sir."

Toby engaged in another silent exchange with his brother, then looked back at her. "But you want to go bareback?"

She did. She really, really did. Even though she knew it was reckless, even though the common-sense part of her brain screamed at her to change her mind, Lucy wanted to know what it felt like. Just once.

Forty years old and she'd never had unprotected sex.

Then again, she'd never wanted to before now. But something about Toby and Charlie—mostly Toby—told her she'd be safe with them and had been all night.

Maybe it was the sheer size of them or the way they hadn't hesitated to come to her aid earlier, but not a single warning bell had gone off in her head, and not once had she looked for the exit. Not since Toby had thrown her over his shoulder and waltzed her out of that pub, anyway.

Hell, she'd achieved *subspace* in his hands. She wanted more of that. She wanted more of him. And if one night was all she had to indulge her baser desires, she wasn't holding anything back.

"Is that all right?" she asked, her gaze flicking between the brothers. "It's just that I've never done it before, you know? Not used a condom? I want to know how it feels." Then she shook her head, realising what she was asking of them. "You know what? Forget about it. It was a stupid idea. You're right. Safety first."

There was a moment of silence, then, "I haven't been with anyone since the last time I got tested," Charlie offered with a slight shrug.

"Me either." A smile lifted one corner of Toby's mouth.

Lucy let go of the breath she'd been holding. "That makes three of us."

Charlie chuckled quietly and scratched his head. "I guess we should have had this conversation earlier, huh? Possibly *before* we started going down on each other."

Toby's smile slipped. "Birth control?"

She pointed to the inside of her upper arm. "I have the rod. I'm good to go."

Toby gripped her upper arm and slid his thumb back and forth over the matchstick-sized implant resting just under her skin. His gaze flicked back to hers. "Are you sure —*really* sure—you want this? You can change your mind at any time."

Letting her legs fall open in blatant invitation, she smiled and held out her arms to him, beckoned him to join her. "Yes." Begged him to fuck her. "*Please.*"

Toby smiled down at the gorgeous woman in his bed, loving the sultry tone of her voice. Next to the words 'yes' and 'sir', hearing the word 'please' fall from Lucy's lips was like a shot of pure adrenaline.

"Please."

It was the catalyst that set everything in motion.

In the time it took between one breath and the next, Toby was on top of her, slipping his tongue inside her mouth as he fisted his cock and fed the hard length of it into the tight, silken embrace of her cunt. She was so wet, so warm, and as he moved his hips and began the slow erotic glide of his body inside hers, he felt ten feet tall and bulletproof.

He felt like he could conquer the world.

Never had a woman responded to him as beautifully as Lucy Barton. Never had he wanted a woman as much as he wanted her right then in that moment.

"Heaven," he whispered as he pulled his mouth away from hers. "Sweet fucking heaven."

Kissing and nibbling, he followed the line of her jaw, then bit down hard on her earlobe. He enjoyed her cry of pain. "You're perfect," he whispered in her ear.

Lucy groaned. "And you're... huge!"

Toby chuckled. "I'm not *that* big."

"Nine inches at least, if I had to guess." She gasped, her back bowing, pushing her breasts against his chest. He smiled lazily at the feel of her tightly pebbled nipples rubbing against him, teasing him with sensual possibility.

"Ten, actually." He thrust deep to prove his point. "But who's counting?"

Charlie snorted and shook his head. "Stop bragging and give me a hand."

Toby grinned at his twin, then kissed Lucy hard. "Come here, baby."

It was the work of a moment to reverse their positions and settle her weight on top of him, and he groaned as she sank down on his cock, all the way down until he bottomed out inside her.

"Oh God," she breathed, right before another orgasm took hold of her.

Her body clamped down on his, squeezing him like a vice. She shuddered and moaned and was so lost to the pleasure, Toby doubted she'd even noticed Charlie join them on the bed. Settling in behind her, his brother kissed her shoulders and neck, but when he slid his hands around her waist and up over her ribs, Toby saw red.

"Don't touch her tits," he snarled. "They're mine."

His brother laughed but reversed the direction of his wandering hands.

Keeping his pace steady so Charlie could do what was needed, Toby rolled his hips as Lucy rocked hers, groaning every time they met in the middle and she ground herself down on him.

He loved the feel of her tight little body wrapped around his, revelled in the feel of her fingers curling into his flesh, her fingernails leaving tiny weals in his pecs where she leaned on his chest to hold herself up. Her dark golden hair fell down her back and around her shoulders, and her head lolled forwards as she moaned his name.

"Toby, Sir. Touch me. *Please.*"

His breathing came in harsh bursts, the sound of Lucy's plea, the sight of her riding him like Lady fucking Godiva so erotic he couldn't resist her any longer. Every thrust of his hips made those twin globes of pierced perfection dance before him—*sexy as sin*—and he slid his hands up her body until he cupped them in his palms. He loved how soft she felt. Not just her skin but her. Soft and warm and pliable. Even her little metal piercings had been warmed by the heat of her flesh.

"I feel like a giant," he said, staring at his big hands and how they completely enveloped her petite breasts.

Lucy laughed, put her smaller hands over his, and encouraged him to massage her flesh, then moaned low in her throat when he gave in to her silent demand and squeezed them hard. His cock swelled and twitched inside her, the sound of her pleasure doing indecent things to him.

Charlie, of course, chose that precise moment to peer over Lucy's shoulder. "She's ready."

None too gently, Toby tugged on Lucy's nipples until she lay flat against his broad chest. Then he wrapped his arms around her and held her down, groaned when her lips found his.

She kissed him at a leisurely pace, only stopping for a moment to breathe through the act of Charlie slowly filling her arse with his cock. Her eyes fluttered closed, and her teeth sank into her lower lip.

Toby petted her, soothed her. "Look at me, baby."

She obeyed and opened her eyes, then sucked down a breath that appeared to restore her equilibrium, because the next words out of her mouth had both brothers grinning from ear to ear, a grin she returned without reservation.

"Let's fuck."

It didn't take long to find their rhythm, for the three of them to match their thrusts, their moans, and their cries of pleasure.

Lucy's mouth was on Toby's again, her tongue slipping along the length of his own. His hand was wedged between their bodies, alternately fingering her clit with rough strokes that made her whimper and pinching it hard until she screamed. Charlie gripped her hips in his strong hands, his fingers spread wide, anchoring him to her. He pumped his body into hers, relentless in his task.

They both were.

And when Lucy shattered all around them, when she cried out her pleasure and Toby saw tears slip down her cheeks, and when her body shook again as another orgasm gripped her in its thrall, he knew he'd never be the same again.

"Fuck!" Charlie chanted quietly. "Fuck. Fuck. Fuck."

Then Charlie slammed his body against Lucy's and held still as he came, and Toby followed only seconds later, his climax so intense it almost hurt.

For a long moment afterwards, the only sounds he heard were those of Lucy and Charlie breathing, kissing, and that of the blood still rushing through his own ears as his heartbeat slowed to normal.

Cupping Lucy's head, he took in her blissed-out smile and her hooded whisky-coloured eyes that called to him in their own intoxicating way.

"Mine," he breathed across her cheeks, kissing away her tears. "You're all mine."

Chapter Ten

L ucy felt rather than saw Charlie slip from the bed. She was exhausted, completely and thoroughly fucked—literally—and could barely keep her eyes open, but she felt like she should say something to him. Call him back for a cuddle, at the very least thank him for helping his brother rock her world. But then she heard the sound of a shower running and found herself being lifted in Toby's strong arms.

"What the—"

The big man nuzzled her cheek, and a shot of something warm and fuzzy speared right through her. "Time to clean you up, dirty girl."

Good God, she loved the sound of that. Not just the part about getting clean but the part where Toby called her a dirty girl in that sexy baritone. Yeah, that was pretty awesome too.

And that wasn't good.

One night only.

That was the rule.

Getting attached was a bad idea.

Sure, Toby was a sensual, Dominant sex god who just happened to be hung like a freaking horse, but it really didn't matter that she hadn't signed the employee contract yet. He was, for all intents and purposes, her boss. He had power over her that had nothing to do with freaky sexy fun time and everything to do with a paycheque and a diminishing level of respect.

Before she could process the negative thoughts that had suddenly resurfaced now she had nothing more pleasurable to distract herself with, Toby walked them inside the biggest shower she'd ever seen in her life and put her on her feet. Taking a moment to look around proved almost as awe-inspiring as the first time she saw Toby's dick, and one word sprang to mind.

Enormous.

His shower was as big as her entire bathroom, decorated entirely in black stone and sleek chrome fixtures, and had a staggering array of directional showerheads lining both sides of the open-ended space.

"I feel like I'm about to be decontaminated and checked over for alien implants."

Toby laughed and Charlie smirked, no doubt a retort about anal probes on the tip of his talented tongue.

"Hopefully this will be a little more enjoyable than that," Toby said.

Lucy groaned. "More sex?"

Judging by the tone of her voice, anyone would be forgiven for thinking she was unwilling to bang the Bennett brothers again so soon after their last bout.

Nothing could be further from the truth, but she ached in places she hadn't ached in years. And as interested as she was by the prospect of having mind-blowing sex in the shower, her pussy needed a rest. The poor girl had earned it.

"No more sex for now, baby. Just relax and let me take care of you."

A prickling sensation in her nose warned her more tears were imminent, only this time they weren't from an orgasm so intense it threatened to send her blind.

"Let me take care of you."

No one had said those words to her in a very long time, and they'd never been said with such... affection.

That warm, fuzzy feeling rose up in her again, shoving her doubts out of the way and daring her to take a chance on this intriguing man.

No. Rules exist for a reason.

Her days of taking chances with her heart were long gone.

Gentle hands directed her under a spray of hot water, and Lucy closed her eyes and turned her face into the cleansing stream. Firm hands worked her over from the tips of her toes to the top of her head, cleaned her skin and washed her hair, then massaged her tired muscles until she didn't feel quite so tired anymore.

By the time Toby shut the water off, a spark of wanting had bloomed inside her.

More than a spark.

Taking his hand, she followed him out of the shower and let him wrap her in a huge bath towel. She almost felt like a doll, letting him take care of her that way, letting him dry her and touch her. Play with her.

When she looked up at him, she saw a softness that hadn't been there earlier. It was... not unnerving exactly, more that it frightened her how much she liked him looking at her that way. Like she was precious to him.

A girl could get used to being looked at like that.

If only it could last.

When Toby finished drying her, he pressed a kiss to her forehead and held her tightly, his naked body notching against hers in a most enticing way.

"I owe you an apology."

Lucy frowned, confused. "What for?"

"For being reckless with your safety. Charlie's right. We should have had that conversation well before we did anything else, but I was just—" He growled low in his throat. He looked annoyed.

"You were just what?"

"I was just so fucking eager to have you that I ignored everything else." He huffed out a laugh, a disbelieving sound. "I guess I could blame it on being out of practice, but the truth is I was selfish. And I'm sorry. It won't happen again." He pecked her on the lips. "Your safety comes first."

Lucy smiled, sliding her hands over his chest and around his neck. "Whoever said chivalry is dead has obviously never met you." She chuckled. "You're not infallible, Toby, and I'm a big girl, quite capable of accepting my portion of the blame." When he frowned at her, she added, "You weren't the only one who was too eager for their own good, and to be completely honest, it wasn't the most reckless thing I've ever done without my clothes on."

Toby's frown melted away, a grin taking its place. "I'm guessing there's a story in that."

She opened her mouth to say something witty, but warm lips crashed down on hers and she moaned instead, parting her lips and letting herself get carried away—all the way back to the bedroom.

He released her with a hard smack on her arse that

made her flesh burn and her clit throb. "I'll be back in a sec."

He disappeared through the bedroom door, and she listened to his heavy footfalls as he jogged down the timber stairs. With a quick glance around the room, she realised Charlie wasn't there either. Where had they disappeared to? What were they doing? And...

"Where are my clothes?" The pile of belongings Charlie had dropped on the floor earlier had magically disappeared. Rubbing her arms to ward off a chill, she walked to the doorway and called out, "Toby? Charlie?"

Charlie's voice drifted up from downstairs. "We'll be back in a minute, beautiful. Just make yourself comfortable."

"Um... okay," she said to the empty room. Except now that she had the opportunity to look around without the distraction of two huge, sexy men sucking up all her brainpower, she saw the room wasn't all that empty, and it wasn't exactly a room.

Toby's bedroom, like everything else about the man, was bigger than most. It was more appropriate to call it a suite with its large en suite bathroom, the huge bed, a tall dresser, and a wide bay window with a built in seat big enough for two.

An intricate bonsai tree in a beautiful red pot was the only splash of colour in the otherwise grey and white room. It sat in the centre of the coffee table in front of the window seat, beside a pile of gardening books stacked neatly and organised by size.

In fact, besides the sex-rumpled bed, everything was neat and tidy and in its place. Even the dark timber floorboards looked squeaky clean. And it reminded her of home. Was this what her house looked like to outsiders? Not just tidy but almost... sterile? She'd almost say it was devoid of character, until she remembered *the wall*.

Spotting the riding crop on the floor, Lucy picked it up and returned it to its home amongst the rest of Toby's collection, then stood back and tried to take it all in. There were so many different whips and floggers, paddles made from leather, wood, and a particularly nasty one made from metal. Handcuffs and leather restraints, ball gags, leg spreaders, and canes of various thickness all lined up in neat rows like kinky soldiers on parade.

And all of it made her imagination soar and her thighs clench around an empty pussy. Well, all except that metal paddle. That thing was the stuff of nightmares.

"Here we go."

Toby walked through the door, gloriously naked, carrying a platter of food. Charlie, who was completely dressed, followed him in with a tea tray and set it down on the coffee table.

"There's only two cups?"

"I'm off to bed," Charlie said with an apologetic smile. "I have a lot of work to do this weekend and need my beauty sleep." He kissed Lucy's cheek and took her hands in his, giving them a tiny squeeze. "Thanks for tonight, beautiful. I had a lot of fun." Then he looked at his brother. "See you for breakfast?"

"You better," Toby said, pouring tea. "You're cooking."

Charlie laughed, then left the room, and Lucy suddenly felt very... exposed.

It wasn't so bad with Charlie there to act as a buffer against the quiet intensity of Toby—that was why she'd agreed to let him join them in the first place, why she'd asked him to stay—but without him, her nerves slowly worked themselves into a frenzy until her hands fidgeted by her sides and she gnawed on her bottom lip.

It wasn't until he spoke that she realised she was still staring at the empty doorway, wondering if it was too late to drag Charlie back into the room and hide behind him.

"Come and sit with me."

Lucy turned to find Toby sitting on the window-seat, looking completely at ease with one ankle resting on the opposite knee, his flaccid cock nestled between strong thighs and a fine china teacup with roses painted on the side in his big hands. He was a grown man having a tea party.

A naked tea party with his doll.

No, not his doll. His *fuck toy*.

His fuck toy.

"You're mine."

Suspicion slid through her mind, and she narrowed her eyes. "Does Charlie really have to work this weekend, or did you tell him to leave?"

Toby raised one stern brow and her knees felt weak. *So sexy*. She reached out and placed her hand on a bedpost to steady herself and hoped it looked casual.

"Are you afraid to be alone with me?"

She didn't miss the challenge in his voice.

Yes. "No."

His other brow joined the first as he continued staring at her, as though he could sense her lie and was looking for confirmation. Whatever he saw, he didn't seem worried by it. He patted the seat cushion beside him. "Then come here. Sit down and let me take care of you."

Unable to think of a reason to refuse and uncertain she even wanted to, Lucy took the seat beside Toby and accepted the cup of tea he'd made for her.

She felt... weird. The whole situation was weird.

Since when did she stick around for a cup of tea and snacks after sex? Hell, since when did she stick around for a shower? Once the deed was done, she'd always been happy to leave, and the bloke in question had always been happy to let her. More than happy. So what was with the tea and crumpets? And why did she feel... flattered?

Still, all the niceties in the world didn't change the fact that this was a one-and-done deal. She'd told him as much at the pub.

"After this cuppa though, I really should go too," she said, staring at the fruit and cheese platter he'd brought for them to share, drool pooling in her mouth at the sight of the finely cut prosciutto, blue cheese, and— "Honey-roasted macadamias!"

Before she could put her teacup down and grab a handful of assorted fare, Toby snatched up the nuts and offered them to her lips, smiling serenely as she accepted them, as though she were doing him proud by letting him feed her. Her cheeks heated and she looked away from him as she chewed, away from the intensity of his stare.

"You're not used to this, are you?" Deep yet soft, his voice soothed her anxiety, if not her embarrassment, as he fed her a bite of cheese atop a thin slice of pear. The delicate flavours exploded in her mouth, and she closed her eyes and moaned, Toby's question shoved aside by the sudden rapaciousness of her stomach.

"More."

Holding another morsel in front of her mouth, Toby said, "Answer my question." Lucy leaned forwards to take the fruit from his fingertips, but he snatched it away, grinning when she growled at him. *Shit. What was the question?* "You're not used to this, are you?"

Caution warred with hunger, and she sounded snippy as she asked, "Used to what?"

"Being intimate with someone."

Lucy snorted and crossed her arms. "I'm intimate with people all the time." And she wasn't going to apologise for it no matter how much society said she should. Sex gave her what she needed: an hour or two of physical interaction with another human being and a bit of mindless pleasure. It cleared the cobwebs from the body, mind and soul and best of all, nobody got hurt. She lifted her chin in an obstinate tilt.

What more could she possibly need?

"I'm not talking about sex," Toby murmured. He stroked her hair, her cheek. Leaned in and kissed her with slow and deliberate purpose. Left her panting for more when he pulled away and finally fed her the plump strawberry he'd snatched away. "I'm talking about the stuff that comes between the orgasms."

She cocked one brow. "Like having tea?"

"Amongst other things," he said, grinning as though he could see through her cunning disguise of false bravado, which she realised as his pale gaze drifted languorously over her from head to toe, he probably could.

Swallowing hard, Lucy felt her cheeks heat again. How did he do that, see right through her bullshit? Men were not supposed to be that insightful. Not in her experience. It frightened her. Intimacy frightened her. Toby's version of it anyway.

"I need to go." But she couldn't find the will to move.

Toby growled quietly, the sound unsettling in its softness. "Stay with me."

Lucy straightened her spine against her need to submit to his demand. "One night only, remember?"

"The night isn't over yet, baby."

"Then why did Charlie leave?"

Slow and wicked, a smile stretched across his face, and Lucy went very still. "So I can defile you in all the ways my brother can't handle," he said. "In all the ways I've dreamed of doing since you walked through my office door." His grin turned predatory. "Or did you think my toys were all for show?"

Chapter Eleven

———————————————

Toby awoke with a yawn and stretched his long body, then rolled over and smiled at the warm bundle of woman sleeping on her stomach beside him. Her long dirty-blonde hair splayed out in all directions, as did her limbs. Lucy was a bed hog. Easily forgivable, as he supposed that she, like he, lived and slept alone most of the time.

The sheet was bunched around her waist, exposing her back, and one arm hung over the edge of the bed. She had one leg on top of the covers and one leg under them, but her foot still poked out from the bottom of the sheet. She wasn't just a bed hog, she was a restless sleeper too. More than once he'd heard her mumble in her sleep, like she was talking to someone, only to suddenly cry out and then promptly fall silent again.

Perhaps that was why she didn't want to stay the night. She didn't want him to witness her nightmares. Which begged the questions, how often did she have these nightmares, and who was she talking to before she cried out? And would she let him keep his promise to take care of her beyond what they'd already done?

He may have seen to her physical needs, but through the night it had become obvious she needed more care than that.

Lucy Barton was a fascinating and complex woman, the sexy submissive he'd pleasured all night long totally at odds with the uptight totalitarian he'd met in his office. And he wanted to know more. He wanted to know everything about her. But right now, his dick was rock-hard, and he wanted to fuck.

Brushing her hair aside, Toby leaned over her and kissed her back, trailing his lips along her spine and around the jagged edges of her scars. She shifted and moaned but didn't rouse more than that. With a smile, he tried harder to wake her and pushed the sheet down to expose the glorious rounds of her perfect arse.

He'd gone to great lengths not to mark her during their play session, to leave her skin clean and clear of bruises, but he knew she'd still be tender and smiled knowing she'd think of him every time she sat down.

Toby stroked his hands over her body and enjoyed her softness. She was fit and healthy, and he could feel firm muscle under her soft skin. He was tempted to spank her but leaned down and continued trailing kisses instead. He paid close attention to the crease at the top of her thigh, right where her leg joined her arse.

During their play session, he'd discovered that crease was a particularly ticklish spot for her, and when he lightly ran the tip of his tongue over the area, she kicked her legs and twisted her body as she suddenly sat up, almost sitting on him in the process.

Two dark amber eyes glared up at him, and her voice was a sleep-roughened snarl. "What are you doing?"

"Time to wake up, baby."

She flopped back on the pillows. "Just gimme five more minutes, and then I'll get out of your hair."

Toby chuckled. "Get out of my hair?"

Lucy threw her arm over her eyes and groaned. "I promise I'll leave, okay? I just want a few more minutes to enjoy this big comfy bed."

"Just the bed?"

Her arm shifted just enough that she could peek out from behind it, and her lips curled up in that wicked way he was coming to recognise as a prelude to her surrender. A smile that said she was interested, didn't want to appear too eager, but was open to persuasion.

"Depends. Is there something you think I'd enjoy *more* than the bed? I mean, come on, this is a pretty freaking awesome bed."

It was too. His older brother and interior designer extraordinaire, Crispin, had designed and built the entire suite of bedroom furniture, from the tallboy and the bedside tables to the coffee table and the enormous custom bed. A bed built for someone of Toby's size and sleeping habits.

Lucy wasn't the only one who liked to spread out when they slept.

Returning her grin, he said, "I can think of one or two things you might like." Then he slid farther down the bed and positioned himself between her thighs so his chin rested on her hairless mound. She giggled when he brushed his stubble over her soft skin, and the sweetly feminine sound ignited his lust.

A flick of his tongue against Lucy's clit was all the warning he gave before devouring her sweet pussy. He'd gone down on her twice the night before and would have happily spent most of their play session eating her out. Her flavour was like a drug. A highly addictive narcotic that had slipped through his veins and sent his passions into overdrive. But after he'd forced her to orgasm multiple times, she'd begged him to stop, her pleasure/pain response edging more into pain than pleasure and her whole body twitching like one giant exposed nerve.

He'd quietened her need and settled her down with one final fuck, had filled her arse with his cock and slowly spooned her, had cradled her body against his chest and committed every curve, every hollow, and every blessed imperfection to memory.

He'd petted her and soothed her and told her what a good girl she was, and she'd come undone so beautifully, mewling his name. Then she'd turned in his arms, a sweaty, graceful, tear-stained mess, and snuggled against him. She'd shivered and clung to him, and he'd stroked one big hand up and down her back until her shivering stopped, until she'd lifted her head, smiled at him, and whispered, "Thank you, Sir."

Now as he ate her out, as he drank in her sweet scent and lavished her clit with pinpoint accuracy, she gripped his hair and bucked her hips against his face, and Toby was in heaven. That was the only way he could describe it.

Sex with Lucy Barton was his own personal heaven.

He'd never been with a woman as responsive as her, as open as she was to all he had to give her. And her appetite for sex rivalled his own.

That was one of the reasons he'd chosen to be single for as long as he had. He'd never found a woman who'd enjoyed sex—his brand of sex—as much as he did. And to find one now was... *exhilarating.*

"Toby!"

Lucy's thighs clamped around his head, and he chuckled against her pussy as she came. Charlie hadn't been wrong when he'd said Lucy had thighs of steel. He could feel his brain being squished inside his skull. And he didn't care. Not if it meant listening to his woman's husky cries of pleasure as he lapped at her cunt and drank down her essence. Fuck, he could stay between this woman's thighs all day.

All week.

Forever.

One night with this woman and he was hooked.

But her? Not so much. *"One night only."* That was what she'd said, and more than once. And she'd just followed that up with *"I promise I'll leave"*, as though now they'd had their fun, he was counting down the minutes until he could be rid of her.

Nothing could be further from the truth.

"I don't want you to leave."

She snorted. "Said no man ever."

He sat back on his heels. "I'm serious. I want you to spend the weekend with me."

Lucy blinked up at him, her eyes narrowed with caution. "Why?"

Was *she* serious? For hours they'd shared the most mind-blowing sex of his existence, and she wanted to know why he was asking her to stay?

Not sure what to make of her reaction to his proposal, Toby yanked her into the centre of the bed and straddled her hips. Instinct told him if he pushed her too hard, she'd run. But if he didn't push, at least a little, he'd be doing them both a disservice.

He shot for the middle ground and told her the truth,

just not the reasons behind it. Because if he were being completely honest with himself, he didn't fully understand his reasons either.

"Because I promised to take care of you, Lucy. I promised to give you what you needed, and I haven't done that yet. Not completely. So I want you to stay for the weekend." He leaned forwards and threaded his fingers through hers, pinned her hands to the bed and stared down at her pretty face. Longed to lean in closer and kiss that tiny sneer at the corner of her mouth. "Allow me to keep my promise."

Lucy chewed on her bottom lip, her whisky gaze searching his face with an intensity he rarely saw directed at him. "Is that an order?"

Toby arched one brow. "Do you need it to be?"

More lip chewing was quickly followed by a brief yet vigorous nod. "Yes."

He fought to hide a smile, then shook his head. "I can't make that decision for you. If you stay, it's because you want to be with me. No other reason. Do you understand?"

Lucy understood perfectly.

If she wanted to spend the weekend with the sex god formerly known as Tobias Bennett, she had to overcome her own personal demons and trust a virtual stranger not to fuck her in the arse, figuratively speaking.

You trusted him with your body. Trusted him enough to ride him bareback.

The thoughts whispered through her mind, then circled back and skated through again with more confidence and volume.

That was lust, not trust, she reminded herself before the

traitorous thought could become an endless loop designed to mess with her sanity.

Lust required getting naked.

Trust required being stripped bare.

Big difference.

And the look in Toby's eyes as he stared down at her, stern and silent as he waited for her answer, left no room for doubts. He'd already shown her he'd settle for nothing less than the latter with their intimate tea party the previous night, and he didn't just want her naked.

Eventually she nodded. "I understand, Sir."

"Good," he said, then pressed a kiss to the corner of her mouth. "Now I'm going to fuck you. I'm going to make you scream as you come all over my big dick, and then I'm going to come all over your gorgeous tits. And when I'm done fucking you, I'm going to pull on my jeans, go downstairs, and help Charlie make breakfast. And you're going to do one of two things."

"I am?" Lucy gasped as Toby slid deep. Her body clenched around him, and they both groaned. *So goddamn big.* She was never walking straight again.

His words were punctuated by the powerful glide of his body against hers. "Either you'll have a shower, dress, and take a seat at the table, in which case I'll assume you want to go home after breakfast."

"Or?" He slammed into her and her breathing stuttered, the first flutters of an orgasm making themselves known deep in her belly.

"Or you'll come downstairs *exactly* as I leave you, sit at my feet, and eat from my hand. You do that and I'll know you've chosen to stay."

It seemed absurd to be having this conversation while they were fucking, but Toby had proven the night before that he had his own way of doing things, and every single one of them was designed to keep her off-kilter.

Designed to push her boundaries.

Or test her resolve.

"What about my 'one night only' rule?"

Toby grabbed her knee and hauled her leg around his waist. "Fuck your rule," he growled, sinking deeper inside her. "One night with you is not enough. I want more. And so do you."

Before she could give the idea any credence—or any thought at all—Lucy's orgasm stole her breath, and anything she would have said dissolved into a wanton plea. "More, more, more...."

Toby slammed home twice more before pulling out of her, straddling her body and taking his cock in hand, then grunting as he came all over her tits. Just as promised.

His come was warm against her skin, and she laughed quietly when he used the end of his dick to write something across her chest.

Mine.

Pushing herself up on her elbows brought her within licking distance of Toby's cock, and the man wasted no time in putting her ready mouth to good use.

"Open up, baby. Lick me clean."

He smiled as she obeyed his command, and Lucy's insides quivered at the sexy sight. Then he closed his eyes and groaned as she snaked her tongue around the smooth head of his dick. The scent of sex hit her, a heady combination of his come and hers, but before she could suck him any deeper into her mouth, he pulled away and left the bed.

Lucy's sounds of pleasure morphed into disappointment as she watched him cross the room and disappear into what she guessed was a walk-in wardrobe. Her assumption proved correct when he returned wearing a pair of faded blue jeans, also as promised.

"The bottom line is this, Lucy. I don't like many people, but I like you. A lot." He fastened his jeans and came to stand before her. "And you're not the only one with rules. I don't fuck my employees. I never have. Not until you."

She knelt on the edge of the bed and fisted her hands in the bedding, her heart racing a mile a minute as his confession swept through her, filling her with long-forgotten emotions, feelings that made her chest tight and her breathing stagger. Her voice was quiet as she stated the obvious and told him the same thing he'd told her before she'd gotten in his truck.

"But I'm not your employee."

"Not until Monday." He stroked the blade of his finger down her cheek, the gentle gesture causing her to lean towards him in the hope of more, but he stepped back and cleared his throat, then nodded towards the wardrobe. "Your clothes are in there," he said. "I left a T-shirt for you too. And I'll replace the blouse I ruined last night." His ice blue gaze lingered on hers for so long she thought he was going to say something else, but then he seemed to think better of it and turned away. "I'll see you downstairs."

Then he disappeared through the doorway, and Lucy heard the now familiar creak of timber as he descended the stairs. The creaking stopped about halfway down, and her heart leapt into her throat.

Was he coming back? Would he say what he hadn't said before? Would he command her to stay and take the decision out of her hands?

One heartbeat passed. Then two... three....

The footsteps continued downwards, quicker than

before, and Lucy's breath shuddered out of her, her momentary excitement quickly dissipating.

Wow. Okay. So he isn't going to be of any help here. Well, no matter. Lucy had been making life choices grander than the one before her now for a very long time. She had this, so she lifted her chin and drew in a calming breath. "Decision time."

The question was, did she take a shower, get dressed, eat breakfast, and go home? Or did she submit to the sex god and stay where she was? All that awaited her at home was Netflix, leftover pizza, and a gut-churning sense of regret. Even just thinking about it, she could feel it swooping around in her belly, stirring things up. But it had never been this intense before.

Probably because the men she usually went home with were as dominant as a paperclip, and doing it doggy-style was about as kinky as they got. There was nothing to regret leaving behind.

But if she stayed, if she broke her one-night-only, no-strings-attached rule—which was pretty much the only thing that had kept her safe for the last seventeen years—then she ran the risk of an even greater regret.

Sometimes knowing something for certain was worse than what you thought you knew before you knew it, you know? And if Lucy spent the entire weekend with the man, she would know—truly know—what he was capable of. And after the intensity of the night they'd already spent together, that was a frightening thought.

But then... she already knew, didn't she? And now that she knew, she certainly couldn't know any less. Right? She couldn't go back to a time when she didn't know that sex with Tobias Bennett was out-of-this-world amazing.

Honestly, the man was a machine. A well-hung, inventive and insatiable machine.

Pressing her fingers to her temples to ease the sudden headache she felt forming there, she realised she was talking herself in circles. She knew what she wanted to do, and she knew what she should do, and really, how many times was an opportunity like this going to come along?

Tobias Bennett was a smart, gorgeous, sexy, funny, deliciously tall, stunningly built man who wasn't just great in bed but was nice too. No, not nice. Nice was too... *nice* a word to describe Toby. He was something, she just wasn't sure what. All she knew was she'd wanted him from the moment she'd met him. And now that she'd had him...?

Ah, hell. She knew he was right.

One night was *not* enough.

Chapter Twelve

"You look nervous."

Toby glanced at his brother across the break-fast table and glared at his smug expression, then realised his leg was bouncing uncontrollably. He forced it to stop. "I asked Lucy to spend the weekend with me."

His brother's smile was surprised but genuine as he gave a decisive nod. "Good. I haven't seen you this excited about a woman since we were nineteen. The smile's barely left your face since you tossed her over your shoulder and walked out of the pub last night."

With a non-committal grunt, Toby rose and walked to the daybed nestled amongst the potted palms. He grabbed a cushion, the big one he used to prop himself up when he was reading or taking a nap, then returned to his seat and dropped it on the floor.

"So?" Charlie urged him on. "How will we know if the lovely Lucy accepts your offer of a debaucherously dirty weekend?"

A slow smile stretched across Toby's face. "Trust me, we'll know."

"And I assume you'll want me to vacate the premises as quickly as possible if she does?"

"I'll let you finish breakfast first, but yes, I'd appreciate it."

"You're too kind," Charlie drawled, then took a bite of croissant, narrowed his eyes, and studied Toby for what felt like an eternity.

Toby fought the urge to squirm in his chair. "What?"

"Nothing."

Huffing out an impatient sigh, he demanded again, "What?"

"You really like this woman, don't you?"

Toby snorted. "What was your first clue?"

"Besides the fact you couldn't wait to get rid of me last night?" When Toby said nothing, Charlie continued. "You didn't have to share her, you know? I would have been more than happy to leave her in your capable hands, if that's what you'd wanted."

"I know."

"Then... why?"

He shrugged and shook his head. "I don't know."

"You don't do anything without a reason, Tobes."

It was true. He didn't. There was a reason behind everything he did every single day, but if he admitted to his brother the reason he'd shared Lucy, he'd never hear the end of it. So he'd lied and said 'I don't know'.

But Charlie was a persistent fucker. "You know, if I didn't know you better, little brother, I'd swear you were falling in love with this woman."

"Good thing you know me better, then, eh?" Toby replied, ignoring the tiny voice in the back of his mind telling him Charlie was right.

Because Charlie was *not* right.

The fact of the matter was, Toby had been in love before, and this, what he felt for Lucy, was not it. Nope. He'd been there, done that, and was not looking to do it again any time soon.

That's why he'd shared her, to keep some distance between them, to keep them focused on the physical. Love was hard. Painful. It sucked a man's soul dry. Nope. He liked Lucy—a lot—but he wasn't looking for love. Hot sex with an even hotter woman? Sure. But *not* love.

Charlie grinned and sipped his coffee. "Uh-huh." Then his brother paused and his grin slipped.

Eyes narrowing, Toby said, "What?"

Clearing his throat, his twin shifted in his seat as though trying to get more comfortable, then said something Toby really didn't want to hear. "I got a call from Isobel."

Spine snapping to attention and his lip pulling up in a sneer, Toby growled, "What the fuck does she want?"

"The same thing she always wants," Charlie said. When Toby remained silent, brooding, his brother continued. "Maybe we should hear her out? She's never been this insistent before."

Toby was about to argue when he heard footsteps—soft, shoeless footsteps—and he rose from his seat at the table. Glancing back at his brother, he murmured softly, "I don't want to hear another word about her."

Then he gave his full attention to the woman standing in the doorway of the conservatory.

"Good morning, Sir."

Gloriously naked, and with his come still drying on her tits and her bottom lip pinned between her teeth, Lucy was a vision. And the breath Toby had been holding since he'd heard her footsteps escaped his lungs in an audible rush of air.

Holding out his arms, he smiled at her, indulgent pride swelling his chest. His cock thickened against his thigh, and he thanked God he'd worn his loose-fitting jeans. "Come here, baby."

She was staying. Lucy had chosen to stay with him, and for some stupid reason, when she went to him and let him wrap her up in his arms, he rubbed his cheek against her hair and pulled the faded scent of gardenias into his lungs with every breath. He felt like he'd won the lottery. Then his brother's words echoed through his head.

Was he "falling in love"?

Christ, no. That was the last thing he needed.

Letting her go, he held her at arm's length, put some distance between them.

Charlie grinned, smug. "Good morning, beautiful."

And Lucy turned her head to greet his brother. "Good morning, Charlie."

Toby liked that she'd used his brother's name and hadn't called him Sir.

He would be the only man she gave that title to from now on.

"Are you hungry?" he asked, leading her around the table to the large green cushion on the floor. The one sitting right by his feet.

"I'm famished," she said, licking her lips as she took in the spread on the table. She reached out one slender hand to snag a strip of bacon, but Toby slapped it away. She yelped, then narrowed her eyes at him and stuck out her tongue.

"Careful, beautiful." Charlie chuckled, snagging the bacon for himself. "You don't want to poke the bear before he's had his coffee."

She breathed deeply and smiled. "Mmmm, coffee."

"Sit," Toby ordered, holding her hand as she lowered herself onto the cushion and tucked her feet under her arse. "Good girl," he said, taking his seat. He was rewarded with a lopsided smile.

Fuck. That smile made his cock hard.

Charlie was right about one thing: Toby *really* liked this woman. Hell, he'd already told her as much himself. And it wasn't her willingness to please him, or that she came apart so beautifully in his arms—he could get that action anywhere, if he bothered to look. It was in the pure joy that lit up her lovely eyes when he praised her, the way she held herself, as though she were unsure if she should feel proud or shy or honoured that he'd even acknowledged her presence, let alone praised her for it.

He'd witnessed uncertainty like that before, like she didn't know if she could take him at his word, if she could trust him, and behaviour like that never came from a good place.

Someone had hurt her. She was vulnerable. And that called to the primal part of him, that animal part of man that needed to protect and defend and comfort his woman. Even if it was only for a weekend.

"How do you like your coffee?"

"Black, please."

Toby poured her a cup and handed it to her, watched her mouth form a pretty pout as she blew on it, then took a sip. Her eyes rolled back as she swallowed it down, and she moaned, the sound one of pure decadence.

"That's really good coffee," she said. "Thank you." Then she passed the cup back and wriggled in her seat, pressing her thighs together and avoiding his gaze.

"Is there a problem?"

Lucy fidgeted again. "No. Not really," she said. "I can hold it."

"Hold it?" Toby shared a look with his twin, identical grins mirrored in their expressions. "Baby, do you need to pee?"

She threw him a pained expression, then nodded. "Yes, Sir."

"And you didn't go upstairs because...?"

Pained turned to peevish, and her hands fisted in her lap. "Because you told me to come downstairs *exactly* as I was, and exactly as I was included a full bladder. So yes, I need to pee."

Never in his forty years of living had Toby felt so triumphant. So jubilant. So dominant. And yet to all outward appearances, he knew he looked like a man who was completely at peace. Because he was that too.

"You're perfect," he said, smiling down at her.

She raised one brow. "I'm really not."

"Up," he said, chuckling. "On your feet." Then he led her through the kitchen to the laundry and downstairs bathroom.

Lucy stared up at him, her gaze cautious. "You're not going to watch... right?"

For a split second, he thought about teasing her, but the way she was hopping from one foot to the other told him he didn't have time. The woman really needed to pee. He shook his head. "No. And there's a lock on the doo—"

He didn't even finish speaking before she'd slammed the door in his face and engaged the lock. Two minutes later, Lucy reappeared looking sheepish as she walked to the sink to wash her hands.

"I'm sorry I shut the door on you, Sir."

Damn, he liked it when she called him Sir.

It made his dick twitch and his balls ache with the need to bend her over the breakfast table and fuck his way into her. "I'll let it slide. This time," he said, lightly slapping her arse and enjoying her little gasp of surprise. "Now come here."

This time when she clenched her thighs together, Toby knew it was for a whole other reason than needing to relieve herself.

Grabbing a washcloth off the laundry bench, he ran it under warm water, then rang it out. "I'm very glad you decided to stay," he said, washing his dried come off her breasts. "It saves me the hassle of kidnapping you and tying you to my bed."

Lucy laughed. "That's me. Hassle free."

His mouth twitch up at one corner. "You think I'm kidding?"

"No, but I thought you said you couldn't make that decision for me."

He shrugged. "Let's call it plan B."

Grinning, Lucy added, "I also think I missed an awesome opportunity to play another round of catch by not coming downstairs dressed and ready to go."

Toby laughed, then bent his head to kiss his woman. Yes, *his* woman. Fuck it. He was conceding defeat. Not that he'd fought very hard. Lucy had been his from the moment he'd met her. He just hadn't realised it then.

He rinsed the cloth again, then got down on one knee.

"Lift your foot onto my thigh. Open up for me."

The laughter dropped from Lucy's face, panic darkening her eyes. "You shouldn't be kneeling for me." She shook her head.

When he could see she wasn't going to obey him, he sighed heavily, hooked his hand under her knee, and lifted her foot for her, causing her to grab his shoulders or risk falling on her arse. When she was steady, he reached between her legs and gently cleaned her. "Do you think me less dominant for kneeling down to wash your cunt?"

She dropped her gaze and shrugged. "At this point, I don't know what to think."

"Would you like to know what I think?"

Lucy nodded, her bottom lip pinned between her teeth.

"I think being dominant isn't just about playing with pretty subs, and it sure as hell isn't just about fucking." Toby set her foot back on the floor and got to his feet. "Being dominant means taking care of my submissive in any and every way she needs me to. It's all those little in-between things, those everyday things like tucking in the tag on the back of your dress before taking you out to dinner, or holding you tightly after you wake from a nightmare, or getting on my knees to wash between your legs. I'm never so dominant as when I'm taking care of you, Lucy. Never forget that."

In a blur of movement, Lucy was suddenly pressed against him, her arms wrapped tightly around his waist and her head buried against his naked chest. She sniffed and her body shook. Was she was crying?

"Hey," he said gently, lifting her chin so she had to look up at him. "What's wrong?"

She sniffed again, her cheeks damp with freshly shed tears and a grimace twisting her lips. "You were right last night. I'm not used to this."

He remembered their conversation on the couch. "Intimacy, you mean?"

She nodded. "I've had a lot of sex with a lot of people, but I'm only just realising I've never been intimate with any of them. Not like this. Not like you." She pulled away and he let her, gave her the space she needed to feel safe. "I'm sorry," she said. "I'm messing this up." She swiped her hands over her eyes, sniffed as she brushed away her remaining tears and pressed her hands to her cheeks.

Toby grabbed her wrists and pulled her closer again, wanting to show her she wasn't alone. "No you're not. This is new territory for me too."

Lucy smiled weakly. "I guess we both suck at following the rules, huh?"

"Some rules are meant to be broken," he said, lowering his mouth over hers but not quite touching.

Her warm breath brushed over his lips when she said, "Like sleeping with your staff?"

"Or sleeping with your boss."

"Or only spending one night."

"Or no-strings sex."

Her breathing quickened. "Strings are messy. They get tangled and tie you up."

Toby grinned wolfishly. "You should've realised after last night, but I like tying you up." He kissed her deeply, thoroughly, then slipped his jeans-clad thigh between her legs and swallowed her moan when she rubbed against him. With a groan he pulled back and then smoothed Lucy's hair away from her face, enjoyed the way the soft strands tickled his palms. "We should get back before Charlie eats all the bacon."

Smiling, she nodded. "Yes, Sir. And how should we punish him if he has eaten all the bacon?"

"I'm sure we'll think of something."

Toby slapped her arse again and sent her ahead of him, giving him a few moments to think. He barely knew this woman who had come into his life, yet he felt like he'd known her forever.

How was that possible? Why did he feel so protective of her, so possessive? How could it feel so right so fast?

And how long would it take before it all fell apart?

Because it would.

It always did.

But until that time came, he'd enjoy the fuck out of her. Even if it was only for a weekend.

Chapter Thirteen

The weekend flew past in a blur of sex and intimacy and everyday things.

Saturday bled into Sunday, time ceasing to have all meaning as they talked and slept and fucked in accordance with their own wants and needs. No schedule, no dinner at eight or bed at eleven, they just were. They just did. And the outside world was all but forgotten.

Lucy had never had so much fun or been so universally satisfied in her life.

Not that they'd spent all of their time in a bed.

It turned out Toby was a fan of fucking anywhere, anytime, anyhow.

Like standing in the middle of his enormous shower with her legs wrapped around his hips and his fingers digging into her arse as he thrust up into her like the devil was on his tail. Or a long, slow fuck on the couch, her legs straddling his as he spent a seemingly endless amount of time worshipping her breasts with his hands and teeth and tongue. Or when he bent her over the desk in his home office and pounded into her while he smacked her arse and pulled her hair and told her she was a naughty girl. Or a quickie on the breakfast table on top of plates of half-eaten pancakes and maple syrup.

Thankfully the shower sex had immediately followed the pancake sex, because Lucy had gotten syrup in places that syrup just shouldn't go, no matter how much Toby protested otherwise as he'd attempted to lick her clean.

Now it was Sunday afternoon and they were enjoying his beautiful garden, lazing on a handmade quilt spread out in the shade of a grove of jacaranda trees. Toby had propped himself against the trunk, a pile of cushions protecting his naked body from the rough bark, and Lucy lay with her head in his lap, staring up at the little sprays of purple flowers that were beginning to poke out between the bright green leaves overhead.

"They're flowering early because of the drought," he murmured. "It's a survival mechanism." He sounded like he was about to doze off.

Lucy turned her head and saw him looking up at the canopy, little spots of sunlight that broke through the leaves decorating his handsome face. Reaching up, she drew her fingertip in a line from one dot to the next, chasing them as they danced across his cheeks and nose until he grabbed her hand and kissed her fingers.

And that was all it took for his eyes to heat, the icy blue giving way to something stormier in nature. His lips lifted in a sly grin, and he didn't sound sleepy anymore when he ordered, "Turn around."

From under the cushions, he produced a length of silken rope, and Lucy's heart sped up. She licked her lips. "Yes, Sir."

Scrambling to her knees, she turned away and placed her hands behind her back, repressing a whimper of need when she felt the velvety softness of the rope as Toby wound it around her wrists and forearms and bound them firmly. When he was done, he instructed her to straddle his lap, which was easier said than done without the use of her hands. She laughed when she toppled to one side and nearly face-planted in his crotch.

Toby helped position her where he wanted her, then stroked his cock in his big fist, coaxing it from its semi-hard state to a fully erect monster again, readying himself to pleasure her. To pleasure them both.

Lucy had lost track of how many times they'd fucked since Friday night. All she knew was that every part of her body ached in the best way possible. Her pussy had been filled again and again, sometimes with Toby's cock, sometimes his fingers or his tongue. Her arse ached every time she sat down, and the skin there had turned what she was sure would become a permanent shade of red. And he'd given her nipples more attention in one weekend than every other lover she'd ever been with had combined.

More than once it had been on the tip of her tongue to call him Master instead of Sir. She'd wanted to moan the word when he made love to her, wanted to scream it when he put her in chains and caressed her body with the tender lash of his whip, to whisper it in his ear when he'd held her afterwards and stroked his big callused hands over the welts on her flesh and made them sting for a second time.

Toby made her feel special. Cherished. Wanted. He made her feel everything she'd feared he would, everything she'd feared he would take away from her when the weekend came to a close, and calling him Master would only make it worse.

Because calling him Master would mean admitting she

had feelings for him that went far beyond anything she'd felt before.

And that scared the shit out of her.

"Up, Lucy. Get on my dick."

She did as commanded, pushing up on her knees so he could notch the head of his gorgeous cock against her cunt, then slowly lowering herself down to a chorus of gratified groans. He grabbed her hips in his vice-like grip and moved her body in time with his, ground her down on him like he had their first night together, mashed her clit against the hard plane of his pelvis and made her writhe in ecstasy.

"Toby," she moaned. "Please."

"Please what, baby?"

"Please use me, Sir. Please make me come. Please... *oh...* God!"

It didn't take long for Lucy to find her release. After an entire weekend of Toby's gentle caresses, hard fucking, and even harder play sessions, her body was beyond primed. Her clit was so sensitive she was sure he'd just have to blow warm breath across the tiny nub of flesh and she'd go off like a rocket. And she couldn't ever imagine growing tired of the way his big cock stretched her pussy so exquisitely, or how he filled her over and over with his come, or splashed it across her tits and arse.

Not for the first time she'd dared to imagine what would happen if her contraceptive failed and she fell pregnant. She'd never thought she'd have kids. Never figured she'd find anyone worth having kids with, but the way Toby had cared for her over the past two days had her convinced he'd make a good dad. He was kind, honest, and firm but fair. Everything her own parents weren't.

"What are you smiling about so dreamily?" he said, thrusting up into her with the force of a battering ram.

Shit. She couldn't tell him she'd been daydreaming about having his kid. *Geez, talk about bunny-boiler territory.* Toby might be more accepting than most men, but Lucy would bet her house the thought of having a baby with his weekend hook-up would still freak him the fuck out. No one was *that* accepting.

"I was thinking about the day we met," she said instead. It wasn't a lie exactly, just a more palatable topic of conversation.

"Oh?"

"I wanted to fuck you from the moment I saw you, and it took every ounce of my self-control not to beg you to take me."

Toby groaned. It was a pained sound that matched the anguish in his eyes. "I wanted you too. I wanted to shove that damn pencil skirt up over your arse, bend you over my desk, and drive my cock so deep inside you you'd feel me for a week."

Lucy whimpered. "To think we could have been fucking all this time."

"What a waste," Toby agreed. "Of course, we can always make up for lost time and keep fucking each other after today."

Swallowing hard against a surge of excitement, Lucy said, "What about our rules?"

"Fuck our rules," he growled. "I want you."

She closed her eyes and moaned, a second round of pleasure swelling inside her, bigger than the first, more intense. Then she yelped when Toby slapped her tits.

Thwack, thwack.

"Don't you dare come yet," he growled. "Not before me. Not this time."

Gritting her teeth, Lucy clenched her pussy, clamped

her body down on his, and smirked. She couldn't come before him? Fine. Then she'd just make him come quicker. But when he returned her smirk and cocked one brow at her, she knew that look.

Game on.

The more Lucy tried to make Toby go faster, harder, the more he slowed his pace and touched her gently. Instead of gripping her hips, he stroked them, slid his hands back and forth and then drifted his touch higher, over her belly, her ribs, her breasts.

He toyed with her nipples, but he didn't pinch them or flick them, just lightly ran the pads of his thumbs over the sensitive little buds, circled them over and over until her eyes fluttered closed and she couldn't see him lean forwards to take one between his soft lips.

Her eyes flew open at the erotic touch. She gasped, arching her back and stuffing more of her breast in his mouth. Banding his arms around her, Toby locked her to him as he thrust upwards and increased his pace.

"Baby," he murmured, his face buried in the crook of her neck, his staggered breaths a warm caress against her scars as his big muscled body began to shake beneath her.

His thrusting lost all rhythm, his breath stuttered against her throat, and he twined his fingers through hers where they were bound behind her back.

"Come with me, baby. It's so goddamn good when we come together."

The tenderness in his voice and the hint of longing in his words were enough to make Lucy let go, and the orgasm she'd been fighting for crashed over her as she surrendered to his will. She broke apart, she shattered, she screamed. And the one word she absolutely did not want to say slipped past her lips on a cry of ecstasy. "Master."

It sounded so right to say it, and she couldn't take it back. Wouldn't take it back.

But that didn't mean he'd welcome it.

When their breathing evened out, Toby leaned back and stared into her eyes, his piercing stare as intense as ever. But the way his lips lifted in a slight smile that looked to be part bewilderment, part awe, and the way his eyes crinkled at the corners as that smile grew broader, made those icy orbs a lot less cold.

He looked... *happy*.

She felt her cheeks heat and ducked her head, dropping her gaze for a moment before looking up from under her lashes. She felt shy.

Vulnerable.

"Lucy."

When he said her name in that deep timbre of his, it did things to her. Inconvenient things. It tempted her to say other words she wasn't sure he'd welcome. Words that made her breathing stutter and her hearth clench as they bubbled up from deep, forgotten part of her. Then he slid his big hands into her hair and pulled her forwards for a kiss and everything inside her relaxed, she could breathe again. But before his lips could make contact, they were interrupted.

"Toby!"

Toby blinked slowly. "Not. Now," he growled through gritted teeth.

"Toby?"

Then he pulled back and sighed heavily. "I'll kill him."

Lucy worried at her bottom lip and turned her head in the direction of the shouting. "He sounds upset."

Toby sighed again and tilted his head to glance over her shoulder. "Agreed."

Leaves crunched under Charlie's feet as he marched

towards them at the bottom of the garden, and whatever Toby saw in his brother pulled his eyebrows together sharply in a deep frown. "Up you get," he said, helping her to her feet and unbinding her wrists, the rope falling away just as Charlie reached them.

"I've been looking everywhere for you," he said, resting his hands on his hips, his breath heaving in and out of him like he'd just run the hundred-metre dash. "We have to go."

Toby pulled Lucy in front of him, pressed his chest against her back, and rested his chin on her head. She shouldn't have felt as happy as she did, considering the sombre mood Charlie had brought with him, but the emotion bloomed inside her anyway, filling her up to over-flowing as she leaned into her lover and sighed quietly, content.

"What's up?"

"We have to go. Now," Charlie said, his gaze darting from Toby to Lucy and back again. His tone was urgent, his voice sharp, panicked. Over the course of the weekend Lucy had interacted with Charlie often and she'd only ever seen him relaxed and jovial. It felt strange to see him this way. He was agitated, almost... angry.

But then she'd seen people behave this way before. When she was a firefighter and attended to people on what was often the worst day of their lives, she'd seen them collapse under the weight of their despair, saw families ripped apart, and watched in awe as others straightened their spines and simply got on with it. Charlie's change in behaviour told her something had happened. Possibly something life-changing.

"Charlie, what's wrong?"

His gaze darted to hers again, and she saw his pain. "I'm sorry, beautiful, but Toby and I are needed elsewhere." His gaze drifted over her head and presumably met his brother's. "Ollie rang. There's been an accident."

His senses suddenly on high alert, Toby tightened his grip on Lucy. "An accident? Where? The Forge?"

Charlie shook his head. "No. Just outside of town." He shoved his hands through his hair and began to pace, so Toby let go of Lucy and moved to comfort his twin, rested his hands on his shoulders and held him firmly. Made his brother look at him. "It's Rafe," he said, the name stuttering out of him before he swallowed hard and added, "And Janie. Someone ran them off the road."

"No." Shock, swift and cold, swept through every vein in his body, freezing him from the inside out. His family was in trouble, and what was he doing? He was standing in his garden completely naked with his dick still wet from the best sex he'd ever had. Shame tightened his gut. "The baby?"

"I don't know. Ollie just said to meet them at Nambour Hospital."

"Fuck." Anger chased away his shock, the heat of it melting the ice and forcing his brain to react. But before he could take action, Lucy was shoving a stack of cushions into his arms and the folded-up quilt into Charlie's.

"Let's go," she said, the commanding tone of her voice cutting through the plethora of questions hanging in the air unasked. Unanswered. When neither he nor Charlie moved, Lucy stared at them like they were the crazy ones. "What? You want a written invitation? Move it." Then she spun on her heel and strode towards the house, breaking into a jog about halfway up the garden path.

Toby stared after her, his mouth hanging open and his anguish momentarily forgotten, then looked at his twin. "What the...?"

Charlie looked as bewildered as Toby felt. "Don't look at me, little brother. She's your woman." Then he did as Lucy had told him to and followed her to the house, Toby close on his heels.

By the time he got inside and dumped the cushions back on the daybed, Lucy was jogging down the stairs with her panties on and a bundle of clothes and shoes in her arms.

She shoved a pair of jeans and a T-shirt at him. "Get dressed, then lock up the house," she ordered before turning to his brother. "Charlie?" But Charlie just stared at her, his face blank and the quilt still clutched to his chest. Lucy took the quilt and placed it on the dining table. "Do you have everything you need?" she asked, her voice gentler than before.

Charlie blinked. "What?"

"You'll need your keys, wallet, phone, and a jacket," she said carefully. "Hospital waiting rooms aren't exactly the warmest places on Earth. Why don't you grab what you need while Toby and I get dressed, okay?"

"Yeah. Yes. I can do that." He disappeared into the conservatory, and Toby heard the door slam at the other end of the space.

"You're good at that," he said, fastening his jeans. "Calming him down. Thank you."

"I guess you never really forget your training. Keeping people calm so they didn't do something stupid and make the situation worse was a part of the job."

Toby frowned. "Isn't that what the cops are for?"

Lucy dragged on her jeans. "Not if the fieries got there

first. Mostly people get to safety and stay there, but sometimes people get out of a fire only to turn around and try to go back in. And often it's because they forgot to grab their waffle iron or their footy trophy from when they were twelve or something equally insignificant that in their panic their brain has told them they just have to have, and the fieries have to stop them." She dropped her gaze. "And they don't always succeed."

The misery in Lucy's voice had Toby itching to pull her back into his embrace, to comfort her and draw the details out of her and ask if that's how she got burned, but they didn't have time. Not now. And that was something he was beginning to regret.

He'd wanted to earn her trust, to ease her into telling him about herself naturally instead of playing twenty questions, so over the course of the weekend, they'd avoided talking about anything deeply personal, preferring instead to stick to favourite foods and books and sexual positions.

Or not talking at all.

In fact, Toby had discovered the silent moments they'd shared had been surprisingly comfortable. And she'd not pushed him for information either, or forced him to participate in meaningless small talk, for which he'd be eternally grateful.

But as a result of that lack of conversation, he knew nothing of her family life and she knew nothing of his, and yet when Charlie had come barging in and intruded on their burgeoning moment of true intimacy, she'd not complained nor interrupted, not even to ask who they were talking about.

She'd just quietly sized up the situation and taken charge. And as much as it had shocked him at the time that his sweetly submissive woman had dared to order him around, Toby was smart enough to be thankful too.

By not letting him ask the hundred and one questions that swirled around inside him still, she'd gotten them moving in the right direction, and now they were almost ready to go.

Lucy pulled one of Toby's T-shirts over her head. It was far too big on her shorter, slimmer frame and slipped off one shoulder, exposing her scars.

Toby smoothed his palm over the ruined flesh and wished he had more time with her. Time to ask her how she'd earned those scars, to listen to her stories and kiss away her hurts. Time to explore her fantasies and help her discover new ones. Time to make her irrefutably his.

But they were out of time.

For now.

"We good to go?" Charlie said, joining them again.

"I think so," Toby said, his mood sobering. The house was locked, and everyone was wearing pants. They were good to go. He took Lucy's hand and walked towards the front door. "We'll drop you home before we head off."

Lucy shook her head. "You don't have to do that. I'll order an Uber. My house is out of your way, and the drive to Nambour is already going to take you close to two hours, especially with Sunday afternoon traffic."

Toby clamped his hands on her shoulders and gently pressed his thumbs into the base of her throat. Just enough to focus her attention on nothing and no one but him. "We're driving you home, baby."

"But—"

"No buts," he argued, his tone sharp as his frustration rose to the surface. "I may have let you take the lead when we needed it, but make no mistake. When you're in my house, I'm in charge. Now you will do as you're told or the next time I put you over my knee won't be pleasant."

Why didn't she understand? She was his to take care of. His to keep safe. Even if it was something as simple as driving her home.

What did she think would happen? That he'd leave her sitting on his front stairs—or worse, drop her off by the side of the road—to wait for a car driven by God knew who, with no bra under her oversized T-shirt and a pair of stilettos in her hand?

Not going to happen.

And what the fuck kind of treatment was she used to from men if she expected him to essentially abandon her?

Even with his family in crisis, Toby thought to her well-being first.

Her cheeks pinkened, her jaw clenched, and she glared up at him, her eyes the colour of fire whisky. *So fierce.* "I'm only trying to help."

Hooking a knuckle under her stubborn chin, he lifted it. "I know you are, baby." He buzzed his lips over hers. "But I'm still driving you home. Come on."

Everyone was quiet on the twenty-minute drive to Lucy's place in Cleveland, two suburbs away. The air in the truck was thick with things unsaid. Toby was tempted to bypass her house altogether and just head for the hospital with his lover in tow. Of course, if he did that, he'd be forced to explain who Lucy was, how he knew her, and why he'd broken his age-old rule about fucking his employees.

Not to mention how pissed off his father would be that Toby had invited a stranger into their midst at such an unfortunate time.

An ER wasn't the best place to meet anyone's family for the first time, let alone the Bennett brood, especially since he wasn't sure he could keep his hands off her for more than five minutes. That definitely wouldn't go over well with his father.

Ulysses Bennett might be an artist and live up to the stereotype of all that entailed, but he was also fiercely protective of his children and wouldn't hesitate to take Toby to task for being a lecherous arsehole when Rafe and Janie needed him most.

So maybe it *was* time to surface and take a breath. Time to evaluate everything that had happened since Friday night.

Besides, if Lucy's stiff posture and the way she was avoiding touching him were any indication, kidnapping her for his own gratification wasn't the smartest move anyway.

When he pulled up in front of Lucy's modest house, she quietly thanked him for the lift, wished them luck with their family, then practically scrambled over Charlie in the passenger seat, issuing apologies in her haste to leave the truck. Toby jumped out the driver side and hauled arse after her, catching her at the front door.

Damn, she moves fast.

"Lucy, wait." He grabbed her wrist, frowned when she tried to yank it free of his grip. "Baby, what's wrong?" His gut sank to his feet as one thought hit him hard. "You're not pissed I have to leave, are you? Because I will not apologise for putting my family before—"

"Sex?" she said, shaking her head. "And of course I'm not mad you have to look after your family, geez. Be grateful you even have a family to look after. But sex is all this was, and now it's over, so, you know, back to our regularly scheduled programming." She turned away, but he saw her hands shake as she fumbled to get her key in her front door.

Toby reached over, took the key, and unlocked the door

for her, mainly to give himself a few more seconds to process her words, but his brain was struggling to make sense of them. He'd thought they were on the same page. He'd thought she wanted him. And for something more than a good time. Obviously, he was mistaken. Still, he'd be damned if he walked away from her without making his own feelings known.

He caged her against the door. "I meant what I said earlier, Lucy. Fuck our rules."

"No." She refused to meet his gaze. "Rules exist for a reason. And I was wrong to break mine. I'm sorry."

No. He tried again. "Lucy—"

"You should go," she said, looking past him to the street. "Charlie looks like he's about to chew through his seat belt."

Scowling, Toby glanced over his shoulder and saw she was right. His brother was getting panicky again.

Pushing away from the door, he slowly walked backwards towards the truck, refusing to stop looking at his infuriating woman sooner than he had to. "This conversation isn't over, Lucy," he said. "I'll call you later."

"Just focus on your family, okay? And I'll see you tomorrow. Boss."

Before he could issue any further protests, she disappeared inside and her front door closed with a slam.

Fuck.

Chapter Fourteen

The drive to Nambour took a little less than two hours, and Toby spent the whole time trying to sort through his feelings for a woman who apparently felt nothing for him.

"Rules exist for a reason. And I was wrong to break mine. I'm sorry."

She was sorry?

Fuck sorry.

He couldn't believe this was happening. Didn't want to believe it. This was why he didn't date. This was why he kept to himself, why he only fucked women when his body absolutely demanded it, and why he never, ever let himself get too close to anyone who wasn't related to him.

Except the tightness in his chest every time he thought about the sexy blonde with the sassy mouth and intoxicating eyes made him think that maybe, just maybe, he'd gone and done exactly that. He'd gotten close to someone without meaning to.

And that gorgeous creature had not only gotten under his skin, she'd dug in deep.

A woman who apparently didn't want him.

The last time he'd let that happen had been more than twenty years ago, when he'd been a naive nineteen-year-old kid, flattered by the attentions of a thirty-three-year-old woman. He'd rushed headlong into that relationship—if it could even be called that—too. But he'd been able to blame that disaster on the inexperience of youth.

Not this time.

This time Toby knew better. At least he thought he had.

Charlie had barely spoken a word in the truck, just stared out the window or texted back and forth with their youngest brother, Oliver. Not that the messages ever changed.

Charlie: *???*

Ollie: *Still waiting. No news yet.*

As they entered the ER waiting room, they were confronted by chaos. A fight had broken out between two young women, and security guards were attempting to break it up. A small boy was wailing at the top of his lungs and clutching his arm to his chest, and another kid had just thrown up on the floor while his mother juggled an infant on one shoulder and dug thorough the large purse she had slung over the other.

From the back corner of the room, a familiar woman waved to them, and they hurried over the meet her.

"What took you two so long?" Abby said, their little sister frowning even as she hugged them in turn. "Slower than a wet week, the pair of you. We expected you half an hour ago."

Toby stumbled to reply. "I... we... ah...."

"We had to drop a friend at home first," Charlie said, coming to Toby's aid.

He shot his brother a grateful look.

Abby didn't question them further. "Well, you're here now. That's all that matters."

"Has there been any news at all?"

"Not since the last time you asked," Ollie piped up from his seat beside their father.

Looking around their little group, Toby also saw Abby's fiancé, Wolf, and Jane's mum, Mary.

He crouched down in front of the older woman. "How are you holding up? Do you need anything?"

Mary leaned forwards, and Toby hugged the woman who was like a second mother to him and his siblings. "I'd be better if everyone would stop asking me that."

"Yes, ma'am. How long have you been waiting?" he asked, easing himself into a chair opposite them.

"About two and a half hours," Ollie said. "I called Charlie within ten minutes of the crash."

Toby shoved his hands through his hair. "What the hell happened? Why would anyone want to run Rafe off the road?"

"It wasn't Rafe they were after," Mary said quietly.

Then Ollie got Toby and Charlie up to speed with everything they knew so far, which included Mary's patisserie getting hit with graffiti and Jane's old clunker of a Jeep being set on fire in front of the Bennett family home. And this was on top of Jane's ex-fiancé/business partner stealing her life savings and leaving her at the altar only a week before.

"I need chocolate," Toby said as Oliver finished filling them in, and he went in search of a vending machine. Charlie tagged along, and he was glad for the company. The last thing he needed was to be left alone with the jumble of anger, fear, and longing swirling in his gut.

"Thanks for the save before. With Abby."

"No problem."

He rubbed the back of his neck, hoping it would ease some of his tension. It didn't. "My head's still spinning from all of this."

"From the news about Rafe or from Lucy dumping your sorry arse?"

Toby clenched his jaw against the memory. "I can't believe she blew me off so easily. Not after everything we did this weekend."

"Uh-huh." Charlie chuckled and shook his head. "You can't believe Lucy blew you off after you snapped at her? Really?"

"What the fuck are you talking about?"

His brother sighed. "For a control freak, you really are clueless sometimes, aren't you? When we needed help, Lucy stepped up. She got our butts in gear and out the door in less than half the time it would've taken us on our own, and you scolded her for it. How did you think she'd react, you big moron?"

Toby blinked slowly. "What? I wasn't mad at her for that. I was grateful."

"Then why did you tell her off?"

"Because she was being stubborn." He shoved his hands through his hair again. "All that bullshit about taking an Uber instead of letting me take care of her. She—"

"She what, Tobes? She offered to save us time so we could be with our family sooner? Wow," Charlie drawled, sarcasm dripping from the word. "What a bitch."

Toby glared at his twin. "You don't get it. You're not into power exchange like me and Lucy. I'm her Dom. She's my responsibility. She's mine to take care of, to protect. Not just her body but her reputation too."

"Ah." Charlie's expression softened. "I think I understand now."

"Do you?"

"That kid on Friday night, the one who insulted her."

"He called her a hooker." Toby's glare intensified. "And that's when she was wearing a bra and a reasonably modest blouse. No way was I letting her get in a car with some random bloke with no bra and a T-shirt four sizes too big. Because you know as well as I do what he'd be thinking, and I'll be fucked if I let that happen. Not if I can protect her from it."

Charlie watched him closely. "You really do like her, don't you?"

"I told you I do."

"What I mean is, this is more than just sex for you, isn't it?"

Toby took one more look around, then gave up on finding a vending machine. "It doesn't matter," he said, heading back to the waiting room. "It was just sex for her, and now it's over." He huffed a sardonic laugh and shook his head. "Back to our regularly scheduled programming."

"*Sooo*, does that mean you're *not* going to call her, then?"

Toby stiffened. "What?"

"Well, correct me if I'm wrong, but you did say you'd call her later."

"What's the point?" he said, shoving his hands in his pockets. "She's already made up her mind."

"Because women *never* change their mind, right?"

He really didn't want to talk about this anymore. "Charlie, just... let it go."

"Did it ever occur to you that she might be scared?"

That got his attention. He stared at his twin as a trickle

of dread slid down his spine. "Of me?" It wouldn't be the first time a woman had found him frightening to be around.

Charlie shrugged. "In a way. I mean, think about it. Here's a woman who's used to being treated a certain way because of how she looks. She even told that little shit-stain on Friday night—what did she say?"

"At least I'm only ugly on the outside," Toby quoted, remembering how ferocious she'd been as she'd stood up to that entitled twat, how fascinated he'd been by her show of strength, and how much he'd wanted her.

"And then you come along and tell her she's beautiful and treat her like a queen, even when she's kneeling at your feet. That's gotta be confusing for her, don't you think?"

And then he'd added to that confusion when he'd scolded her for trying to help them. Assuming of course that Charlie was right. Which—annoyingly—he tended to be.

Shit. He really was a clueless arsehole.

Oblivious to Toby's inner turmoil, Charlie continued. "But I suppose if you've given up all hope that she'd ever change her mind, then I guess there's no point calling her. 'Cause, you know, the absolute best way to win a girl's heart is to make promises you have zero intention of keeping."

His brother's sarcasm hit way too close to home, but just as Toby opened his mouth to respond, the doors to the emergency room swung open and Rafe appeared, his arm in a sling, his wrist bandaged, and his face looking like he'd just gone three rounds in a boxing ring.

And lost.

"Rafe!" Their sister ran to Rafe and threw her arms around him. When he hissed in pain, she pulled back, issuing apologies and bombarding him with questions at the same time.

Charlie nodded at Toby, and in three long strides they

were at Rafe's side, bracketing him with their big bodies and making sure he didn't face-plant into the floor. They walked him across the room, then parked his arse in a chair. Their father sat on one side of him, Jane's mother on the other, and everyone waited with bated breath for him to speak.

"Is she... how is she?" Mary asked quietly, her face tight with concern. "They're not telling us anything."

"There's no news yet," Rafe said, taking the older woman's hand in his. His voice was steady and sure, his words efficient and clipped. He sounded like he was performing in a courtroom, and Toby realised that was probably the only thing stopping him from falling apart. He couldn't imagine the chaos inside his brother's head, inside his heart at that moment. "They're still running tests," he continued, "but when they're done, the doctor said they'll take her to a room in the maternity wing."

Rafe scrubbed a hand over his face. He looked about ready to collapse with exhaustion. "All we can do now is wait," he said. Then Toby watched helplessly as his younger brother broke, as the always-in-control lawyer dropped the charade, fell apart, and let his tears cascade down his face as he sobbed like a small child. "I can't lose her," he cried, his body shaking and his shoulders slumped. "I just got her back. I can't lose her again. I can't do this without her."

"Rafael," Mary said sternly. "She's made of tough stuff, our girl. She'll be all right. You'll see."

His brother turned to the small woman beside him, enveloped her in his arms and clung to her tightly, and Toby knew they were all clinging to the hope they'd heard in Mary's voice.

A throat clearing grabbed everyone's attention, and Toby turned to see Scott Turner, the police sergeant assigned to their tiny home town, the man he was trying very hard not to knock on his arse for letting this happen to Rafe and Jane on his watch.

"I have information I think you should hear," he said, flipping open a notebook and scanning the page. He then proceeded to explain that the graffiti at the patisserie, Jane's Jeep being set on fire, and the car crash had all been the work of Jane's ex-fiancé's ex-girlfriend, retaliation for being dumped and left for broke.

Rafe stared at Scott, the confusion on his face mirrored by pretty much all of them. "Why come after Jane when it was Sam who screwed her over? What could she possibly hope to gain from any of this?"

Scott shook his head as though he were having trouble believing it too. "She claimed Sam left her because of Jane."

Mary snorted. "Surely this girl doesn't think he actually *loved* Jane?" she said, one brow raised in a you-must-be-joking gesture.

"Nothing like that," Scott continued. "According to Rachel, before Jane came along, the most she and Sam had ever scored from one con was about fifteen thousand dollars. Obviously, Jane was worth considerably more than that. If I had to guess, I'd say Sam got greedy and didn't want to share. Figured now he'd hit the big time, he didn't need Rachel any more and ditched her."

"How the hell is that Janie's fault?" Oliver demanded.

Scott shook his head. "Ollie, I've been a cop for twenty years and I still don't understand half the things criminals do. She's been caught, and she can't hurt Jane anymore. Focus on that."

"Mr Bennett?" a large man in dark blue scrubs called out from the ER doors.

"Yes?" Toby, Charlie, Rafe, Oliver, and their father all answered at once.

"Ah... Mr *Rafael* Bennett?" the nurse clarified. "You can see Miss Melville now."

Toby watched his brother and Mary disappear into the hospital and rubbed at his chest, at the persistent ache over his heart. He felt so empty in that moment.

So alone.

He'd never loved anyone as deeply as Rafe loved Jane, had never known that level of devotion to another human being who wasn't related to him.

Then an image of a certain blonde with whisky-coloured eyes and legs for days burst through the gloom around his heart and he ached for a whole other reason.

Lucy had been everything he'd never known he'd wanted in a woman, and everything he had. She was sweet and clever and funny and beautifully submissive, but she was also strong and independent and fierce. And she'd been his. For a whole weekend, he'd known how it felt to care for someone so deeply he thought he'd never get her out of his system. And then he'd lost her.

Because... rules.

And because he'd been an arse.

Charlie gripped Toby's shoulder. "All joking aside, call her," he said quietly. "You deserve to be happy, and Lucy gave you that. Don't wait, little brother. Call her. Tonight."

Toby shook his head. "You heard her this afternoon when we dropped her off," he replied, surprised by the gruffness of his voice. "She made her views about dating the boss very clear."

"All I heard was a woman protecting herself from hurt. She doesn't know it yet, but you'd never hurt her. Not intentionally."

A small smile tugged at the corners of Toby's mouth. "Well, no more than she begged for, anyway."

Charlie laughed and shook his head. "If Lucy being a masochist isn't a sign from the universe that you're meant to call her, then I don't know what is."

"Who's Lucy?"

"It's impolite to eavesdrop, *liebchen*," Wolf said, sliding his arms around Abby's waist as they joined the twins.

"Our future sister-in-law," Charlie told her, grinning, "if he can manage not to fuck it up."

Abby's eyes grew to the size of saucers. "Seriously? You sly dog."

"Easy, kiddo. I'm not even dating her yet. It's...." His mouth twisted. "Complicated."

"Oh for pity's sake, why do all the men in this family have to make everything so damn complicated?"

"Why do you assume it's me at fault and not her?"

Abby cocked one brow and smiled indulgently. "You're adorable."

He grimaced. "Shut up."

"But seriously, who is she?"

Charlie laughed again. "His new office manager."

All around him, his family said things like "wow" and "what the fuck, man".

But it was his father who spoke last, his craggy voice disconcerting in its calmness. A sure sign he was disappointed in his son. "I thought you had a policy against sleeping with your employees."

Toby clenched his jaw so tightly he thought he felt his molars crack. *Charlie is a dead man.* Breathing deep, he slowly shifted his gaze to meet his fathers. "Technically, she's not my employee," he said with a heavy sigh. "She hasn't signed the employment contract yet."

Ulysses stood, his eyes narrowed. "Outside. Now."

With a parting glare at his twin, Toby followed the old man out into the chill of the late evening air. "Dad—"

"What the hell were you thinking, Tobias?" his father whisper-raged. "Taking advantage of a woman you have power over? I raised you better than that."

Fists clenched tightly, Toby felt every word out of his father's mouth like the sting of a single-tail whip. Heat blazed under his skin as he listened to Uly's hushed tirade, and it joined forces with the embarrassment of being scrutinised by his siblings and the hurt of being rejected by Lucy, building and building until it spilled over and words flew out of his mouth on a roar.

"I did *not* take advantage of her!"

"You sure about that?"

He scrubbed a hand over his face. "I made it clear from the very beginning that her job was never in jeopardy. She could say no at any time. She could leave at any time. I asked her more than once if she was certain she wanted to continue and she always said *yes*."

His father was unflinching in his cause. "Are you *sure* about that?"

Toby wasn't sure of much at that moment, but he had no questions about Lucy's consent. "Yes. I'm sure."

They stared at each other in silence for a minute before Uly spoke again. "Do you have feelings for this woman?"

Toby nodded. "Yes I do."

Uly rubbed his jaw, then sighed heavily. He looked tired, more than a man his age should. "Take your brother home. You both have work in the morning, and it's a long drive."

"We can stay," Toby said quietly, feeling less like an adult man who owned his own business and more like a kid being dismissed by his father.

He knew what was coming next.

Uly shook his head. "Jane isn't coming out of there any time soon, and neither is Rafael. Go home, son. Get some sleep."

And there it was.

He was being sent to his room.

A little while later, he and Charlie were back in his truck, heading home along the Bruce Highway.

"What did Dad want?"

"To ream me out for taking advantage of Lucy."

Charlie snorted and shook his head. "That's not what happened and you know it."

Toby grunted. "Do I?" He gripped the steering wheel tightly, his knuckles blanching with the effort. His father had raised some valid points.

"What? You think Dad is right?" his brother, ever the mind reader, said. Charlie's voice bristled with irritation. "I've met the woman, remember? I doubt anyone could take advantage of Lucy unless she allowed it. And I know the old man means well, but he wasn't there. I was. And I can tell you without a doubt in my mind that Lucy wasn't there for fear of her job. She was having fun."

Toby swerved suddenly to avoid a suicidal kangaroo. Bloody beasts had zero road sense. "Some women are better at pretending to be something they're not. You know that."

"I also know you shouldn't let your past dictate your future," Charlie shot back, proving he knew exactly where Toby was taking this conversation. Then he sighed and scrubbed a hand over his face. "Listen to me, Tobes. I know you better than you know yourself. You're the guy who always does the right thing, even if it's not in your best interest." Toby opened his mouth to argue, but Charlie held up his hand to stop him. "And I know your version of doing the right thing is making all the decisions by yourself like the control freak you are. But here's the thing—are you listening to the thing?"

Toby spared Charlie a moment to shoot him a brief glare. "I'm listening."

"Okay, here's the thing. If you're really that unsure of every special moment you shared with that magnificent woman over the weekend, then you need to talk to her about it. And then you need to respect her enough to assume whatever she tells you is the truth. Don't let Dad get in your head. I mean, let's face it. The old man doesn't exactly have a stellar record when it comes to women. I mean really. Take our mother for example."

"I know," Toby said with a snort. "But it was the old man who taught me to always do the right thing, even if it's not in my best interest."

His brother chuckled. "All I'm saying is talk to her. Find out if you're on the same page."

Until she'd blown him off that afternoon, he'd already thought they were. "And if we're not?" Toby asked, pulling off the highway into the service centre to refuel.

"I'm sure you'll think of something."

"I'm not so sure. Before she slammed her door on me, she'd been pretty adamant that rules exist for a reason and she was sorry she'd broken hers," he said, disgusted with himself for making her feel that way. Christ, it had been a long time since he'd worried about shit like that. He didn't miss it, the feeling of always being on edge, wondering if he was screwing everything up. Finding out too late that yes, actually, he had.

Charlie unfastened his seat belt and shrugged, clearly unconcerned about Toby's inner battle for control over his uncertainty. *Bastard.* "I remember she was pretty adamant about only staying for one night too," he said, reaching for the door handle. "And look how that turned out."

Toby was halfway out the driver side door when his brother's words hit their mark.

Well, shit.

Chapter Fifteen

It was Monday morning, and Lucy pulled into the carpark of Bennett's Gardens and Landscaping at seven o'clock sharp, ready to begin her new job.

Toby was already there. His truck was parked beside the entrance, and the sight of it immediately filled her stomach with a riot of butterflies. Partly because she remembered the way he'd touched her the first time she'd been in his truck, how nice it had felt to be wrapped up in his arms, and how easily he'd gotten her off using nothing but his fingers.

Mostly the butterflies were in a tizzy because of the second time she'd been in his truck, when he'd driven her home and she'd been rude to him because that had been easier than dealing with her feelings.

To make matters worse, when he'd unexpectedly kept his promise and actually called her, she'd fobbed him off and refused to answer her phone, letting his call go straight to voicemail.

It had been a childish decision she was sure would come back to bite her in the arse, but in her defence, she'd still been upset with him for being a dick to her when all she'd done was try to help.

Just because she was submissive didn't mean he could yell at her for no good reason.

Later that night, she'd gotten over herself, did some adulting, and checked her voicemail. And almost swooned at the sound of his rich baritone saying her name and calling her "baby". Toby had apologised for his "ungrateful attitude", then asked her to come in early so they could "talk".

That was the other thing jacking up her heart rate. Nothing good ever came of people wanting to "talk" to her.

The main gate was still locked, but just as she was looking for another way inside, Toby appeared and waved to her.

"Over here." He held open a smaller side gate and ushered her through, but with his big body partially blocking the entrance, Lucy had to practically squeeze past him. She tried desperately not to breathe him in as she passed, not to lean even closer than she already had to and inhale his scent.

Well, she pretended to try.

He smelled so good, like crisp linen but with an undertone of something she'd come to recognise as being all Toby —cut grass and morning dew and freshly turned earth after the rain. The man smelled like spring, and it did things to her.

So many inconvenient things.

"Good morning, Miss Barton."

Miss Barton? Crap. That didn't sound promising, even if his voice did sound like liquid sex, all smooth and deep and tempting.

She swallowed, her throat working overtime to push even one word out. "Morning," she finally stammered. She'd reserve the right to decide if it was good or not after their talk.

Awkward silence stretched between them as she followed him inside the administration building, separated into three main areas. The front section was the reception area. The desk was hidden behind a curved half-wall, the company name and logo displayed across the front of it. A small sitting area filled with comfortable chairs, a small coffee table and a water cooler occupied the space between the desk and the floor-to-ceiling windows that looked out over the garden centre. This would be her workspace. To the side of reception was a small conference room.

Toby had explained during her interview that he used the room primarily for the landscaping side of the business, for meetings with clients and his work crew. The third area was Toby's office and was situated directly behind the reception area.

Toby's workspace was different from the others in that there were no windows, only a back door and a large skylight. When she'd asked him why, he'd explained he worked better without distractions, but after spending the weekend with the man, she had a hunch it also afforded him the privacy every introvert craves and gave him a safe space to retreat to when it was too peopley outside.

"I'm glad you got my message," he said without even a hint of censure.

Keeping her gaze pinned to his broad back and defi-nitely *not* the magnificence of his firm arse packaged almost sinfully in a pair of cargo shorts, she followed him inside his office and quietly closed the door.

"I'm sorry I missed your call last night," she said. "I didn't—" She was going to lie and say "I didn't hear it ring" or "I didn't answer because my hands were wet", but when

Toby folded his arms across his chest and raised one brow, practically daring her to lie to him, the truth spilled out of her, revealing her spite. "—want to talk to you."

Toby's lips twitched. She could tell he was trying not to laugh, but then he let it out anyway, and some of the tension eased from the room.

"It's okay, baby. I deserved that."

Baby. Her heart did the same weird little flippy-floppy dance move it had done the night before when she'd listened to his voicemail. As though nothing had changed since they'd made love in his garden on Sunday afternoon.

Before the Uber incident.

The thought made her stupidly happy, and she bit her lip in an attempt to hide her excitement, then let out a slow steady breath. It wasn't true, of course. Something had changed, something important, and she needed to get herself on even ground before she threw herself at him and destroyed any leverage she might have had during their talk.

"How are your brother and his friend doing?" Because nothing screamed even ground like a family tragedy. *Stupid, Lucy.*

He gestured for her to take a seat, then did the same. "Rafe's okay. A sprained wrist, a few bumps and bruises. He'll be fine." He rubbed his hand across the back of his neck, and she had to grip the arms of the chair to stop herself from going to him and rubbing his shoulders to ease his stress. "It's Jane we're worried about," he said, and he gave her a rundown of the incident.

"They were still running tests when we left last night, and my sister, Abby, sent word this morning that she still hasn't woken up." Then a small smile tugged at his lips and his expression softened. "The only good news so far is they discovered Jane is having twins, and both babies appear to be in good health."

Lucy relaxed into the chair and let go of the tension she'd been holding onto as Toby spoke, then leaned forwards and touched his hand where it lay on his desk. "I'm sure Jane will be okay too. By the sound of things, she got her head rattled pretty well by the airbags and has possible bruising on her brain. Once that heals, I'm sure she'll be fine."

"And how long does that take?" He scowled, but she saw the worry underscoring the ferocious expression.

"It varies," she said gently. "Brains are weird, and every person is different. But if the doctors aren't worried, then you shouldn't be either. I've seen people bounce back from far worse." Toby slid his hand out from under hers and leaned back in his chair, so she did too. Then she readjusted herself and lifted her chin, refused to acknowledge how much the removal of his touch burned a hole through her chest. "Now, what did you want to talk about? Or did you call me in early just to finalise the paperwork?"

Toby straightened the items on his desk until they sat perfectly square to one another. She'd noticed him do it every time they ate too, probably more so because of her vantage point from the cushion at his feet which put her line of sight almost directly level with the tabletop. The cutlery had to be aligned just so, and his brow pinched every time Charlie didn't put the salt and pepper mills back in their little caddy in the centre of the table.

The tiny smirk on Charlie's face every time he did it led her to believe he did it on purpose. *Arse.*

Towards the end of the weekend, she'd started directing a steady glare at him every time he did it, which only made him smirk at her in turn.

"We'll get to your employee contract," he said, patting a set of papers to the side of his blotter. "But first, I wanted to apologise properly for how I spoke to you yesterday. I know you only wanted to help us and I'm thankful you felt... comfortable enough around me to do what you did."

She raised one brow. "You mean boss you around?"

"Yes." A small smile lifted his lips. "Charlie doesn't handle bad news well. I usually spend so much time calming him down that it takes more time than it should to get going. But you settled him so quickly. Thank you."

Heat infused her cheeks, and she had to bite her lip to stop herself from smiling like a git at his praise. "I'm used to dealing with high-maintenance men," she said, then realised she'd just insulted her boss's twin brother. "Not that Charlie is high-maintenance," she rushed to add.

Toby's smile widened. "No, he really is." His smile turned rueful. "But I'm also sorry for being a dick when you offered to find your own way home. I appreciate that you were trying to save us time—hell, by handling Charlie, you *did* save us time—and we got to the hospital sooner than we would've."

Lucy shifted uncomfortably in her seat and lifted one shoulder in a half shrug. "Family is important." Not that she'd know. Her parents disowned her after she was injured, and even before that they weren't winning any Parents of the Year awards.

"Yes. But so are you." Toby stared at her across the table, and her gut clenched at the yearning she saw in his pale eyes. "That's what I wanted to talk to you about." He took a deep breath. "I like you, Lucy Barton. I *more* than like you. And I'm pretty sure you more than like me too."

That wasn't what she'd expected him to say. She didn't

really know what she'd expected Toby to say, but that definitely wasn't it.

He *more* than liked her?

Before she could stop herself, she whispered, "How much more?" Then her breath hitched in her chest at her own audacity. *Did I really just say that out loud?*

A lopsided smile stretched across his handsome face. "Much, *much* more." He licked his lips and she tracked the movement like a hawk, knowing exactly what he could do with that tongue when he had a mind to. "In fact, if I thought for a second you'd say yes, I'd ask you to move in with me."

Say what now? Lucy's whole body snapped to attention, and she swallowed hard. "What makes you think I'd say no?"

He chuckled and leaned back in his chair, laced his fingers together and rested them on his lean stomach. "Because you're as stubborn as I am, and you like your rules too much."

That's because rules existed for a reason. "Rules protect people, keep them safe." She tapped a finger against her scarred cheek. "I'm walking proof of what happens when you don't follow the rules."

A flicker of shock danced across his face but was gone a moment later. She wasn't surprised by his reaction. They hadn't exactly shared their deepest, darkest secrets with each other, and she wondered if he would still "more than like her" if he knew the truth of how she came to be disfigured.

If he knew about Michael.

"Do I make you feel unsafe?" His brow was bent in an expression of concern mixed with genuine curiosity.

Lucy shook her head and offered him a small smile. A

secret smile. "No."

At no point during their weekend sex-fest had Toby done anything to make her think she'd be unsafe with him. Not once, from the moment he'd carried her out of the pub until he'd dropped her at her door, had she felt anything but protected by him. Not even when he was cross and telling her off for wanting to take an Uber. And she still wasn't sure what the hell that had all been about.

What she did know was that it had been a long time since anyone had made her feel the way Toby had. She'd completely forgotten what it felt like to know someone else was watching over her, and she knew now she'd confused his concern with bullheadedness, which had made his dominance seem more like bullying. And after the shit she'd had to put up with towards the end of her last job—something else she had yet to discuss with Toby—she'd decided the best sex of her life wasn't worth it and called it quits before it could go any further.

Before her heart could get involved.

But as he'd driven away from her, the crushing feeling in the centre of her chest, the one that had nearly brought her to her knees, had made her realise she was too late.

She more than liked him too.

Her heart was involved.

He leaned forwards. "I know I fucked up, Lucy. I've been alone most of my adult life, and I'm not used to having to explain myself to anyone." He snorted. "Not even Charlie. But that's no excuse for the way I spoke to you, and as much as I'd like to say it won't happen again, I can't make that promise. But I promise I'll try."

It wasn't the greatest apology in history, but at least he was being candid.

Lucy studied Toby for a long minute, her eyes narrowed

and one brow cocked, and decided she'd forgive him—depending on the answer to her next question.

"Why were you so insistent about driving me yesterday?"

Toby ran his tongue over his teeth and studied her in turn. "I was being selfish." He rubbed the back of his neck again. "And I didn't want anyone to see you."

A sudden chill sent goosebumps skittering over Lucy's flesh, and the blood drained from her face so fast she felt faint. "You didn't want anyone to see me," she repeated slowly, her grip tightening on the arms of the chair as she digested each word individually, hoping she could string them together again in a way that didn't sound so awful.

He didn't want anyone to see her.

He didn't want anyone to see the monster he'd fucked.

He was beginning to have more in common with her old boss than she'd ever thought possible. She'd forgiven him too quickly.

Lucy levered to her feet and locked her knees to stop them from wobbling. She kept her gaze glued to a point just above Toby's head, knowing if she looked at him directly, she'd probably burst into tears. When was she going to learn her lesson? Rules were there for a reason. And every time she broke them, she got hurt.

"I'd really hoped there'd be more to it than you wanting to keep me as your dirty little secret," she said, her voice brittle even to her ears.

"What?" Toby sounded confused, but he couldn't possibly be. No one was that naïve.

She straightened her spine. "You didn't want anyone to see me," she said again, only this time her skin heated with anger and chased the chill from her blood until she positively boiled with rage. "Fuck you!"

Chapter Sixteen

Bewilderment was not something Toby had a lot of experience with, but since meeting Lucy Barton, he almost felt like he was on a first-name basis with the emotion. Usually it was a good thing, making him realise the things he craved in life were not only possible but very much within his grasp.

But not now. Because Lucy was glaring at him with the force of a thousand suns and looked like she was about to explode.

"Fuck you!" Her voice shook with rage, her words stained with hurt.

What the fuck?

This was why he liked plants.

They didn't have messy emotions. Or talk. Or swear at him for no apparent reason. Why was she so upset? And how did he make it stop so they could get back to the place where she was smiling and he wasn't feeling like a gigantic, clueless arsehole?

He clenched his jaw and stared at Lucy as his brain

cycled through their conversation until, like a low-hanging branch, realisation slapped him in the face.

"You didn't want anyone to see me."

Suddenly understanding how that must have sounded to a woman who was used to people brazenly calling her ugly in public, he winced at his own stupidity.

Then leapt to his feet to stop the understandably irate woman from storming out of his office.

Toby wrapped his arms around Lucy's waist and yanked her away from the door. "Baby, I didn't mean it like that. When I said I didn't want anyone to see you, I just meant—"

"What?" She struggled against his hold, but he refused to let her go, even when she swung her elbow and caught him in the ribs, causing a pained grunt to burst from his lips. His woman was fierce.

But so was he. "The way you were dressed."

"The way I was dressed?" The venom in her voice would've made a lesser man's balls shrink to the size of raisins. "I was wearing jeans and a T-shirt, you pompous arse."

Somehow, he managed to spin her around so she was facing him, then gripped her wrists in one hand and pinned them to the door above her head. His lips pressed together in a thin line of frustration, but he kept his voice even, his tone low. "No way in hell was I letting you get into a car driven by Christ only knew who while you were wearing one of *my* T-shirts and *no* bra."

He shoved his other hand through his hair. "Every time you leaned forwards, even a little, I could see straight down the top of that shirt, right to your goddamn perfect breasts, piercings and all. And I didn't want anyone else to see you like that, didn't want to give them the chance to treat you with disrespect. Especially after the way that little shit-stain spoke to you the other night." He let out a slow breath and stared her down. "I told you I would put your safety first, and I meant it. I was only trying to protect you, Lucy. Your reputation as well as your body. And I won't apologise for that."

She sucked down a shallow gasp, then licked her lips. Toby felt his dick begin to thicken against his thigh, the memory of that tiny sound, of Lucy's sweet gasps when he fucked her hitting him right in his balls. *Fuck.* He repressed a groan, even as he wished they could wrap up the talking part of their talk and get to the part where there'd be make-up sex and a lot more gasping.

Lucy stopped struggling and watched him cautiously. "Well... maybe you should explain how wanting to protect me was selfish."

He leaned his forehead against hers. "By driving you home myself, I got to spend more time with you, simple as that." He released her hands and cupped her cheek. "I don't know about you, but I didn't want the day to end. You were so determined that we'd only have the weekend together that I wanted to spend every possible second with you. It was selfish because I should have been doing everything in my power to be with my family." He shook his head and locked his gaze on hers, hoped she'd see his remorse. "It was selfish because all I wanted was to bury myself deep inside you and never come out again."

"Oh." Lucy stared up at him with her very own look of bewilderment. "So... you weren't trying to hide me?" she said, her voice soft and unsure, her brow tugged down and her gaze marred by shadows of doubt. "You weren't ashamed of me?"

"No." Toby shook his head. "God, no. And I'm sorry I

made you feel that way." He'd wanted to protect her from arseholes, not become one himself, and it just highlighted how far he still had to go. How far he was willing to go. For her. "I could never be ashamed of you, Lucy. But I am—"

"A prude?" she said, then immediately pressed her fingertips against her lush mouth and widened her eyes as though she couldn't believe she'd just said that.

A slow smile spread across his face as he relaxed and leaned down to kiss her. "Not a prude. Possessive," he said. "I didn't know how possessive I could be until you came along. You're mine, and I don't want anyone else looking at you the way I do."

She scoffed and shook her head. "I really don't think you need to worry about that. Nobody's looked at me the way you do in a very long time."

When his brow scrunched in a look of confusion, she pointed at the scarred side of her face, raised one brow, and grimaced with an expression that said "exactly how dumb are you?"

Toby's eyes narrowed and his body zinged with a flash of anger. If he ever got a hold of the people who'd made this gorgeous creature feel less than worthy of every good thing in this world, he'd make them hurt. "No. You won't be doing that anymore."

Lucy frowned. "Doing what?"

"From now on, every time you belittle yourself, you will be punished. You, Lucy Barton, are a clever, sexy, gorgeous woman. Say it."

The blood drained from her face. "What?"

"Say it."

Swallowing hard, she mumbled the words. "I'm a clever, sexy, gorgeous woman."

His hand landed on her arse with a sound wallop and

he sighed even as she yelped. "Hmm... we'll work on that." Then he leaned down with every intention of kissing his woman properly, of getting the make-up sex part of the morning under way, but she turned her head and his lips landed on her cheek.

"We're at work."

Toby chuckled and nuzzled against her instead. "Is that another one of your rules? No nooky at work?"

She snorted. "Nooky? How old are you?"

"Same age as you, but we do try to be family friendly around here. Besides, you and I both know when I say 'nooky' what I really mean is 'fuck you senseless'." Then before she could argue he captured her mouth with his and kissed her, thoroughly, deeply, until she pressed her palm against his chest and gave him a playful shove. Not that it actually moved him anywhere. Still, he leaned back a little, gave her some space.

"Well nooky will have to wait," she said, looking a little less resolute than she did a minute ago. "We really should finalise that paperwork first. Then maybe you could take me on a tour of the place before we open?"

Toby took her mouth again, grinned when she didn't resist, and teased her with little pecks of his lips between every other word. "Only if that tour includes bending you over my desk and fucking you until you scream my name."

Lucy mock-glared at him, even going so far as to fold her arms over her chest and tap her foot. Then she rolled her eyes and said, "Fine. But only if there's time."

"Baby, I'll make fucking time. In fact, let's do that first. Before the tour."

"Second, after the paperwork," Lucy countered, pulling her T-shirt over her head and tossing it on the chair."

"Paperwork, nooky, tour," Toby said. "In that order."

"Exactly. If only because the last thing I need is to get caught by your staff and have everyone assume I only got the job because I'm screwing the boss. Also, I need a work shirt."

Toby froze, Lucy's words running through his head with all the subtlety of a herd of stampeding elephants. He'd hoped to take their burgeoning relationship public, to be as open and upfront about it as possible. But he hadn't really thought it through, hadn't thought about the ramifications to Lucy and her reputation. And while he knew most of his staff wouldn't give two fucks either way if he was sleeping with Lucy, one or two of them may have an issue with it. *Fuck. Why can't anything ever be simple?*

He sat heavily and yanked Lucy's employee contract closer, flipped over the top page.

"What's wrong?" Lucy asked, her voice sounding miles away. "Toby, you're scowling. What did I miss?"

Her question snapped him out of his daze and he focussed his attention on the paperwork in front of him. "It's nothing. Don't worry about it."

Straightening to her full height, she folded her arms across her chest and shook her head. "If this relationship is going to work, both privately and professionally, then we need some rules." He opened his mouth to speak but she held up her hand and cut him off. "I'm not Charlie. I can't read your mind like he does, or whatever it is you two do when you talk to each other without actually talking to each other."

Toby smiled. "You noticed that, huh?"

"Kinda hard not to. I assume it's a twin thing?" When Toby nodded, Lucy continued, "Well that won't work with me. I need you to talk to me, to tell me what's going on inside your head."

Leaning back in his chair, Toby scrubbed his hand over his jaw then matched Lucy's gesture and folded his arms. "I'm not great at talking to people. Never have been. And I'm not used to having to explain myself, either. In fact,"—he huffed out a laugh—"this is probably the longest conversation I've ever had with anyone not directly related to me."

"So, I guess the whole quiet caveman act over the weekend wasn't actually an act, huh?" Lucy asked. "You really are that quiet all the time?"

He nodded. "Yes. Even my family refer to me as 'the stoic one'. But... I feel different around you. I don't know why but I *want* to talk to you." He shrugged. "I just don't know what to say." Then he held out his arms and beckoned her to him, relaxed when she eased into his lap and put her arm around his shoulders. "Being with you over the weekend felt...." He licked his suddenly dry lips and searched her eyes, though for what he wasn't sure. "It felt like finding an oasis at the end of a very long walk through the desert. And you made me want to dive in head first. It was a little overwhelming, to be honest." He smiled, almost to himself. "Overwhelming, but not unwelcome."

Her eyes grew glassy with tears and his gut tightened.

I've said the wrong thing again.

Then she cupped his cheek, and a tiny smile teased the corners of her mouth. "For a man who doesn't talk much, that was the perfect thing to say."

A rush of breath escaped him, his relief palpable. He took her hands in his and rubbed his thumbs over the backs of her lean fingers. "Can you forgive me, Lucy? For the dumb shit I said? And for the dumb shit I'm bound to say in the future?"

She pursed her lips like she was holding back a grin. "Only if you promise to practice talking more."

Toby's lip curled in disgust. "Talking?"

"Yes."

"More?"

"Yes."

"To actual people?"

Lucy snickered. "Yes, to actual people." She kissed his cheek. "But you can start with me."

Tucking her head under his chin, he said, "You're the only person I want to talk to." Then he nudged her thigh with his thickening erection.

Leaning back, she cocked an eyebrow at him. "Hmm... I'm pretty sure 'talking' is the last thing on your mind right now." She sighed and shook her head, a gentle laugh easing out of her. "Why do I get the feeling every conversation with you is going to end in sex?"

"Because you have very good instincts."

Lucy wasn't ignoring the way Toby had cunningly avoided answering her question about why he'd suddenly flopped into his chair, looking like he really wanted to hit something.

She'd just decided there were more important things to think about at that point in time, like his thick cock slowly teasing her with every measured thrust of his hips, or how every stroke of his tongue over her sensitive scars made her whole body shiver with awareness.

Or how every damn word out of his mouth made her pussy clench and her heart race full tilt ahead.

"Christ, I missed you last night," he murmured, his warm breath tickling the shell of her ear. "You have no idea how hard it was not to drive back to your place and kidnap you, take you home, tie you up and snuggle all night long."

After they'd signed her contract and discarded their pants, Toby had bent Lucy over his desk as promised. His warm weight pressed against her back and his thick fingers entwined with hers, curled over the edge of the wooden surface and held her in place. She felt completely surrounded, shielded. Safe.

Cared for.

"Sounds like I missed out on some pretty serious snuggling." She managed to push the words out between gasps and moans.

He chuckled by her ear. "Snuggling should always be taken seriously." Then he levered himself off her and grabbed her hips and it was all she could do to remember to breathe as he ploughed into her from behind, hard and fast and unrelenting. A bubble of laughter burst out of her when she noticed the desk move, inching its way across the floor with every thrust of Toby's hips, then moaned when he reached between her legs and found her swollen clit.

"Toby, Sir," she moaned, her orgasm building inside her, winding her tighter and tighter like a spring about to snap.

"You ready, baby?"

Lucy whimpered, her brain unable to form words. But a sharp slap on her arse was just the jolt she needed to snap her out of her daze.

"Yes, Sir."

Toby picked up his pace, slamming their bodies together in a heated frenzy until her body clamped down on his, milking his cock of everything he had to give her. Her breathing was loud and ragged and her blood pumped in her ears as the intensity of her orgasm ripped her lover's name from her throat. But Toby didn't stop. Lucy knew he'd climaxed, could feel his come slipping down her inner thighs. So why did he still feel hard inside her? Not that she was complaining—fuck no! It felt incredible. *He* felt incredible. And it was only after she'd screamed his name a second time that he let loose a roar of his own.

"Lucy!" His weight came over her again, his heavy breaths cooling her sweat slicked skin. "I fucking love making you come," he panting quietly by her ear, then sank his teeth into her earlobe.

Lucy's eyes rolled back, the pain prolonging her pleasure, then Toby fisted his hand in her hair, messing up her ponytail and hauled her backwards. He pulled her up off the desk and landed them both squarely in his big leather office chair, his thick cock still deep inside her as she squirmed in his lap.

"I could stay buried in you all day," he said, punctuating his words with little thrusts of his hips. Lucy smiled like a contented cat, especially when Toby began nipping at her and licking her with the tip of his tongue, teasing the sensitive flesh of her scars. "Whaddaya say we skip work, go home and fuck some more?"

Awareness and anticipation sent a shiver through Lucy and she'd be lying of she said she wasn't tempted. But she wanted—needed—to prove to herself that she wasn't going to repeat her past mistakes. Their little tryst had been fun and Toby's offer was enticing, but it was also completely inappropriate. Especially in the office. "This," she said, swallowing thickly. "This is why we need rules."

Toby growled. "No more rules." Then he turned her slightly towards him, cupped her cheeks in his hands and lowered his mouth to hers.

"I thought... you liked rules," Lucy said between kisses.

"I do," he said. "I like *my* rules. Like, whenever you're in my house, you will be naked." He slid his hand between her legs again and ground the heel of his palm against her clit. Her mouth fell open on a moan and she squirmed against him, then he pulled away abruptly, leaving her wet and needy. "And, you don't come unless I say so."

Lucy quivered against her lover's naked thighs then pouted, exaggerating the action. "You're mean."

Toby's grin sharpened. "I think you mean, 'you're mine'."

Lucy bit back an excited grin then cocked one brow. "Isn't that you're line?"

He gently chucked her under her chin. "I think we both know I don't mind sharing."

And just like that her blood ran cold and she was shoving her way out of his lap, his cock and his come slipping free of her body as she scrambled away. But he caught her wrist and held her fast.

"Hey, where are you going?" When she refused to look at him, he rose to his feet, gripped her chin in his strong hand and made her look at him. "Talk to me, Lucy. Why'd you shut down on me?"

"You don't mind sharing." She repeated his words, hoping they didn't sound as pissy as she felt, hoping he'd understand why she was upset without having to explain, but when he continued staring at her, she sighed. Her shoulders sagged. "I'd hoped there wouldn't be any more sharing." Then she lifted her gaze and stared up at him beseechingly. "I don't want to be shared again. Not by you."

In an instant she was being wrapped in Toby's arms and squashed against his chest. "Baby, no. That's not what I meant at all. I am never sharing you again. You hear me? Not with Charlie, not with anyone." Then he leaned back and stared down at her, a frown creasing his brow. "Wait, you did *want* to be shared the other night, yes? You didn't feel like you had to?"

"What? No," she assured him, shaking her head. "I absolutely wanted what we did, but that was when I thought we'd only be together for one night. Now...." She shook her head again.

"Now?"

"I only want you."

Toby's features softened and he reached up to smooth back the hair that had come loose from her ponytail. "I promise you, baby, sharing you was a one-time deal and even then...." He smiled and her breath stalled in her lungs. He was so goddamn handsome. "Well, I think we both thought it would prevent what's happening now, didn't we? That Charlie would act as a buffer against our attraction to each other. But it didn't work. You're mine, Lucy Barton. *Only* mine. And I'm yours. Absolutely only *yours*." He pressed a kiss to her forehead then breathed out sharply through his nose. "In fact, that's what I was pissed off about earlier, when you asked what was wrong."

So, he wasn't avoiding the question after all. "Oh?"

"I want to tell people about us. I don't care who knows we're fucking or dating or whatever we want to call this thing between us." He sighed and scratched his head. "But you're right. There are some people who will think the worst of you and speculate about how you got the job if they know we're together. And I promised I'd protect you from that crap."

Lucy sighed in relief and huffed out a laugh. "Oh, thank God. For a moment there, I thought it was something serious."

Now the big man just looked confused. "What?"

Lucy straightened his shirt collar and brushed the backs

of her fingers over his shoulders then smoothed the fabric down. Tidying his work shirt seemed ludicrous considering he wasn't wearing any pants, but it kept her hands busy in a way that prevented her from taking advantage of said pant-lessness. "You can't protect me from everything, Toby." She sighed quietly. "I know what I said earlier, but gossip about the new girl is inevitable. That's just how these things go, and I've been doing this long enough to handle almost anything they can throw at me. I do appreciate the thought, though." She slid her hands lower and wrapped her arms around his waist. "No one's ever looked out for me the way you do."

Not even Michael.

He narrowed his eyes. "Does that mean I can tell people about us? That you'd be okay if I pointed you out in a crowd and said 'that's my girlfriend'?"

Would she be okay?

No one had ever called her their girlfriend before, even before she was scarred. She was always just Michael's 'annoying little sister', at least until she'd became a fully-fledged firefighter and then she was known by all as 'that uppity bitch'.

Yeah, being one of only two full-time female firefighters at the station was loads of fun because God forbid you go up a ladder faster than the men. *Geez.*

No one had seen her as girlfriend material back then, at least not the men she was interested in. It didn't help matters that her father was the station chief.

Not that he would have cared one way or the other if any of the guys had wanted to date her, but they hadn't known that. And she'd been in no rush to tell them the main reason she'd joined the family business was to make it harder for her imposing hulk of a father to ignore her.

Fuck that for a joke. The last thing she'd wanted was a pity date. But a pity date was the last thing Toby Bennett was offering.

As soon as that thought sank into her brain and made itself cosy, she tightened her arms around him and knew that yes, actually, she would be very okay with people knowing she was his girlfriend. The gossips could go fuck themselves.

"Okay," she said, smiling. "No hiding."

"Perfect," Toby said, smiling down at her. Then his gaze flicked to his watch and he sighed. "We should probably put on pants. The staff will be arriving soon."

Lucy grabbed Toby's arse and snickered. "And you don't want them to see your sexy bum?"

He copied her action and squeezed her backside in his big hands until she yelped, then hauled her closer. "Depends. Do *you* want them to see my sexy bum?"

Her eyes narrowed as a spear of jealousy stabbed at her and she bared her teeth in a snarl.

Toby laughed then nuzzled her cheek. "I'll take that as a no," he said, then slapped her arse.

Lucy pulled on her underwear and jeans. "I still need a work shirt," she reminded him, watching with a hint of regret and more than a little longing as he tucked himself away and zipped up his cargo shorts. Even at work the man went commando. *Naughty.*

"I have spare shirts in there," he said. Then nodded to the cupboard beside the bank of filing cabinets lining one wall of his office. "There should be something in there that'll fit you."

Lucy opened the cupboard and pulled out the shirt on top. It was a deep green polo shirt with the garden centre's logo embroidered on the top left. She checked the tag for a size then put it back and searched for something a little larger. She was trim and fit, and her breasts were on the smaller side, but her body was long. Unless she wanted to expose her midriff—and the scars on her back—every time she stretched her arms above her head, she needed something a little bigger.

"Is it okay that I'm wearing jeans?" She removed the polo from the plastic wrapper. "I forgot to ask the other day."

"Jeans are fine," Toby said, manoeuvring his desk back into position. He straightened his belongings. "As long as everyone wears the company shirt, I don't have any preference about pants." He snorted. "Hell, one of my weekend guys wears a utility kilt."

Lucy laughed and a minute later she had her uniform sorted, her employee contract signed and was feeling cool, calm and confident. Today was the beginning of a new day, a new career and a new relationship. "Do we still have time for that tour?"

Toby opened the door and shook his head. "Not this morning, baby. Maybe after lunch?"

She knew she'd find her way around by then, especially as the first thing on her to-do list was a fire safety check, but she also knew seeing the business through Toby's eyes would help her sort out an action plan for how she ran the office, would help them both form a more enduring partnership.

Hopefully both professionally and personally.

Toby quickly showed her his current operating software and gave her a brief run-down of the day-to-day operations of the business. As Lucy listened and catalogued the new information, she freed her hair from its ponytail, finger-combed the fresh tangles it'd earned during their bout of office sex, then pulled it back again. She was about to loop the hair-tie around her hair when Toby cleared his throat.

"Leave it down," he said, his voice rough again. "I like it down."

Lucy didn't move. She kept her grip on the thick bundle at the back of her head and pursed her lips. "It's not professional to leave it down."

Toby grinned. "You need to relax, Lucy. You're not working for some uptight security firm anymore. It's okay to let your hair down."

"Wearing my hair in a ponytail at the office is me letting my hair down," she explained as she looped the elastic tie around her hair and secured it neatly. "If I wanted to be uptight, I'd wear it the same way I did to my interview."

But instead of ending the conversation as she'd hoped, Toby's grin became feral and he pinned her against the desk. "Can't say I'd be sad to see the return of that skirt and the way it hugs your gorgeous arse," he said. "But if you ever show up here again with your hair in that obnoxious bun, I'll make damn sure to mess it up as thoroughly as I did your ponytail." He pressed closer, forced her to grab the edge of her new desk as he leaned her back her over it. "Take it out."

The growl in his voice made her own voice shrivel to nothing. Gone. In the face of all that dominating hotness it had simply fled the scene, and the urge to submit to her lover came screaming to the forefront of her mind. Her knees felt weak, her mouth was dry and her panties...?

Soaked.

But the office was her domain, not his. And it was time she let him know it.

"No."

Toby's only response was to cock one eyebrow, his feral grin still entrenched on his face.

Lucy lifted her chin. "This is what you hired me for," she said, proud of the fact she didn't sound as aroused as she felt. "And this,"—she waved a finger between them—"is why we need rules."

"So you keep reminding me," Toby said, letting out a long, slow breath. "Fine." He gave her a sliver of space. "Rules." Then he yanked her against him, gripped her arse and pressed what felt like a fresh erection against her belly. "We'll discuss your rules over dinner." Then he leaned down and whispered in her ear, "And for dessert we'll go home and discuss mine."

Chapter Seventeen

L ucy swallowed hard then sank her teeth into her bottom lip, holding back the whimper desperately trying to escape her. She was incredibly turned on. So much so she feared the combined power of her arousal and his would soak through her jeans.

Toby eventually stepped back and gave her some much needed breathing room, and the second he turned away, she sucked down the oxygen her brain had momentarily forgotten it needed to function at full capacity.

"I have to open everything up now," he said, then lifted his hand and waved at two men walking past reception. The staff were arriving. "I have a landscaping client coming in at nine. If I'm not in the office when they arrive, show them into the conference room and offer them coffee and—"

Feeling more confident now there was more than an inch of space between them, Lucy held up her hand and cut him off. "Not my first rodeo," she said, then just to reinforce her viewpoint from earlier, she added, "Boss."

Toby scratched his head and smiled. He almost looked bashful, which was so fucking cute Lucy wasn't sure how to react. She doubted *Toby* and *cute* got used in the same sentence very often. Hot, sexy, gorgeous, absofuckinglutely the most amazeballs sex god of all time—those were words she could easily associate with Toby Bennett.

And yet, there he stood looking apologetic and shy. *Cute as fuck.*

"Sorry. I haven't had any help in here for months and even before that, well, Bec was better with paperwork than she was with people."

"Kinda like you?"

He grimaced but his eyes danced with amusement. "It's hard enough talking to people about their garden designs without throwing small talk into the mix." He shuddered. "But just because I don't like talking to people, doesn't mean I don't know how. And yes, I'd rather avoid it when I can. Talking to people is exhausting."

Lucy chuckled and smiled up at him, resisted the urge to touch him and stroke the sculptured curves of his biceps, the muscles bulging and pulling his shirt sleeves tight.

"Then it's a good thing you have me for that now. So relax and let me do my job so you can focus on yours."

Toby stepped close again and Lucy didn't resist when he bent his head down and kissed her cheek. "I fucking adore you."

Lucy ducked her head as the tell-tale heat of a blush crept up her neck and into her face. Then she pursed her lips. Annoyed at how easily he distracted her from her purpose. "Yeah, you say that now, but just wait. By the time I'm done with this place, you may not think me quite so adorable."

But Toby didn't seem worried. "Do your worst, baby. I look forward to seeing what solutions you come up with. Oh, and this," he said, reaching around her to pick up the tiny flowering cactus sitting beside her computer, "is for you. Welcome to BGL, Miss Barton." Then he gave her one last slap on her arse and left her alone in the office.

"After lunch" came and went and Toby still hadn't taken Lucy on a tour of the garden centre. As expected, she'd made her own rounds of the place about mid-morning when she'd conducted a fire-safety review, audited the security system and introduced herself to the staff.

All of them were welcoming, if a little wary, and eager to discuss their roles in the business. Ashley, the young woman who ran the tiny café inside the main building, seemed very appreciative of Lucy's arrival.

And very chatty.

"Don't get me wrong," she said, "Toby's a top bloke, but it'll be so good to have someone here who actually knows what they're doing in the front office. I volunteered to fill in while Bec was away but the boss said "no". Besides some friend's wedding or something he went to last weekend, I don't think he's had a day off in months. And yeah, I'm sad Bec's not coming back, but it'll be nice to get things back to normal around here."

Lucy had sat in the café for a good half hour, sipping coffee and talking to Ashley between customers, and by the time she returned to the office she had a pretty good handle on company gossip mill, who was secretly banging whom, and who to keep an eye on for one reason or another.

She also wondered how long it would take the staff to figure out she was banging their boss, and if any of them truly had a problem with it.

She was pretty sure theories about her scars would be flying thick and fast though.

More than one employee had *the look* while she spoke to them. *The look* being what Lucy called the expression people always displayed the first few times she spoke to them, before they became comfortable enough with her appearance they either stopped noticing her scars as something out of the ordinary, or stopped caring about how she came to have them and simply accepted they were there to stay.

And it didn't matter who the person was, *the look* was always the same: head tilted, mouth slightly open, eyes filled with a mixture of pity, horror and morbid curiosity.

Eyes that never made contact.

Except Toby's. He was the first person she'd met in a very long time who'd looked at her differently. Not once from the moment she'd met him had he looked at her with pity or horror, and his curiosity had never been morbid, simply curious. He found her fascinating and it had nothing to do with her scars at all.

Lucy figured it had more to do with the challenge she'd presented him that had made his head tilt, and the thought of fucking her tight body that had made his lips part.

Yeah. She'd liked Toby's *look* one hell of a lot.

By the end of her first day at Bennett's Gardens and Landscaping, Lucy was quietly confident she could get the place back to peak operational condition—and back under budget, something she'd have to discuss with Toby—within a month. Two, tops.

"Ready to go, baby?" Toby asked, locking his office door.

Lucy shut down her computer and picked up her notebook, the one filled with a to-do list twelve pages long. "We have a lot to talk about over dinner," she said, holding the notebook aloft.

Toby grabbed the book and tossed it back on her desk. "Not tonight we don't. Work stays at work, where it belongs." She opened her mouth to protest but he cut her off before she could speak a single word. "That's one of *my* rules."

When Toby arrived at Lucy's house, he was surprised to find her waiting in her underwear. As surprises went, it wasn't a bad one, but he distinctly remembered instructing her to wear a dress to dinner.

As he followed her through her meticulously kept house, he took the time to appreciate the white lace of her bra and panties, the way the sumptuous fabric clung to her smooth, soft skin, the way it accentuated her toned physique and luscious arse.

When they reached her bedroom, he pushed her up against the wall, slipped his hand between her thighs and found her panties wet. And almost changed his mind about going out.

Which he was pretty sure was Lucy's plan all along, and wasn't one he'd let her get away with.

He may have conceded defeat in the office and let Lucy take the lead—she was right, that was what he hired her for —but outside of work, Toby was in charge.

Still, the downcast direction of her gaze and general gloominess in the air didn't put him in a punishing frame of mind. Something was wrong with his girl. So he ignored the urge to pull her underwear to one side, sink one thick finger into her eager pussy and fuck her into submission, and followed her advice from that morning.

Toby decided to give talking a go instead.

He smoothed one hand over her hair, petted her, kept his voice soft. "Why aren't you dressed, baby?"

Lucy's long hair fell all around her, shrouded her face as

she stared at the floor. But Toby didn't want to talk to the top of her head so he hooked a knuckle under her chin and lifted her face to his.

The misery in her lovely whisky-eyes almost brought him to his knees. An hour ago she'd been eager to see him again, excited for their dinner date. What had happened to make her so miserable?

She swallowed hard. "I was dressed," she said quietly. "Just as you wanted." She cast her pitiful gaze to the dress discarded on the floor. The froth of fabric looked like an oversized serving of pink fairy floss and was the only thing in the room out of place. "But I—" She took a deep breath and straightened her spine, lifted her chin higher and looked him dead in the eye. Toby's chest swelled with pride. His girl was tough. Determined. "I know we said 'no more hiding', but that dress made me feel too... exposed."

"How do you mean?"

"My scars," she said, sliding her hand over her right shoulder, covering the mottled flesh. "Everyone will see."

Confusion furrowed Toby's brow. "Everyone can already see your scars." He felt like an arse pointing out the obvious, but it was true. Lucy had made no attempt to hide her face and neck from him, the scars there quite prominent and not easily hidden. So why was she upset?

"Not all of them," she said, her hand tightening on her shoulder.

That one small gesture screamed volumes, and a kernel of understanding burst open in Toby's mind. From what he'd seen so far, Lucy had a tendency to dress modestly in jeans and T-shirts or knee-length skirts and high-buttoned blouses. Not that she was opposed to flashing a little flesh— the plunging neckline of her blouse on Friday night was proof enough of that.

But even that sexy blouse had covered her shoulders and back, had hidden her other scars from prying eyes.

"The scars on your face," he said, gently brushing the backs of his fingers over her cheek, "They're your armour, aren't they? You use them to keep people at bay until they either cut and run or earn your trust."

Lucy nodded but said nothing, so he kept going.

"And this,"—he moved her hand from her shoulder and replaced it with his own—"and these,"—he slid his hand down her back—"they're your soft underbelly. Your vulnerable spots. The bits of yourself you hide from everyone." *Everyone but me.* Lucy had not only shown Toby those soft spots, she'd willingly rolled over and let him play with them, with her. All of her. "Why?"

Gnawing on one corner of her bottom lip, Lucy lowered her gaze again. "Like you said, the scars on my face and neck are like armour. People stare at me but social niceties dictate they keep their opinions to themselves. But for whatever reason, as soon as people see my other scars, those niceties fly out the window." She raised her face again and fire burned in those whisky-coloured depths. Bitterness stained her voice. "Wow! What happened to you? How far down does it go? Can I see it? Can I touch it?" Her eyes filled with tears and her voice broke. "I'll give you a thousand dollars if you let me film myself jerking off over it."

Toby reeled backwards, his eyes so wide they watered with the effort. "What the fuck? Someone actually said that to you?"

Lucy nodded, the fire returning to her gaze. "My scars are like an iceberg. People stare at the bit on top but it's the part lurking beneath the surface they all want to see. And that,"—she jabbed a finger at the dress on the floor—"let's them. Somehow, wearing a strappy dress is more effective than painting a target on my tits. And people never fail to take aim."

Moving to sit on the edge of the bed, Toby tugged Lucy into his lap. She'd revealed a lot of herself in the past few minutes, and as she sat stiffly against his thighs he realised it was his turn to share.

Because that was what people did, wasn't it?

They shared parts of themselves, revealed their soft underbellies bit by bit until they were completely exposed. That was a relationship. Exposing every part of you to someone else and trusting them to take care of you. Trusting them to want you—love you—even after they'd seen the worst of you. Toby wanted that with Lucy.

He wanted her trust.

Fuck. He wanted her *everything.* Wanted to be *her* everything.

Resting his forehead against her temple, he said, "I know what it's like to be stared at."

She scoffed, that one small sound loaded with more disbelief than she ever could have put into words. "People don't whisper disgusting things about tall people. They don't wonder out loud what you did wrong to be so horribly tall."

Toby grimaced. "No, but they do wonder if you're a degenerate like your father."

Lucy pulled back and looked up at him, her brows pinched, forming a tiny crease above her nose. He wanted to reach out and smooth it away, didn't want her to feel sorry for him, only to understand that he knew how it felt to be different. To be singled out. "Your father's a degenerate?"

That made Toby laugh. "I suppose it depends on your definition of degenerate. Dad's an artist, a painter. He has nine children to six different women, and for one reason or another he ended up raising all of us."

Lucy blinked slowly, as if she were waiting for her brain to digest the information. "He raised all nine of you on his own?"

"We're pretty well spaced out in age, so it wasn't like he had nine toddlers all at once. And he had help. My eldest brother and his wife lived with us for a long time, and one or two close family friends would check on us, make sure we had everything we needed."

"But...?" Lucy asked, one brow raised.

"But, when you grow up in a family like mine in a small town like Melville's Cross, you stick out for a whole other reason."

Her grip tightened on his arm. "I'm not going to like this, am I?"

"Imagine being a seven-year-old kid," he said, his gaze unfocussed as he recalled the memory more easily than he liked, "rocking up to the school gates and overhearing the other parents whispering to each other. 'There goes another one of Bennett's bastards'."

"What horrible people!" Lucy gasped, her outrage making her nostrils flare. And in that moment it struck Toby with the force of an atom bomb what a fierce mother Lucy would be, how protective and loving. He almost laughed out loud at the unbidden thought, until his cock twitched in agreement.

He squeezed her thigh, in part to let her softness and the warmth of her body soothe the ache of the memory that never quite left him, but also in part to stop himself from settling his hand over her belly and imagining what it would look like if it was round with his child. *What the fuck is wrong with me?* He was becoming fanciful in his old age.

Shaking his head to clear the ridiculous thought, he focused on their conversation. "They never said it to our faces, but they never hid their dislike of us either."

"But you were just kids. You didn't have any say in who your parents were."

"Exactly," Toby said. "Just like you have no say in whether or not you're scarred. It is what it is and it's up to us to choose what we do with it. My siblings and I could have cowed to the other parents and their ignorance, but we didn't. We held our heads high and refused to give them the satisfaction of knowing they'd hurt us. Just like you did the other night in the pub. I was ready to swoop in and save you but you never needed saving. You stood up for yourself and put that little shit in his place and it was a fucking privilege to watch." He put Lucy on her feet and threaded his fingers through hers. "But you don't have to do it alone anymore. Not if you don't want to. I know you're strong, I've seen it, but I'm here for you, baby. However you want me."

Pink spots rose on Lucy's cheeks and she bit her lip. Her gaze darted down and away.

Toby stared up at her, his brow pulled tight, his eyes narrowed. "What is it?"

Digging her toe into the plush pile of the rug covering the bedroom floor, Lucy gave a half-shrug and an embarrassed smile. "I don't want to diminish the weight of everything you've just said, because honestly, that was just about the most wonderful thing anyone has ever said to me."

Something in Lucy's underlying tone sent a warning to every nerve in Toby's body, made his muscles lock down tight and his jaw clench as he waited for the inevitable blow. "But...?"

Lucy shifted closer and stood between his knees, moved his hands to her hips then placed hers on his shoulders, curled her fingers into the cotton of his shirt. Then she smiled down at him, her eyes bright with need. "I really like it when you call me baby."

Relief flooded Toby and burst out of him on a shaky laugh. "I really like it when you call me master." Lucy's blush deepened and Toby wanted to throw her down and fuck his way into her until she cried out "master" all over again. He rubbed his thumbs over the soft flesh of her hips, just above the lace of her panties. "But I also need you to know I meant every word I just said. I promise I'll be there for you. I'll support you, shield you or just stand back and watch you kick arse. Understand?"

Nodding, she smiled at him. "Thank you," she whispered. "Master."

A spark of wanting crackled through his veins, lighting up every corner of his body and brain as Lucy said the word he'd been longing to hear again. But Toby had other tasks to attend to before he could satisfy his own lust. Like reminding his little subbie who was in charge and that there were consequences for her actions.

"Right now, though," he said seriously, staring her down as he rose to his feet. "I want you to pick up your dress, put it on, then bend over the bed and accept your punishment."

Lucy sucked back a short, sharp breath. "Punishment?"

"You've made us late for dinner, baby," Toby said, unbuckling his belt and pulling it free of the loops on his jeans. "I think five lashes should suffice." He watched her gaze darken and shutter with pleasure, saw her throat bob and her chest rise and fall with a quickened breath. "On each cheek." Lucy whimpered and the pink of her earlier blush crept down her throat towards her breasts. Her thighs were pushed together. Tightly. Toby let his mouth curl up on one side as he folded his belt in half, loving the way her eyes tracked his movements. "Are you turned on, baby? Does the thought of my belt curling around your spectacular arse make you wet for me?"

She nodded rapidly and whimpered again. "Yes, Master."

Ignoring his need to adjust his aching cock, Toby slapped the belt against his palm and watched Lucy tremble. He kept his focus sharp in case her knees gave way and he had to catch her in a hurry, before she collapsed in a horny heap on the floor. "Then you'd better be quick. If we're lucky we might still make our reservation."

Her eyes widened and she swallowed hard as she clutched the dress to her chest. "We're still going out?"

"Yes, we are," he said gently.

Chewing on her lip, Lucy's gaze darkened under a furrowed brow. "People will stare."

"Let them."

"But—"

"But nothing."

Toby understood why Lucy felt anxious, especially after some of the things people had said to her in the past. Seriously, if he ever met the guy who offered to make her a porn star... well, Toby had access to a wood chipper, a state forest and several siblings with flexible morality when it came to protecting their loved ones. And he was pretty sure no one would miss the douchebag.

His belt dangling from one hand, Toby cupped Lucy's cheek with the other and bent to kiss her lips. "If people want to stare at us, let them. They want to whisper about us, who cares? You're mine, Lucy. And I'm proud to be seen with you, scars and all. Trust me to look after you. Please."

Barely a second passed before Lucy straightened her

spine and nodded, that one short, sure bob of her head all the permission Toby needed to continue.

"Good girl," he said, her submission causing a pleasurable warmth to bloom in his chest, then he tightened his hand around her chin. "Now bend over the fucking bed. I'm hungry."

Chapter Eighteen

Lucy closed her eyes and rolled her lips between her teeth. Every time she moved, even the tiniest bit, the welts on her arse rubbed against the lace of her panties and sent a riot of sensation scorching through her body, heating her up in all the right places.

Rolling her lips between her teeth was the only thing stopping her from moaning out loud and announcing to the entire bloody restaurant exactly how horny she was.

Closing her eyes was simply so she couldn't see the smug grin on her lover's face as he revelled in her discomfort.

It wouldn't have been so bad if Toby had fucked her after he'd punished her, helped her burn off all that extra adrenaline, but he hadn't. Apparently making him wait to eat his dinner meant she had to wait for him to eat her pussy. Because that's what he'd promised her as he'd run his fingers over her aching arse then slipped them between her shaky legs.

"You're going to sit on my face and I'm going to make

you come so fucking hard," he'd whispered in her ear as he'd stroked his thick fingers through her arousal. He'd tormented her clit with gentle, taunting almost-caresses, had worked her into a frenzy then left her wanting. Aching. Needing. "I'm going to lick up every drop of your sweet desire, baby. And by the time I'm done with you, you'll never want to leave my bed again."

Lucy opened her eyes, let out a long, slow breath and wondered if it was possible to make it through dinner without making a complete fool of herself. Although, if she was being honest, that ship had already sailed.

She couldn't believe she'd freaked out about a dress. Or that she'd vomited her insecurities all over Toby. And yeah, she'd given him and his brother a glimpse into the world of her anxieties on Friday night, but that had been nothing compared to the shitshow she'd dumped at his feet when he'd picked her up for dinner.

To his credit, he hadn't run away. Nor had he told her to just get over it, because telling someone in the grip of an anxiety freak-out to "get over it" never ended well.

No. Toby had been patient with her. Kind to her. He'd been sexy and sweet and demanding. He'd asked her questions and hadn't judged her answers. Then he'd opened up and told her something about him. Something deeply personal. He'd empathised with her and called her baby and told her he'd be there for her. For whatever reason. He knew she didn't need him, but said he'd be there for her anyway.

He'd made her feel special again, and again she wasn't sure how to feel about that. Usually when someone went out of their way to make her feel good, it was over and done within an hour or two.

One night stands had become so ingrained in her way of

life that she didn't really know what to do on an actual date, which, as she sat there staring blankly at the menu, she realised was part of the reason she'd had her little episode.

Lucy didn't like feeling unsure of herself. And going out to dinner with a man who already knew he could have her in his bed anytime he liked but was being nice to her anyway, was disorienting.

And that in turn made her realise how supremely pathetic her life actually was.

"What's wrong?"

Snapping her gaze up from the menu, Lucy stared into Toby's crystalline eyes. Eyes that stared back at her with concern. She opened her mouth to deny his statement but never got the chance.

His gaze narrowed. "And before you even think about lying to me, don't."

Lucy swallowed against the lump in her suddenly dry throat. "I just realised something about myself."

Toby's eyes lighted with curiosity. "And what's that?"

It was on the tip of Lucy's tongue to tell Toby he was dating a total loser, when she had a second epiphany. One that screamed at her to pull her head out of her arse and take a good look at the man sitting opposite her, to realise how she'd come to be there.

The tightness around her chest eased. "I was thinking about the choices I've made throughout my life. How everything I've done has led me here. To you."

The light in Toby's eyes seemed to spread to the rest of his face, his expression beaming at her. But when he took her hand in his and brought it to his lips, his eyelids shuttered and the light changed, became more sensual in nature, and Lucy was certain had the waitress not chosen that exact moment to ask if they were ready to order,

Toby would have suggested skipping dinner in favour of dessert.

The memory of his whispered words made Lucy squirm and wish she could dull the throbbing in her clit. But her movements rubbed the lace of her panties against her arse which made her moan. Toby chuckled knowingly.

After the infuriating man ordered their meals, he asked Lucy if she'd like a glass of wine. In what she hoped would be the first of many getting-to-know-you moments, Lucy said, "I don't drink alcohol." But instead of the incredulous "Why not?" that usually got tossed her way when she said what was considered the most un-Australian thing ever, Toby simply smiled, then ordered them both a pink lemonade.

"You can have a drink if you want to," she assured him. "Just because I'm a teetotaller doesn't mean you have to be."

And then he said something wholly unexpected. "I don't drink either."

"Why not?" she blurted, then cringed at the incredulous zeal with which she asked her question. She'd turned into one of *those* people.

Toby grinned. "Charlie and I are allergic to alcohol."

Lucy's brain stuttered and for a moment she couldn't form words. "I'm sorry, but it sounded like you said you're allergic to alcohol." But when he cocked one perfectly carved brow and stared at her, she realised he wasn't kidding. "Wow. Seriously, that's actually a thing? People can be allergic to alcohol?"

"Uh-huh."

"What happens if you drink it?" A flitter of panic swelled in her chest. "Do I need to start carrying an Epi-pen around with me?"

Toby chuckled. "That won't be necessary. It's not life

threatening. I just break out in hives. Big, nasty looking ones. It's pretty gross. And itchy."

The exaggerated way he screwed up his face as he described his allergic reaction made her panic recede. She laughed. "Sorry," she said, still chuckling. But then he smiled too and Lucy was struck by how boyish Toby looked, mischievous. Playful.

Gorgeous.

Dinner was served and they ate in relative silence. That was one of the things Lucy admired most about Toby. He didn't talk just for the sake of it. He didn't feel the need to fill the void with the noise of pointless chitchat. Every conversation they had was meaningful. Not necessarily deep, but meaningful.

It made for a pleasant change from the office gossip she endured at work.

Listening to scuttlebutt kept Lucy informed about her staff—who was fighting, who was fucking, who was pulling their weight and who wasn't—but it was also exhausting. And made her appreciate Toby's silence even more.

Toby of course, chose that exact moment to speak. "Should we discuss these rules of yours now?" he asked, then wrapped his big hand around his glass of pink lemonade—the girliest drink in existence—and tilted it to his full, masculine lips.

Lucy bit her lip, hard, stifling her hormone driven squeak of appreciation. Then she took a sip of her own drink. The sweet yet tart flavour bursting on her tongue did not refocus her attention as she'd hoped. Nope. Her imagination went in a whole other direction and she suddenly found herself wondering if pink lemonade tasted as good as Toby would taste after drinking pink lemonade.

When Toby cleared his throat, Lucy realised she'd been

staring so intently at his mouth she'd forgotten to answer his question.

"I'm sorry, what did you say?"

The big man smirked at her, didn't even try to pretend he wasn't laughing at her. *Bastard.*

No. Not a bastard. That was what the horrible people in his home town called him and his siblings when they were just little kids. The townspeople were the bastards. Not Toby. Never Toby.

"I asked if you'd like to discuss your rules. For us, for work."

"Oh, right," she said, and straightened in her seat. Then she snapped her legs together and tried to suppress the flare of heat in her sex as her panties shifted against the welts on her arse. "Yes. Let's do that."

Toby would have to be blind to miss the way Lucy's eyes glazed over every time she moved in her seat. The ten lashes he'd given her before dinner were hard enough she'd feel them for the rest of the night, possibly into tomorrow. And the lace of her panties, soft as it was, would provide just enough friction to stimulate her tender flesh and make her shiver with anticipation, keep her off balance. It would be as if he were continuously stroking her arse with his own fingers.

He knew her pussy was wet and fully expected her panties to be ruined by the end of dinner. *Perfect.* Lucy Barton really was the perfect woman for him. She got off on pain, he got off on control. They were a good fit. Certainly a better fit than he'd experienced with anyone else in a very long time.

"The rules, as far as work is concerned, need to be straight forward, something we'll remember easily. Agreed?"

"Agreed."

"So with that in mind, I propose the following," she said, then cleared her throat. "One, as the business manager, I'm in charge of internal business decisions, day-to-day operations and staffing requirements for the garden centre and café, leaving you to focus on the landscaping side of the business."

Trying his best not to grin at his lovely little submissive being all bossy and adorable again, Toby asked, "Internal business decisions?"

"With your final approval, of course, but yes." Lucy wriggled in her chair again and swallowed hard. "Things such as software and security upgrades, maintaining the business website and social media accounts, staffing disputes, budgeting and supplies are my areas of expertise. Gardening... not so much."

Toby nodded as she spoke, her proposal acceptable so far, but then his brain snagged on something in particular and he frowned. "I don't have any social media accounts."

"You will," Lucy said, her smile full of the confidence she'd lacked earlier in the evening. Toby was relieved to see its return. "Two, if and when I make any changes to the internal operations and/or staff requirements, I'd appreciate your full support. Especially in front of the staff. They need to know I'm their go-to person now, not you. And to that end," she said, pausing as though bracing herself for whatever she had to say next, "please don't call me baby in front of the staff or clients."

Toby ran his tongue over his teeth and pierced Lucy

with his stare. "I thought we were going to be open about our relationship."

"We are," she assured him, "but I don't want our relationship to undermine my authority. I've seen it happen before. My predecessor at the security firm was engaged to the managing director at the time. He always called her by a pet name and soon everyone in the office was doing it too. It completely destroyed her credibility within the work environment and the staff walked all over her. No one took her seriously and in the end she took stress leave, then quit. So, as much as I love it when you call me baby, it's just not—"

"Professional," he said, sighing quietly, remembering their squabble over her hair. Toby reached across the table and took Lucy's hand in his. He understood. Completely. Especially after seeing her house. Lucy liked order, she liked control. Just like him. But that meant they had to learn to compromise. And just like her hair, it was no big thing for him to concede about her name.

"As long as I can call you baby outside of work, I have no problem calling you Lucy at work. And occasionally Miss Barton," he added with a quick grin. An image of Lucy in that arse-hugging skirt, bent over his desk while he spanked her with a wooden ruler formed in his mind. His cock stiffened against his thigh and he shifted in his seat, trying to adjust himself without actually grabbing his dick in the middle of the restaurant. "On second thought," he ground out, "maybe I'll stick to Lucy."

Lucy's perceptive gaze flicked to his crotch and back and it was her turn to grin. When a strangled snorting sound escaped her, he raised a brow.

"Anything else?"

Lucy broke eye contact and the fake candle in the

centre of the table suddenly became the most interesting thing in the room. "Three... no sex at work."

"I beg your pardon?"

"I said—"

"I heard what you said and... no. That won't work for me. Which you obviously knew or you'd still be looking at me." Toby almost laughed when her jaw dropped and her gaze flicked back to his, her eyes wide. He squeezed her fingers and lowered his voice, took on that deeper tone he knew drove her wild. "If you think I can keep my hands off you for that long, you're nuts." Lucy's mouth snapped shut and her cheeks pinkened. Toby let himself smile. He loved making her blush. "But, I can see how that would affect our working relationship so I'm willing to accept your rules with one amendment."

"Only one?" she asked, her eyes narrowed under a disbelieving brow.

"I'll agree to your no sex at work rule, but only during business hours. Outside of nine to five your arse is mine," he growled. "Take it or leave it."

Squirming in her seat again, Lucy's blush deepened and she nodded. "Take it."

"Good. Let's get out of here."

"What about dessert?"

"You are dessert."

Toby paid for dinner then wrapped his arm around Lucy's waist and led her outside. The sun had set and there was a chill in the air, but the sky was clear and the stars bright. The restaurant he'd taken her to was less than fifteen minutes from her house and overlooked the bay.

As they strolled back to the car, Toby listened to the waves gently lapping against the rocky shore, the soothing shushing sound at odds with the chirping and ticking of insects and the chittering squawks and flap of leathery wings as flying foxes passed overhead. But somehow, it just worked. *Like me and Lucy.* All those noises combined to make something harmonious and special. Beautiful.

Effortless.

Lucy shivered against his side and he hugged her closer, rubbed his hand up and down her arm.

Her dress showed off exactly as much skin as she'd said it would, and even with her hair flowing freely down her back and over her shoulders, Lucy had still been anxious, had still worried people would stare at her. Judge her. So before they'd left her house, Toby had told her to put on the matching pink cardigan he'd seen sitting on the end of her bed. It was thin and wouldn't keep her very warm, but it would hide her scars.

The ones she was fretting over, anyway.

When she'd looked at him, questioning, the cardigan clutched in her hands, he'd said, "Baby steps." And she'd thrown herself into his arms and hugged him so tightly he'd thought she'd never let go. He'd also thought he'd be completely okay with that. Toby liked having Lucy in his arms, safe and warm and his.

Or not so warm.

When Lucy shivered again, Toby hurried her to the car and got her inside.

The trip to Lucy's house was short and relatively quiet. He rested his hand on her thigh, she complimented his choice of restaurant. But when he parked his car in her driveway, they both fell silent, the air between them thick with anticipation.

Toby swallowed hard and tried to calm his breathing. He felt like a teenager, sitting there in his car with a hard-on straining against his jeans and a pretty girl only inches away and not knowing what to say to her. He knew what he wanted to do to her, but in that moment words failed him.

And he'd been doing so well too.

Lucy looked so beautiful, sitting there in her pale pink dress and the darker pink cardie, sweet and sexy and so insanely fuckable. He slid his hand higher on her thigh and opened his mouth, but before he could say anything, a bright light snapped on and practically illuminated the interior of the car.

"Busted," Lucy chuckled.

Toby shielded his eyes against the burning white light. "By who?"

But Lucy didn't answer. Opening the door, she climbed out of the car and walked towards the light. "You can stop blinding us now."

What the...?

Toby unclicked his seatbelt and hurried after Lucy, continuing to shield his eyes as he slipped his arm around her shoulders, placed himself slightly in front of her. Between her and whomever was hiding behind the light.

When the light dimmed, he blinked repeatedly to rid his vision of the little blacks dots floating in front of him, then stared at the woman standing on the veranda of the neighbouring house.

"Lucy?" He whispered her name and hoped like hell she heard the underlying "What the fuck is going on?" in his tone.

"Toby, this is my neighbour, Mrs Miller. Maisie, this is Toby Bennett, my bo—"

"Boyfriend," Toby rushed out, just in case Lucy was thinking of saying "boss" instead. "It's good to meet you, Mrs Miller."

"I've known Mrs Miller all my life," Lucy said. "She taught me how to make pancakes."

"Oh, well now I'm *really* glad to meet you," Toby said with a smile, "so I can say thank you. I was lucky enough to sample Lucy's pancakes over the weekend."

Lucy's neighbour looked to be seventy-years-old if she was a day, and stared at him with thin, over-plucked eyebrows raised high over hawkish eyes. Her mouth was pinched in a look of disapproval, causing creases in her skin to flare out around her lips, and her short hair was dyed the same shade as his jacaranda blooms. A pair of glasses sat perched on the end of her nose and she wore an old fashioned apron over her clothes, the type with the pocket in front that he'd be willing to bet good money contained a handful of sour lollies.

Her gaze darted to his arm around Lucy, then drifted slowly from his head to his toes and back again. A sly grin kicked up one side of her mouth, lessening the harshness of her expression, and when she spoke her voice sounded stronger than her appearance would suggest.

"I seriously doubt her pancakes were the only thing you sampled."

"Maisie!" Lucy gasped, her eyes wide in horror. "You can't say things like that. Apologise, please. Now!"

The old woman rolled her eyes. "I'm old, honey. I can say whatever the hell I want and people think I'm adorable."

"You are not adorable, you cantankerous old bat."

"Fine," Maisie huffed. "I'm sorry I insinuated the walking mountain here,"—she gestured to Toby, whose eyes had grown to the size of hubcaps as he held in his laughter —"rocked your world all weekend. My bad."

Lucy closed her eyes and pressed the tips of her fingers

to the middle of her forehead, like she was fighting off a headache, then she frowned at her neighbour.

"What am I going to do with you?"

Toby was captivated by the old woman and couldn't wait to hear what she said next. It was obvious to him, even from their brief exchange, she and Lucy knew each other very well. They were possibly even closer than friends, more like pseudo-family.

He knew of few people who could call an elderly woman a "cantankerous old bat" and get away with it.

"You're not going to do anything with me," Maisie said. "You're going to enjoy the rest of your evening climbing your mountain man." Then she turned to Toby, all semblance of her earlier severity replaced by a kind smile and a knowing gaze. "I'm sorry if I seemed rude, Toby, but I'm always suspicious of new cars in the neighbourhood."

"Rightly so," he said, inclining his head. "Next time I change cars I'll be sure to tell Lucy so she can give you a heads up."

Her expression brightened, bordering on respect. "I would appreciate that, thank you."

Lucy turned her head to direct her frown at him. "Just how many cars do you own?"

"Me personally? Five."

"You own *five* cars?"

"Eleven if you count Charlie's." Her jaw dropped and Toby shrugged. "What? We like going fast."

Lucy snorted. "I noticed."

"Well," Maisie said, interrupting them. "I'll be getting back to my movie. Be good, children," she added, turning back for the door. "And if you can't be good, be good at it."

Toby stared after the old woman as she made her way back inside, his body shaking with silent laughter.

"I am so sorry," Lucy said, her gaze likewise focussed in the direction of the retreating Mrs Miller. "I should have warned you about her."

Toby pressed a quick kiss to her temple and grinned. "I can't wait for you to meet my family."

Chapter Nineteen
____

"So, what's the story with you and Maisie Miller?"

Lucy lay on her back beside Toby, their bodies slick with sweat, their breathing ragged and their come still wet on her thighs.

Using Toby's outstretched arm as a pillow, Lucy felt hot and boneless, and she swallowed thickly against her need for a glass of water. The very last thing she wanted to talk about was the old woman who lived next door.

"Please tell me you weren't thinking about my seventy-two-year-old neighbour while we were fucking."

Toby's bark of laughter was so loud and sudden it made her jump. "Christ, no." He rolled onto his side and draped one heavy leg over hers, pinning her against him, then nuzzled against her neck. His hot breath fanned against her skin and tickled her scars. "I can promise you I will never think about another woman while fucking you. No matter how sassy they may be."

"Maisie is definitely sassy," Lucy said, laughing as she swatted away her lover's wandering hand and shoved at his leg, attempting to rise from the bed. Toby growled at her, the deep, throaty sound vibrating through his chest and into hers. "I'm thirsty," she explained, but he apparently didn't care.

The arm she was lying on curled around her, pulling her closer, and his other hand gripped her thigh, his fingers digging in, cocooning her in his long limbs and preventing her from going anywhere.

"And...?" Dark and thick with warning, Toby's voice whispered across her cheek, that one word conveying more meaning than most men could cram into an entire sentence. A whole freaking paragraph, even.

And that's when she remembered. She'd forgotten the rules. The very simple rules they'd gone over when he'd stripped her naked, bent her over the bed and fucked her senseless.

But brain-melting sex would do that to a girl.

She recovered quickly and cast her gaze down. If she wanted to leave the bed, she had to ask Toby for permission. "May I fetch a glass of water, Sir?"

Relaxing his grip on her leg, he smiled, then slid his hand higher. He skimmed his palm over her pussy, her stomach and between her breasts, coming to rest at the base of her throat. Lucy's breath hitched as she waited for his next move. He didn't make her wait long.

"You forgot the rules, baby," he whispered, tightening his grip around her throat. "Now you have to be punished."

Any normal person would have been terrified by the prospect of a giant man threatening to punish them.

But not Lucy.

Not when the man in question was Tobias Bennett and certainly not when she could feel his gorgeous cock harden against her thigh.

Excitement lanced through her body and she felt it

everywhere, lighting her up from the inside out as it crackled along her veins, heated her blood and ignited her passion. But before she could say a word, Toby dragged her off the bed.

Forcing her to her knees in the middle of the shag-pile rug—that did little to cushion her weight on the hardwood floor—he twisted his hand in her hair. Pain exploded in her scalp. Pain that morphed into pleasure as he held her still, captive to his whims.

Her pussy flooded with warmth.

Toby's semi-hard cock jutted towards her face. Lucy stared at the thing, a feeling of awe bubbling up inside her and escaping on a sigh of appreciation, until the big man dragged her closer, practically shoving it in her face.

"What are you waiting for, baby?" he growled. "It ain't gunna lick itself."

Flicking her gaze towards Toby's, Lucy saw the raw lust in his expression, lust she reflected back at him as she reached up to take his cock in her hand.

Slowly he shook his head. "Mouth only," he said through gritted teeth, his voice harsh. "Put your hands on my legs."

Lucy's excitement spiked again. Toby only sounded like that when he was ready to snap, when he'd take her rough and hard, his face buried in the crook of her neck, his arms banded around her as though he'd never let her go.

When he'd whisper in her ear and tell her how beautiful and perfect she was, and unlike his brother, when Toby told Lucy she was beautiful, she believed him.

Not wanting to appear over-eager, she kept her voice calm and even. "Yes, Sir," she said, then forced herself to brace her hands against Toby's rock hard thighs instead of curling them around his thick length like she wanted to.

Leaning forwards, Lucy snaked her tongue around the broad head of Toby's cock. She could taste them on his flesh, smell the musky aroma of their arousal coating his silky skin, feel the heat of his blood as it rushed to strengthen his cock. Her eyelids fluttered closed.

"Lucy." Toby purred her name like he was confessing a sin.

Lucy shivered with wanting.

The second stroke of her tongue was firmer, less of a tease as she licked along the side of his shaft. Again and again she licked and nipped at him until his cock was fully erect and danced in front of her eyes, silently demanding her full attention.

Which is exactly what she gave him.

Snaking her tongue around the head again, she used her lips to pull his cock inside her mouth, then slowly bobbed back and forth, taking him a little deeper every time. There was little chance she'd ever take all of him—he was too damn big for that—but she'd give him the best goddamn blowjob of her life.

Moaning as she worked his cock, Lucy desperately wanted to slip her hand between her thighs and get herself off, but she knew she'd be earning herself another punishment if she did, and she wasn't confident her next one would be as much fun.

An image of Toby's toy wall sauntered through her mind like it owned the joint, making her shudder. Some of those paddles were nasty. More than even she could handle.

Above her, Toby groaned and anchored both hands in her hair, twisting the strands around his fingers as he tugged her closer, thrust deeper.

The feeling of fullness in her mouth overwhelmed her and when he hit the back of her throat she had to swallow hard to stop herself from choking. Tears leaked from her eyes, slid down her cheeks and caught on her lips, adding to the mess beginning to drip down her chin.

"Beautiful."

One word was all the warning Toby gave before he pulled back and thrust again. Picking up the pace, he fucked her mouth and throat, harder, deeper, faster. He took her, possessed her. Used her.

Eyes wide, Lucy clung to her lover's thighs, helpless as he fucked her face. Helpless and annoyed. At him, at herself, at her needy body clenching around nothing, eager to be filled. Longing to be satisfied.

Lucy liked physical pain. Always had. It soothed her mind when she was stressed, calmed her anxiety and reset her equilibrium. She didn't know why and she didn't care, she just knew it worked for her. Like a balm for her soul.

Toby's hard and fast face fuck didn't hurt, but it also wasn't the most comfortable thing in the world, and the sting in her scalp where he fisted her hair compensated for that lack of pain and she felt it all the way to her toes. *Delicious.*

So why was her brain railing against it?

Her body was responding as expected. Her skin felt tight and flushed, her heart raced, her clit throbbed and her pussy wept. So why wasn't her brain on board for the experience? And why did she feel tightness in her chest? Because it was a punishment?

But that didn't make any sense.

Toby had punished her over the weekend and she'd loved every salacious second of it. Maybe because he'd had taken away her ability to speak, to say her safeword if she needed it? Or was it simply because he'd taken away her control? Instead of giving Toby the sensual blowjob she wanted, Lucy had to make do with being used.

She'd wanted to *give* him pleasure. He wasn't supposed to just *take* it from her.

But now she had to make do with being his fuck toy.

A flicker of understanding tickled her brain.

Lucy was Toby's fuck toy.

His to command and control and dominate. His to protect. He'd been very clear on that point so why would he stop now? And Lucy *knew* she could stop the punishment if she wanted to. Even without the power of speech, she knew all she had to do was tap his leg three times, pause, then tap twice more and Toby would stop everything. It was their secret knock, a silent safeword they'd devised over the weekend.

That's why he'd insisted she place her hands on his thighs. When she wasn't gagged, he tied her hands behind her back.

And as her mind clung to that knowledge, it began letting go of everything else.

Her annoyance at herself for forgetting the rules was forgotten. Her irritation with Toby for making her so goddamn fucking horny—which she realised was the real punishment—vanished. She stopped overanalysing everything.

Lucy didn't need to be in control. Not with Toby. Not while he was there to take care of her. And he'd never been going to let her give him that sensual blowjob.

Because he was punishing her.

"Look at me, baby."

Unable to ignore the command, her gaze instantly snapped to his. And the way he looked at her blew her mind. Pleasure. Reverence. Desire. Hunger. It all swam in the ocean of his arctic gaze, boring into her from above.

And that's when she surrendered.

That was the moment she let go of everything else. Every doubt, every question, every lingering work-related thought she hadn't been able to shut down when they'd clocked out... Lucy let it all go.

She clung to Toby's thighs and stared up at him, allowed herself to drown in the ocean of his eyes, to be present in the moment, to let go of her control and truly submit.

And when she did that, a myriad of things happened.

Her anxiety and the tightness it caused in her chest eased away, she relaxed and breathed more easily, and... she made a decision.

Lucy chose to *trust* Toby.

Trust him not only with her body as she'd done over the weekend, but with her mind too.

And maybe her heart....

Then she swallowed hard and hoped like Hell he didn't turn out like the last man she'd trusted.

Toby groaned. And he was surprised he'd been able to say that much.

The sight of Lucy on her knees taking his cock down her throat, watching her mind blank, feeling her body relax, seeing the fire in her whisky eyes bank into a smouldering flame, incandescent with desire.... And the feel of her lips, her teeth, her tongue, all working together in beautiful synchronicity as he fucked her mouth with hard, demanding thrusts, his hands fisted in her hair, her tears drying on her cheeks....

Bliss. Pure unadulterated bliss.

Her fingers curled into his muscles, her short, practical fingernails leaving weals in his skin, and he relished the tiny bite of pain, let it focus his attention. He was punishing her, sure, teaching her a lesson, but he'd also felt the shift in their dynamic. Had seen the moment she'd given over to him, the moment she'd surrendered, when the sharp focus he always saw in her intelligent eyes blurred around the edges and she'd accepted him. Trusted him.

Completely.

It was a heady feeling, one he'd never truly felt before.

Throughout the twenty odd years he'd lived as a Dominant man, Toby had rarely taken on a submissive for more than a few sessions.

Hell, he'd rarely taken on a submissive, full stop. Mostly because he'd never fully overcome his natural shyness, and while the strong, silent stereotype worked in some situations, the ability to clearly communicate during a play session was a necessary skill. Not only for the submissive's safety, but his own.

While he owned the ability to talk when needed, he lacked the inclination.

His perfect woman was one he was so in tune with, words became superfluous. Unneeded. Unnecessary.

But his laconic demeanour wasn't his only issue. If Toby was being completely honest with himself, he'd admit the real reason he'd avoided forming attachments to any of the willing few who'd crossed his path, was that he feared he'd go too far.

In the heat of the moment when anything could happen, Toby had feared his own dark urges, his need to control a woman's body, to bring her pleasure by inflicting pain, would cause more distress than it cured. Hell, he frightened people simply by walking into the room. Put a whip in his hand and a scowl on his face and he was downright terrifying.

He'd known the trust previous submissives had put in him had been tentative at best, and at the time he'd been okay with that. He hadn't been looking for anything more, anything deeper. So he'd negotiated scenes and discussed boundaries, pushed soft limits, respected hard limits and left his subbies feeling boneless and satisfied. And when they were ready to move on—or they tried pushing for more than he was willing to give—he'd pointed them in the direction of someone more compatible.

His brief—yet ultimately disappointing encounters—had allowed him to keep his personal demons in check without messy emotions getting involved. And he'd seen it as a kindness to push the women away, to isolate them from his inner turmoil before they got it in their pretty little heads that he needed fixing.

There was nothing wrong with him or his dark desires. He'd just never found the right woman to openly share them with. Someone who shared his predilections, who revelled in his heavy handed discipline.

Until now.

Until Lucy.

Toby wanted more than just a few sessions with her. He wanted something deeper than the timidity of a temporary partner. He wanted something permanent and knew in his gut Lucy was her.

The right woman.

She had to be.

She was the only one he'd ever felt 100 percent

comfortable sharing himself with. All of himself, not the watered down version he usually presented to the world. And now that he'd claimed her as his, now they were moving forward in their relationship, she needed to know Toby was in control.

Of everything.

Her body was his. Her mind was his. Her heart....

Toby mentally shook his head. Charlie was right. This wasn't just about sex. This was so much more. He was forty-years-old for fuck's sake and he was tired of being alone. He wanted a partner, someone he could share his life with.

Someone who didn't share his DNA.

He knew Lucy was a strong woman, independent and sure of herself. She had insecurities, like everyone else, but she faced them head on and rose to the challenge day after day. Toby admired her for that. He knew in their day-to-day life he'd offer her support when she needed it and back off when she wanted it, even if his protective instincts screamed at him to do otherwise.

Their misunderstanding Sunday afternoon had brought home that lesson well enough, and it was a mistake he would take care not to repeat.

But outside of their day-to-day existence, Toby would take what he wanted, what he needed. And he would give Lucy the same.

He would give her everything.

Staring down at his lover, Toby felt his chest swell with those messy emotions he tried so hard to avoid. And he let them come, let them wash over him and surround him, drag him down into their murky depths, fill him up and drown him. He had no idea if he had her heart or if he even wanted it. But he knew one thing.

This was about so much more than just sex for him.

His gut tightened and his balls drew up tight. He was going to come. Taking one last look at the goddess on her knees before him, Toby drank in her expression of total submission then thanked the powers that be for putting her in his path. Then he closed his eyes, let out an almighty groan of pleasure and filled her throat with his seed.

Easing himself out of her mouth, he relaxed his grip in her hair and petted her. Stroked the long blonde strands away from her face and smiled.

Lucy wiped her mouth and chin with the back of her hand, her eyes shuttered, her lips curved in a look that said she was entirely too pleased with herself.

Cheeky woman. Toby chuckled and held out his hands, then pulled her to her feet. "I need to find another way to punish you," he said with a sigh. "You enjoy it too much."

She tried looking innocent but it wasn't a look she wore well.

Toby hauled her against his firm body and slapped her arse hard. The loud crack of his big hand against her pliant flesh rent the air and drowned out her sudden intake of breath, but not the sultry sigh that followed.

He chuckled again and shook his head. "See what I mean?"

Completely unrepentant, his woman leaned up and nibbled his jaw. "Admit it. You love it."

But he had no intention of admitting anything. Especially when his feelings on the matter were so new and uncertain.

"Get back in bed," he ordered, his hand delivering another sound smack on her butt. Lucy whimpered and rubbed her body against his—*horny girl*—and he was about to throw her down on the sheets when he remembered why they were out of bed in the first place. Reining in his need, he kissed her forehead. "Do as you're told. I'll get you some water."

Lucy nodded and stepped out of his embrace. "Yes, Sir."

Toby returned from the kitchen with two glasses of water then settled back into bed, propping himself against the padded headboard and wondering how the hell he was going to fit his overly large body in Lucy's regular sized bed. When she leaned into him and snaked one arm across his stomach, he ceased to care.

Lifting an arm around her shoulders, Toby brushed his fingertips over her scars. And curiosity got the better of him. "How did you get burned? You said the other night it was a house fire, but what actually happened to you?"

She stiffened beside him. "I thought you wanted to know about Maisie."

"I want to know everything about you," he said quietly, tightening his hold on her.

She tried burying her head between his pecs, then sighed heavily. Her breath tickled his skin. "Everything?" she mumbled against his chest.

"Everything."

Lifting her head, she stared at him, her eyes darkened by the muted light in the room, and Toby was surprised by what he saw lurking in her golden depths.

Fear.

"I'm not ready for that yet," she muttered quickly, quietly, and tried to move away.

Tightening his arm around her even more, he held her against his chest and prevented her escape. "Just tell me about Maisie, then," he said, keeping his voice low and calm.

She let loose a humourless laugh. "I'm not sure I'm ready for that either."

"Would it be easier if I made it a command instead of a question?"

He felt her lips tilt up where they pressed against his chest. "No, Sir," she said, shifting so she sat fully in his lap and rested her head on his shoulder. "Maisie used to be a nurse. She helped my Nan look after me,"—she waved a hand at her scars—"after this happened. She was bossy and funny and never allowed me to wallow in self-pity."

"What about your parents? Where were they during your recovery?" he asked, then mentally slapped himself when he felt her stiffen against his body. This was why he usually left the talking to Charlie. Toby could boss a woman around in bed like a champ, but small talk—and not so small talk—had a tendency to end with his foot in his mouth. "Were they...? Ah, are they...?"

"Dead?" Lucy supplied.

"Yeah."

"No. But I am. As far as they're concerned." Toby felt her breath stutter against his neck, heard her sniff like she was holding back tears. "They disowned me," she whispered. "After the fire."

Toby stared straight ahead at the bare wall and scowled. He'd cut his own mother out of his life and only because she was a piece of work who didn't deserve the time of day. His father had always had his back though, had always been there for him and his brothers and sister when they needed him, knew Uly would come running when they called.

How could Lucy's parents abandon her when she was hurt and needed them the most? What possible justification could they have for treating their daughter that way?

"Lucy." He tilted his head to look down at her, but she refused to meet his gaze. Gripping her chin with hard fingers, he made her look at him. "Why would they do that?"

The fear he'd seen in her expression only moments ago intensified. Her eyes were open wide and her bottom lip quivered, until she pulled it between her teeth and bit down.

She looked terrified.

But of what? Her parents, or him?

She swallowed hard. "I killed my brother."

Chapter Twenty

"Get off me."

Lucy scrambled away from Toby and pulled her knees to her chest, tried to make herself as small a target as possible.

That's what she'd always done when she felt threatened, when her mother went on another drunken tirade about how everything bad in her life could be blamed on Lucy's distinct lack of a penis.

She could hear Toby pacing back and forth at the foot of the bed but she refused to look at him. His dark tone as he'd spat those three little words at her had cut deep. But what had she expected? That he'd pat her on the head and say "It's okay, baby. I understand"...? How could he possibly understand what she'd done?

How could anyone?

Tears scalded the backs of her eyes but she pressed her lips together as tight as she could, trapping inside the sobs that were desperately clawing their way up her throat, stopping them from escaping. She had no right to cry.

Suddenly Toby sat beside her, the bed dipped and

creaked under his weight. Peeking out through the fall of her hair, Lucy saw his knuckles blanche as his hands clenched on his knees. An odd sensation stabbed at her as she watched his long, thick fingers grip and flex.

A mixture of lust, fear and longing arrowed through her and angled downwards as the memory of those hands on her body assaulted her, making her bite her lip to stifle a moan as she remembered how he'd touched her, caressed her.

What the hell is wrong with me?

Toby cleared his throat. "I'd like to say I won't hurt you," he said gruffly, "but I think I just did. Didn't I?"

Slowly, Lucy lifted her head and stared at him. Toby was so tall that even sitting down she had to look up to meet his gaze, and what she saw there only made her determined to shove her fear back, to push it down and keep it at bay. She'd never get through this if she didn't.

"It's not the worst thing anyone has ever said to me," she said quietly, meeting his remorseful gaze. "And it's not like you didn't warn me."

Toby frowned. "Warn you about what?"

Her lips lifted with a sardonic tilt. "That you suck at talking to people."

The big man let loose a bark of laughter, the rough sound breaking the tension between them. "I'm sorry, Lucy. My mouth ran away from me before my brain could catch up."

"It's okay," she said, wishing she could rewind the last five minutes and explain herself better. Wishing she'd said anything other than "I killed my brother". No matter how true a statement it may be.

"No, it isn't." Toby took a breath, as though he was thinking carefully about what to say next. "I was insensitive to your needs, but I've gotten over myself," he said, his tone repentant, "and now I'll shut up and listen to what you have to say. I asked you to tell me everything. It was unfair of me to push you away just because you said something I'm...."—he paused again—"struggling to understand."

Lucy offered him a small smile and nodded once to acknowledge his apology. "Sometimes I struggle to understand what happened too."

Toby reached out and settled one big hand over hers. "Tell me," he said, the words more request than demand.

Lucy focussed on the feel of his hand, the roughness of his palm where it pressed against her skin, the strength of his fingers as he wrapped them around hers. And she drew strength from him. Toby's quiet presence as he sat beside her filled her with hope and loosened her tongue.

Even if her only hope was that he didn't reject her again once he knew the whole, terrible truth.

"Okay. Well, I can't really tell you something without telling you everything, so here goes." She took a sip of water. "Joining the fire brigade was a Barton family tradition. My pop, my dad and my brother—Michael—were all firefighters and I wanted to join too. Dad told me I could join up, but only after I finished university."

"I'm guessing he didn't make your brother do that?"

Lucy stared at the floor and shook her head. "Dad was never a big supporter of women in the ranks. I think he thought I'd change my mind once I saw what else was on offer."

"But he was wrong?"

Lifting her head again, she let herself grin. "Oh yeah. He was so wrong. The day after I received my degree in business management, I applied to Queensland Fire and Rescue and I got in. Dad was *not* happy about it, but

Michael gave me a high-five and took me out for ice cream to celebrate."

Toby smiled. "Michael sounds like he was a good brother," he said quietly.

"He was," she said, hoping Toby didn't notice the waver in her voice. "Best big brother I could have wanted. He helped me train, and I passed every test with flying colours."

"I remember those tests," Toby said with a grunt. Lucy lifted one brow and stared at him until he got the hint and elaborated. "My family tradition is blacksmithing. My dad made all of us go through the training with our local RFS chief. He wanted to make sure we knew what to do in the highly likely circumstance at least one of us would set fire to something."

A smile curled Lucy's mouth and she chuckled softly. "And did you? Set fire to something?"

"Not me personally, but I may have been present when Charlie accidentally set our sister's teddy bear on fire."

Eyes flaring wide open, Lucy mashed her lips together to suppress her laughter. It didn't work. "Oh no! Was she upset?"

Toby cleared his throat again. He seemed to do that when he was nervous. "She doesn't know about it."

Cocking one brow, Lucy threw him a dubious look. "Surely she would have noticed her teddy was missing?"

A sudden grin jumped to life on Toby's face. Lucy pressed her hand to her chest to still her racing heart. Her lover was one devilishly handsome man when he smiled at her like that.

"Oh, she definitely noticed. Charlie felt so guilty about what he'd done, he got rid of the bear, then told Abby that Mr Poochie had gone on holiday. For six months he sent her postcards detailing Mr Poochie's adventures, until finally he wrote one saying he, the bear, was very sorry but he'd decided to stay with a little boy he'd met in Perth who needed him more than Abby, and that he hoped she understood."

"And she bought that?" Lucy said, gobsmacked by both the ingenuity of Charlie's plan and the depths he'd plumbed to lie to his sister.

Toby shrugged. "She was eight."

"How old were you two?"

"Sixteen."

"Old enough to know better than to lie to your little sister," she said, her lips twisted in annoyance as an overwhelming sense of sisterly solidarity welled up inside her.

"And your brother never lied to you?" Toby said lightly, bumping his shoulder against hers.

"No, he didn't," Lucy said, then shifted uncomfortably as she watched Toby's expression change. His smile thinned and his eyes narrowed in what she recognised as his silent signal for her to explain herself, one she'd seen often enough over the weekend when they'd had a difference of opinion. "He protected me," Lucy added, her voice barely a whisper.

Toby's voice dropped into his familiar growl. "From what?"

Lucy twisted her hands in her lap and took a breath. She'd agreed to always be honest with him. Indeed, she'd insisted upon it, and if this fledgling romance of theirs had any chance of becoming more, she had to tell him everything. Including all the shitty parts of her life she'd rather just forget.

She'd already demanded the same from him and knew she could give no less.

"Not what. Who." She took another breath then lifted her chin and stared Toby straight in the eyes. "Our mother."

The instant Toby heard the quaver in Lucy's voice, he hauled her into his lap and pressed her head into the crook of his neck. He told himself he was comforting her, helping to soothe her, keep her calm as she told him about her past, about her brother.

But the truth was, the haunted look in Lucy's eyes when she'd mentioned her mother had dragged up so many of his own memories, horrendous, dark, despicable memories, that he'd felt physically ill.

He was the one needing comfort.

"Are you all right?" Lucy's soft voice reached him through his panic.

Barely.

"Huh?"

"You're shaking," she said. Grabbing his shoulders for support, she sat up straighter in his lap and stared at him, examined him with a curiosity he found uncomfortable.

Fighting back his own insecurities, Toby cleared his throat and said, "I'm fine. Please, continue."

Lucy stared at him for a moment longer before settling against his chest and resting her head under his chin. And he took comfort in her touch, the way her slender fingers stroked over his skin, the way she pressed her lips against the base of his throat before continuing her story.

"My mother is... unwell. She's bipolar, and when she was in a manic period she... drank. A lot."

Toby stroked Lucy's hair, breathed in her floral scent. "Is that why you don't drink?"

She nodded, rubbed her cheek against his chest. "Yes. It's also why I don't own any bric-a-brac. Or as I used to call it, ammunition."

"Pardon?"

"She used to throw things at me when she was in a foul mood."

Clenching his jaw against the memories of his own bad mother, Toby held Lucy tighter, as if the cage of his arms could protect her from her past. "I'm sorry, baby."

"Don't be," she said, her voice no longer soft, but clear and strident. "Everything she did just made me more determined to succeed. That wasn't her intent, and it was a hard lesson to learn, but when you spend your whole childhood being told you're unwanted, that you're to blame for everything bad that's happening to you, you can either sit there and take it, or you can fight back."

"And you fought back?"

"Not at first." She sighed deeply. "When I was younger and didn't know any better, I sat there and took it. I feared her. Feared her temper and her mood swings. I took to hiding from her, would even walk home from school as slowly as possible just to delay the inevitable. I looked forward to finding her passed out on the couch. Days when she simply ignored me were bliss. Then one day I noticed something."

Toby tilted his head, curious as he stared down at Lucy, as he watched her eyes flicker with memories. "What?"

"Mum never went off at me if Michael was home. So I started finding excuses to hang out with him as much as possible. And he let me. But eventually he told me he wouldn't always be there to protect me, that I had to learn to deal with her on my own. So I did." She huffed out a laugh. "In my own way."

As he listened and digested everything Lucy was saying, Toby rubbed his hand in a circular motion against her back, the action helping to soothe him as much as it did her. He loathed Lucy's mother on principle alone, and instinctively knew if he ever met the woman he wouldn't hesitate to share his feelings with her. He felt close to Lucy, enjoyed the feeling of intimacy that sat so comfortably between them as she shared her past with him.

Was it because they both had shitty mothers? Was he simply feeling protective? Or did it run deeper than that, something more infinite?

All he knew was he wanted to curl himself around her, hold her, keep her safe, shield her from any more hurt. But he also wanted to know why he felt that way.

Desperately.

"Why was your mother so violent towards you?"

"Because I wasn't born a boy," she said matter-of-factly, looking up at him with a sad smile stretched thin across her tired face. "She had a vision of her perfect family and I ruined it."

Toby harrumphed. "And what was this perfect vision?"

"A handsome husband and two strapping boys, all firemen, of course."

He frowned, curious. "And how did you learn to deal with your mother's... disappointment?"

A sly grin tugged at her lips. "By making it as obvious as possible that I wasn't a boy, and by proving anything they could do, I could do better."

Toby chuckled. "I bet you did."

"I grew my hair long and took to wearing pink all the time, and I started working out with Michael and the guys at the fire station after school, and a weird thing happened."

"Oh?"

"My confidence grew. And the more confident I became, the more I stood up to Mum. And the more I stood up to her, the less she picked on me. We fought more, though, and she still threw things at me when she was drunk, but one day I threw things back. I just got so angry with her and I smashed a coffee cup on the floor right in front of her and—"

"And what, baby?"

"I frightened her," Lucy said, her voice dropping to a whisper, her gaze glazing over. "Truth be told, I think I frightened myself more. It was the first time I realised I was stronger than her, that I could hurt her more than she could hurt me." She shook her head as if clearing away the fog clouding her eyes and pasted on a brittle smile. "I think she realised it too. At least, she stopped throwing things at me after that. And I stopped being afraid. I stopped a lot of things."

"Such as?"

She offered him a small, sheepish smile. "I stopped censoring myself, both at school and home. And I stopped worrying about what everyone else thought of me. It was quite freeing actually."

Silence settled over them again and Toby continued circling his hand on Lucy's back. But there were questions left unanswered, and he had to know. He gave her another moment of quiet, then asked, "What happened with Michael? What did you mean when you said you killed your brother?"

Lucy burrowed against his chest and he felt her body expand as she took a deep breath. "We got a call out to a house fire," she said softly. "A big old Queenslander that was being renovated, so lots of flammable shit lying around. By the time we got there it was more a case of containing the flames so they didn't spread to the neighbouring properties. The house had gone up so damn fast, we didn't think we could save it."

She sniffed and sat up straighter, lifted her hand to play with the hair on his chest. He guessed it gave her something to focus on as she spoke, let her hide the tears he could feel wetting his chest.

"Dad was in charge that night, telling the crew where to go, what to do. The family had already gotten out of the house and were standing in front of their neighbour's place. He sent me over to talk to them, to ask if everyone was out, but just as I reached them, the mother became hysterical, started screaming that her little boy was gone.

"Everyone had thought someone else was keeping an eye on him and he'd managed to slip away. The dad explained the kid had been upset because they didn't bring his favourite toy with them. He said they'd looked but couldn't find it, and fearing the fire was getting too big, they'd just grabbed their kids and run for it.

"I was heading back over to tell Dad when I saw the kid. It was just a flicker of movement in the bedroom window, like someone had run past it. A real blink-and-you-miss-it moment. The fire hadn't reached that section of the house yet, but it was close. And the smoke was bad. Thick, black choking plumes of the stuff just billowing out of everywhere."

Lucy paused and took a breath and Toby just kept rubbing circles on her back, not wanting to interrupt her chain of thought again. She needed to get it out and he needed to hear it.

"I knew I could get to the kid. Knew I could get him out. I was fast, faster than the men, and smaller too. I could squeeze in and out of places they couldn't. So instead of taking the sixty seconds or more to tell my dad what I was doing, I shoved my face mask on and ran towards the house. Michael grabbed me, stopped me, but I yelled at him. I said,

"Kid. Still inside." And that was all the info he needed. We bolted up the stairs to the front door, Michael determined it was still safe to enter and we headed for the bedrooms."

Toby frowned, tilted his head to look at Lucy's face. When her eyes met his, he asked, "Was it safe to enter?"

Her eyes almost twinkled with mischief and he had her answer even before she spoke. "Not even remotely." Then her sparkle dimmed. "But there was no way we were leaving that little boy to die alone."

Pressing his lips to Lucy's temple, Toby held her tightly for a moment and pulled her scent into his lungs. Her words caused a sense of pride to settle over him.

My woman.

"I found the boy hiding under his bed," she continued, "a blanket pulled over his face and a floppy blue teddy clutched in his hand. He was crying, terrified. He just wanted his mum." Lucy sniffed and shook her head. "But he wouldn't come out, and every time I reached for him, he shied away even more. It was my mask," she said quietly. "He was afraid of it. So I took it off, my flash hood too. I showed him who I was underneath, that he didn't need to be scared. I told him I'd get him to his mum."

Toby was on the edge of his seat. He'd already pieced together the outcome of Lucy's story—the kid was saved, Lucy got burned and her brother died—but hearing her talk was both thrilling and horrific and he simultaneously wanted to hear more, and didn't. He wanted to crush his lips to hers and silence her, stop the horror in its tracks, stop the vivid pictures her words elicited from forming in his brain and keeping him awake at night.

But he couldn't. Because Lucy couldn't. If just the thought of what happened threatened to keep him up at night, how the fuck did she live through it?

Lucy's thoughts weren't thoughts, they were memories. She didn't just dream it up. She'd lived it. A living nightmare.

A nightmare that haunted her still, if her restless sleeping habits were anything to go by. Habits that again made him feel for her, made him wish his touch alone could soothe all her worries, take away all her pain. If Toby's touch could do that for her, he would wrap Lucy in his arms and hold her forever.

He'd never let her go.

And it was then he realised what he'd been feeling, why he had such visceral reactions to the woman in his lap, his arms.

I love Lucy.

As ridiculous as it was, it was the only explanation that made any sense.

And it both thrilled and terrified him.

Because....

What if she didn't love him back? They barely knew one another. And sure, she was willing to fuck his brains out and call him Sir and Master, and she was willing to date him publically and go out to dinner... but that didn't mean she loved him. Or would ever love him.

And what about kids?

Did Lucy want a family of her own or would she be content to play auntie to his ever increasing horde of nieces? Would she leave him if he couldn't give her a child of her own? If she did have kids, what kind of mother would she be? He'd already fantasised about seeing her belly swell with his child. Would knowing that freak her out as much as it did him? Or would she be on board with adding to the Bennett brood? There was also their age to consider, neither of them getting any younger....

Completely unaware of Toby's inner battle, Lucy continued talking, her soft voice drawing him and his wild thoughts back to the moment.

"I heard a loud crack above us and knew we didn't have long. The roof was collapsing. So I grabbed the kid's arm and dragged him out from under the bed. Little bugger fought me the whole way. By the time I got him out from under there, I didn't have time to put my mask and hood back on, so I just scooped the boy up and ran. He kicked and screamed every step of the way but we made it back to the front room unscathed. I passed him off to Michael who passed him out to someone else but then—"

Her body shook and a wretched sob tore from her throat. "The ceiling collapsed. Right on top of me. I was pinned on my side and couldn't move. The smoke was so thick and I didn't have my mask." She shook her head as if trying to dislodge the memory. Toby held her tighter. "I heard Michael yell my name, I saw him reaching out for me then—" Lucy stared straight ahead, her eyes glassy with tears, staring, unblinking.

"Then...? What happened, baby?"

"He was gone," Lucy whispered, her voice tight as more tears rolled down her cheeks. "The floorboards gave way beneath him and he fell." She shuddered against him. "I could see him—my brother—I could see him through the hole in the floor. He'd twisted around and landed awkwardly on a pile of old Besser blocks. He—" Her breathing stuttered as she tried to control herself and her hands curled into fists. "He broke his neck."

Toby dropped his head back and stared at the ceiling, tears stinging behind his eyes. "Oh, Jesus fuck."

"I... I saw the light leave his eyes." Sniffing loudly, she turned her head and looked up at him, clawed at his shoulders as if she were scrabbling for something to hold on to and when he met her gaze, the look of desperation peering back at him broke his heart and his own tears slipped free.

"Toby, I watched my brother die. I watched him die knowing he shouldn't've even been there, and if it hadn't been for me, he wouldn't've." She swiped at her tears. "That's the last thing I remember before blacking out. Seeing Michael's eyes staring up at me. Eyes like mine."

She took a deep breath. "Next thing I knew I woke up in the hospital. I had a tube down my throat, I couldn't feel half my body, and my mother was screaming at me, saying she wished I'd died instead of Michael." She dragged a hand over her face. "I haven't seen or spoken to either of my parents since."

Toby kissed the top of Lucy's head, then swiped his forearm across his eyes. He blew out a slow, calming breath. "How old were you when it happened?"

"Twenty-three."

"And Michael?"

"Twenty-eight," she said with a sad smile. "He'd just started seeing someone, too. A cute redhead." She shrugged and hiccoughed a laugh. "At least I thought he was cute."

Toby's eyebrows shot up. "Michael was gay?"

Lucy shook her head. "Bi-sexual, like me." Then her tears came in earnest and her words came on a wail of despair. "And I'd give anything to have him back. It's not fair. It's not fair that he died and I got to live. I broke the rules. I didn't follow the chain of command and Michael died."

Toby pressed her head to his chest, tucked her under his chin. "My sweet girl," he murmured, kissing her hair and rocking her in his lap. "Michael broke the rules too, baby, and willingly by the sounds of it. That's not all on you. And if you hadn't broken the rules, if you'd stopped to tell your father what you were doing, would the boy have survived?"

"No," Lucy whispered. "But that doesn't make it hurt any less." Shaking her head, she wiped at her face again then took a deep breath. "And do you want to know the real kicker?"

"What?"

"I don't even have a photo of Michael. Nothing to remember him by."

"What? Why?"

Lucy sniffed. "After my parents disowned me, my mother had the locks changed and gave all of my belongings to charity. Nan had photos in a family album, but there was a spate of burglaries in the neighbourhood about a decade ago. In addition to Nan's tele, microwave and jewellery, the thieves took the photo album." At Toby's curious frown she explained, "It had this ornate gilded cover on it." She shrugged. "It looked worth a lot more than it actually was."

"I'm sorry, Lucy. For everything you've been through."

His lover shrugged again and yawned. "It's not your fault."

He cupped her cheek and made her look at him. "It's not yours either," he said, but the defiant glint in her amber eyes told him it was going to take time to convince her of that.

Lucy had carried the weight of her brother's death for a very long time. Toby couldn't hope to cure her of that overnight, no matter how much he wished he could.

Tugging her down onto the bed with him, he pulled the covers over them both. For the first time since he'd met the woman, the silence between them felt awkward, but just as it was on the tip of his tongue to regale his lover with a tale about his own horrid mother and what she'd done to cause him to cut her out of his life, he heard Lucy's breathing grew heavy and even, and realised she'd fallen asleep. He also realised the awkwardness he felt was all on him.

For the first time since taking her to bed, Toby didn't sleep a wink.

Chapter Twenty-One

Wakefulness tickled Lucy's senses, prodded her awake with the promise of a new day. Yes, that was what she needed. A new day. Time to recover from the emotional upheaval of the previous night and to smooth her ruffled feathers. Time to quietly deal with the memories of her brother's death and put them to rest again. Put *him* to rest again.

Somewhere safe inside her where she needn't fear being overwhelmed by her grief, the depth of which had taken her by surprise.

Until she'd realised it wasn't just grief she'd been feeling.

Lucy had known Toby Bennett less than two weeks, and she'd known him intimately for even less than that. So how in the bloody hell had she developed such strong feelings for the man when she barely knew him?

Telling Toby about Michael had been unplanned, and she'd been unprepared for the heartache that had threatened to crush her as she'd told her tale.

Lucy hadn't spoken about that night to anyone. Not her

nan, not Maisie, not even the psychologist she'd been forced to see every month for twelve months after the fire.

She'd never shared her pain before, never admitted to anyone how much she missed her brother and confidant. She'd always retreated inwards, shut everyone else out. That was how she'd learned to survive in a world where the odds had always seemed stacked against her.

By hoarding her emotions like a dragon hoards gold.

But Toby wasn't just anyone.

True, she'd hesitated to tell him anything, as she did with everyone—no one wants to hear about the time someone killed their own brother—but Toby was different.

Toby treated her like she mattered to him. He was sweet and kind and the sex was beyond amazing. But mostly, she liked that he *saw* her. He saw the real Lucy, not the hard-arse office manager or the speed dating sex-fiend or the stoic survivor.

Toby saw the submissive woman. He saw her need to be owned by him and wasn't overwhelmed by that need. He didn't run away from her. And sure, they'd both stumbled a bit, neither one of them used to being in a proper relationship, but the fact he was sticking around and giving it his best shot spoke volumes.

He didn't make her feel like she was too much.

And she now knew the feeling that rose up inside her every time he walked in the room wasn't just lust. It ran deeper than that. Hotter. Darker. Fuller. More insistent.

It was why she'd been so scared to open up about Michael in the first place, about how he'd died.

Truthfully, Lucy had been terrified by what Toby's reaction might be, that he would reject her, and when he'd pushed her away and proved her right, it had hurt.

So much.

She'd gone into default mode and curled in on herself, protected herself, but then he'd apologised and held her hand and he'd *listened*.

Men always underestimated the power of simply listening to a woman. Of hearing her and understanding that she didn't need him to solve her problems for her. Lucy wasn't sure Toby understood that yet, not completely. He was so used to being in charge, being obeyed. So used to protecting others.

When she'd spoken to the staff at the garden centre, not a single one of them had anything bad to say about their boss. And not in the usual snitches-get-stitches, cone-of-silence way she'd witnessed at the security firm.

Toby's staff had made it clear they had nothing but respect and affection for the man, with "quiet" and "firm but fair" being the most common choice of words used to describe him.

During their little tête-à-tête, the café manager, Ashley, couldn't sing Toby's praises high enough. Not necessarily as an office manager, but definitely as a man. And Lucy was pretty sure the young woman had a crush on the boss.

She wasn't overly enthused about the situation, but she couldn't blame the girl—Toby was hot! But as long as Ashley kept her hands to herself, they wouldn't have a problem.

Smiling to herself about her hot boss and imagining the even hotter sex she was about to have, Lucy rolled over and reached for Toby, but when she saw nothing but bedspread, she panicked.

Scrambling to sit up, she noticed the other side of the bed wasn't just empty, it looked as though someone had tried to make the bed. And Toby was nowhere to be seen.

His clothes and shoes had vanished too, almost as though he was never there.

Maybe he wasn't. Maybe she'd just dreamt him up. Maybe her secrets were still her secrets and she hadn't made a fool of herself in front of her boss. Or maybe she had. Maybe Toby had decided Lucy *was* too much to deal with and had snuck out before dawn. Maybe he was done, finished. Gone. He'd heard her out and decided she wasn't worth the effort after all.

Wrapping her arms around herself, Lucy dropped her chin to her chest and let the tears come. She'd finally found someone she trusted enough to share everything with, someone she could love, and it was over before it had even begun.

"Baby, what's wrong? Did you have another nightmare?"

In an instant Toby was there, gathering her to him, gently rocking her in the cradle of his strong arms and stroking her hair away from her face.

"You're still here," Lucy whispered, bewildered, and swallowed down her panic, forced herself to breathe normally. "I thought you'd left."

What she'd really meant to say was "I thought you'd left *me*."

Hating how clingy and pathetic that sounded, even if it was only inside her head, she tried to sit up and move out of Toby's embrace, prove she wasn't a melodramatic basket case and didn't need his softness and warmth.

That she did need him for anything.

She didn't need him at all.

But Toby was clever. Clever enough to see her defences for what they were. The actions of a scaredy-cat trying desperately to avoid any more hurt.

"Oh no you don't," he said, a warning tone deepening his commanding voice. "Don't go getting all prickly on me now, baby."

If the way he tightened his arms around her was any indication, Toby was definitely more stubborn than her. The more Lucy struggled to free herself, the tighter his hold became. And still tired from her restless night, she quickly conceded defeat and slumped against him. Admittedly she hadn't tried *very* hard to escape, not when what she really wanted was to be exactly where she was.

Toby chuckled softly as Lucy nuzzled against the base of his throat. "You all done now?"

Lucy nodded.

"Good. Want to tell me what that was all about?"

Lucy shook her head. She felt like an idiot. "Why are you dressed?" she asked quietly, her uneasy tone grating on her frayed nerves.

Where was Toby going. And why?

It was too early for work.

Toby kissed the top of Lucy's head and circled his big hand against her back. He'd done that the previous night too and it felt nice, soothing. She liked it. But then, she always liked the feel of his hands on her body.

"I have to pick up Charlie. Dad texted last night. He wants us to visit Rafe at the hospital," he explained. "He's refusing to leave Jane's bedside. Dad's hoping we can convince him to go home for a bit, get some sleep and eat a proper meal."

"Oh," she mumbled, feeling foolish for jumping to conclusions. "Why didn't you wake me?"

"Because it's only five o'clock,"—he kissed her forehead—"and you were finally sleeping peacefully."

Lucy shivered. Thanks to her anxiety, she'd always

been a light sleeper, but after Michael died she'd suffered terrible nightmares which in turn resulted in long bouts of insomnia. For years she'd feared closing her eyes, because every time she did she relived the gut-wrenching horror of losing her brother all over again.

Over time she'd learned to deal with it, but talking about her life, talking about Michael, opening up and exposing her innermost shame to Toby, had reawakened those nightmares.

More than once she'd awoken in a fright and cried out for her brother, only to find Toby instead, waiting with open arms, offering her comfort. Then he'd held her until she'd dozed off again, kissed her cheeks, her mouth, stroked her hair. He'd been tender and kind and she'd clung to him like a freaking limpet. *So needy*. She hated feeling needy.

Lucy didn't *need* anyone.

"I was going to leave you a note," Toby said, "but I guess I don't have to now." Then he rose to his feet, grabbed his car keys from the bedside table and unclipped a smaller set of four keys. "You'll need these to open the nursery and the office."

Lucy stared at the keys as Toby set them beside her phone on the bedside table. "Me?"

Toby smiled. "Of course you. You're my office manager, aren't you?"

Right. Of course she was. It was only her second day on the job with a new system she was only just learning to use, but sure. Why not? It seemed Tobias Bennett was intent on pushing her boundaries both in and out of the bedroom.

"When will you be back?" she said, getting to her feet. She felt small beside Toby most of the time—a novel feeling for a woman of her size—but standing in front of him naked while he was fully dressed, just added a level of sexiness that was hard to beat. Especially when it helped pull her out of her funk and back into the land of the living.

"I'll be back this afternoon," he said, shoving his wallet in his back pocket. His phone buzzed on the bedside table. Reaching around her, Toby grabbed the device and stared at the screen, his lips flattening as he shook his head.

"What is it?" Lucy asked, her chest tightening with fear for Toby's family. Had something awful happened? "Is everything okay?"

Toby showed her the screen.

It was a text from Charlie. *Stop fucking Lucy and hurry the fuck up!!! I want to hit the road before we hit traffic.*

A bubble of laughter escaped Lucy and the tightness in her chest eased. Then another message popped up on the screen that brought the tightness roaring back with a vengeance.

Also, Isobel called again. We can't keep avoiding her.

"Who's Isobel?"

Toby snatched his phone away and glared at the screen, then clicked it off and shoved the device in his pocket. "No one," he said, his voice flat and tinged with anger. But who was he angry at? Charlie for sending the message, Lucy for reading it, or himself for letting her see it?

Lucy straightened her spine and stared Toby down. His mouth had thinned and the blue of his eyes had turned ice cold. "Who is Isobel?" she asked again, her voice made stronger by Toby's attempted deflection.

Her lover glared at her for a moment longer before blinking slowly and letting out an even breath. He ran his tongue over his teeth. "No one you need worry about."

"Which is exactly the type of thing you should say if you want me to worry," she said, folding her arms across her chest, refusing to back down.

Toby's lips twitched into a devilish smile and he wrapped his arms around her again, pinned her against his chest and trapped her arms between them. "You're not jealous, are you, baby?"

"Of course not," she said, diverting her gaze from his before he detected her lie.

Okay, so maybe she was a little bit jealous. But who the hell was this woman that he and his brother were avoiding? Someone else they'd shared? Someone who maybe had a little trouble letting go, who'd expected more than a one night stand and wasn't thrilled by the fact the twins had moved on and left this woman—whoever she was—behind?

"Good," Toby said, as though the matter were closed. "Because she is absolutely no one you need to be jealous of." Then he fisted his hand in her hair and bent his head to kiss her, his lips firm and hot and unyielding as they met hers, demanding her surrender. And it was only when she capitulated and melted against him that he finally broke the kiss.

Toby's passion made Lucy feel a little better, but her past experiences still niggled at the edges of her rational mind and her unease refused to settle. Fiddling with the buttons on Toby's shirt, she shifted her weight from one foot to the other. "Just... don't play games with me, okay?"

"No games. I promise."

Continuing to stare at his shirtfront, Lucy cocked one brow, and said, "So Isobel is...?"

Toby chuckled and rubbed the back of his neck. "You're not going to let it go, are you?"

She shook her head and lifted her gaze to meet his, direct and unwavering. "Nope."

"Fine. Isobel," he said, grimacing, "is my mother. And the reason Charlie and I are avoiding her is because our mother makes your mother look like the Tooth Fairy. But I don't have time to discuss it right now. I have to go."

It was on the tip of Lucy's tongue to demand he make time "right now" but knew he had more important places to be. More important people to be with. "Right," she agreed, pasting on a smile. "Family first."

"Don't do that, baby." Toby's voice was dark, his eyes narrowed.

"Don't do what?"

"Don't think you're less important than my family." Toby settled his hand around her throat and gently squeezed. "You listen to me and listen good. You're mine, Lucy Barton. *Mine.* You are special to me. Do you understand?"

With her eyes wide and her breaths coming short, fast and excited, Lucy nodded.

"Say it," Toby demanded, his icy gaze darkening in a look she was intimately familiar with. He was getting worked up, excited. And so was she.

Heat bloomed low in her belly and her earlier troubles were all but forgotten. Pressing herself closer, Lucy felt her lover's erection straining against his jeans, but she knew better than to reach for it without permission.

Holding her hands by her sides, she clenched them tightly to ward off the urge to live dangerously. "Yes, Sir. I understand."

Toby relaxed his grip around her neck, stroked his thumb over her pulse. "Good girl." Then he looked at his watch and smirked. "Charlie can wait a few more minutes," he said, reaching for his belt buckle. "Bend over the bed. I'm going to give you something to think about while I'm gone. Make sure you really do understand."

As Lucy turned away and braced her hands on the

mattress, she realised she understood perfectly. She understood she was in far more trouble than she'd ever imagined.

Charlie was waiting at the front gate of their property when Toby arrived to pick him up. "Where the fuck have you been? It doesn't take that long to get here from Lucy's," he complained as he buckled his seat belt.

Toby picked up one of the take-away coffees he'd stopped for on the way and jiggled it in front of his brother's face. "You're welcome."

"Mmm... liquid magic," Charlie said, accepting the coffee and taking a sip. "Also, you smell like sex."

Toby grinned unrepentantly as he put the car in gear and headed north. He wasn't going to apologise for enjoying himself, for being happy and in love. Christ knew he'd spent most of his adult life avoiding those exact emotions, preferring instead to focus his efforts on building his business and taking care of his family, things he could control.

But from the moment he'd met Lucy Barton, Toby had known he was no longer in control. And for a control freak like him, the sensation was not one he enjoyed.

In truth, he was terrified.

"How is the lovely Lucy, anyway?"

Toby's grin softened and he fought to stop his mind from drifting away on an erotic daydream. "She's perfect."

"Oh, God." Charlie chuckled and shook his head. "There's no such thing as a perfect woman, Tobes."

"Maybe not," Toby conceded with a chuckle, "but she's perfect for me."

Charlie's smile was broad. "She really is, isn't she? I'm

happy for you, little brother. If anyone deserves a good woman, it's you."

A good woman.

That's exactly what Lucy was. And Toby wasn't letting her go.

Which was exactly what he'd explained to her in no uncertain terms when he'd removed his belt and painted three fresh stripes across her spectacular arse. He'd considered fucking her too, but stopped short of the act. Not because he was running low on time, and certainly not because he didn't want to—he couldn't get enough of her gorgeous body—but because he wanted her to focus on the pain, the reminder that she was his and all that entailed.

He did slip two fingers deep inside her pussy though. Just to tease her.

A little pleasure to help define the pain.

When he'd left her, she'd been a weak-kneed mess, frustrated and needy and glaring daggers at him as he'd walked out the door. Toby smiled to himself, knowing he'd make it up to her later. It had also taken the whole of the drive from her place to his for his erection to go down, so it wasn't as if she was the only one suffering.

Suffering....

That reminded him of the other reason he felt no guilt for making his brother wait. It was a just punishment for upsetting Lucy with that stupid text message about Isobel. And while she seemed relieved by the news the message was about his mother, he didn't like the swiftness with which she had assumed otherwise.

Admittedly, he probably should have been more up front instead of trying to dismiss her query, but after the emotional upheaval he'd nursed her through the night before, the last thing he wanted to do was turn the tables on her and unpack his own baggage at her feet. He would though. Eventually. Just not at five o'clock in the morning.

"While we're on the subject of women, why the fuck did you text me about Isobel? I told you the other day, I don't want to hear another word about that conniving bitch."

"I know," Charlie said, avoiding eye contact. "Hence the text message instead of voicemail. No hearing required."

Toby shot a quick scowl at his twin. "Semantics."

"Bless you!"

"Fuck you."

Charlie turned in his seat and stared at Toby for a long silent minute. "You know we have to deal with her, Toby. She's not going to go away and the longer we ignore her the—"

His brother's sudden silence was troubling. "What?" Toby demanded.

"What if she tries to grab our attention the same way she did with Dad?"

Toby's vision narrowed and his grip tightened on the steering wheel to the point of pain. "If she hurts a single hair on their heads, I'll kill her myself."

"If she goes after my daughters," his brother snarled, "you'll have to get in line."

Chapter Twenty-Two

Lucy couldn't get comfortable. Every time she moved in her chair, heat flared across her backside and she had to bite her lip to stifle her moans.

The belting Toby had given her before dinner the night before had been very carefully and evenly spaced out across her arse. No two swats in the same place twice.

The burn in her flesh had been delicious and sexy and teasing. But the lashes he'd administered before leaving to pick up his brother had all landed in the exact same spot—right where her thighs met her arse. There was nothing teasing about it.

Toby's strikes had been deliberate and precise and her skin felt hot and tight. There was no possible way she could move without feeling the burn of his belt.

And while she understood that was his intent—to make it impossible to ignore and therefore reinforce his stance that she was special to him—it didn't make her life any easier when it took every scrap of her determination and self-control to focus on her job, and not the near constant throbbing of her clit or the wetness of her panties.

So unprofessional, she thought as she continued scouring the financial records. *But so freaking hot!*

Toby had left her in a state of total wanting with no hint of relief on the horizon.

"He is so gunna pay for this," she vowed as she worked through her to-do list. "I don't know how and I don't know when, but he is *sooo* going to pay."

"Who's going to pay for what?"

At the sound of Ashley's voice, Lucy straightened and looked over the top of the privacy barrier that hedged the front of her desk. Her wet, unprofessional panties had her so distracted she hadn't even heard the girl come in. Throwing on a hurried yet hopefully pleasant smile, she said, "Knowing my luck? No one and for nothing. What can I do for you Ashley?"

Lucy had learned a long time ago to keep staff on topic. When she'd first started working as an office manager, she'd made the mistake of trying to be everyone's friend. She'd lost countless hours of productivity to gossip and idle chit-chat, and she'd already discovered Ashley's propensity for both.

"I have the post for you. The postie left it with me when he came in for a coffee."

Reaching out for the proffered stack of what was most likely bills, Lucy frowned. "That's weird. He had to walk past the office on the way to and from the café. It would have taken literally thirty seconds or less to pop in here and hand me the post."

Ashley shrugged then shoved the door open again to leave. "Hey, don't ask me. I just work here. See ya'."

Lucy put the post in her in-tray, then scribbled a note to speak with the postman on a Post-It and stuck it on the inside of the privacy barrier, lining it up perfectly with the other notes she'd written. She sighed softly as she scanned her ever increasing to-do list. Had she really thought it would only take a month to get on top of this mess? There was so much to do. And she still had to talk to Toby about her plans.

As if on cue, her phone dinged with an incoming message. *On my way back to the office. See you soon, baby.*

She bit her lip to rein in her silly, schoolgirl grin, but could do nothing about the jump in her heartrate. Lucy was absolutely crazy about the man.

Head over heels... *in love?*

She'd felt something like it that morning, thought maybe, possibly she *could* love Toby. But no, it was too soon to be sure. Too early. Too... immense. And suddenly her heart was thumping against her ribs for a very different reason.

Panic.

But when her phone dinged again, she realised her panic was the excited kind and her smile broadened. *I know it's against the rules between 9 and 5 but I really need a hug. Meet me in my office at 12:30 sharp.*

Another ding. *Bring snacks.*

Checking the time, Lucy saw it was already 12:17, and remembering Toby's weekend confession to being a chocoholic, she popped over to the café, grabbed two fresh coffees and the last two chocolate muffins. She was just placing the treats on a plate on Toby's desk when he strode through the door, then closed and locked it behind him.

A quick glance at the clock on the wall and she saw he was right on time, then without a word her lover pulled her into his arms and sealed his mouth to hers in a deep and passionate kiss.

When Toby pulled back, Lucy noticed he looked tired

and worn, but underlying that was something else. Something she couldn't define. It wasn't hope, nor was it hopelessness. It wasn't frustration or anger or determination. He was just... off.

He leaned his forehead against hers. "You're so beautiful," he whispered.

Tilting her head to one side, Lucy frowned at him. "Are you all right?"

Toby lifted his head and raised one brow. "I tell you you're beautiful and you wonder if there's something wrong with me?"

She sent him a withering glare and poked a finger into his belly. "Not because of that. You look... I'm not sure how you look. Agitated, maybe?" She shook her head. "You're not yourself."

Toby kissed the top of her head and tightened his arms around her. "No, I'm not. And I love that you know that." Then he leaned back and stared down at her, his face as serious as she'd ever seen it, and she'd seen his I'm-going-to-whip-you-until-you-come face. "I need to talk to you about something. It's not work related but, fuck it. I don't really care about the rules today."

Lucy's frown turned curious and her lips quirked up on one side. "Okay," she said, drawing out the word. "What do you want to talk about?"

Planting his arse in his chair, Toby pulled Lucy into his lap. He was quiet for so long Lucy wasn't sure he would ever speak again. Then he sighed and scrubbed his hand across his jaw and said, "I want you to move in with me."

I'm sorry... "What?"

Chuckling suddenly, the seriousness ebbed out of his expression and Toby tucked Lucy against his chest. He stroked his hand up and down her arm. "You heard me, baby."

She had heard him. She just wasn't sure she understood him. They'd been dating for less than one week and he wanted her to move in with him? Not that the offer wasn't tempting, but did she really want to throw away every last scrap of her freedom just because she'd found a man who was sweet and kind and clever and sexy and oh, yeah, a certifiable legend in the sack?

Still, it was an odd request and she had to question his timing.

"Where is this coming from? Why do you suddenly want to live together?"

He was quiet again for a moment, and when he finally spoke, his words sounded careful, as though he was thinking them through as he was saying them.

"Seeing Rafe with Jane today, seeing the love, the devotion and the soul-shattering anguish on my brother's face as he sat beside the love of his life, really put things in perspective for me."

"How so?"

"Rafe and Jane have had this on again, off again, push and pull relationship for sixteen years. They've been in love for *sixteen years*, but do you know how long they've officially been dating?" Lucy shook her head. "About as long as we have."

Pulling back so she could see his face, Lucy saw as clear as day the sincerity in the man's expression. "Holy crap. It's taken them sixteen years to get their act together?"

"Yes, and I don't want that to be us." Toby's gaze bored into hers and her pulse went into overdrive, especially when he slid his hand along her thigh and under the hem of her skirt. "I know how lucky I am to have found you, Lucy, and

I don't want to waste a minute of our time together." He squeezed her thigh with bruising intensity, and staring into his icy blue gaze was like watching an oncoming storm. "Move in with me, baby. Be mine. Be my girl 24/7."

He was freaking her out. Toby could see the panic in Lucy's eyes as easily as he felt the thunderous pulsing of his heart.

He wanted this. He wanted her. And seeing Rafe with Jane had only reinforced exactly how much. He was done with screwing around, with one night stands that never satisfied his wants or needs.

He was tired of his most meaningful relationship being with his twin brother, a man who already had the children and the family he craved.

And he was absolutely done with loneliness and filling his life with work and pretending he wasn't the biggest sad-sack on the planet.

Toby had found the woman he was meant to be with—a woman who both inspired and calmed his passions—and he wanted to get the show on the road. But now that he knew what he did of her upbringing, he suspected the woman in question would need convincing.

"What do you need, baby," he murmured, nuzzling against her before biting the soft skin below her ear, marking her flesh. "Talk to me."

She made a little moaning sound and snuggled closer, dug her fingernails into his bicep as she held on. "Just yesterday you said you weren't going to ask me to live with you because you knew I'd say no."

He shrugged. "And now I'm hoping you'll say yes."

She was quiet for a moment, then said, "Admittedly, the thought of waking up every day in that big, luxurious bed of yours does hold a certain appeal."

"But...?"

"It's a big step, Toby. And as you pointed out, we haven't been dating very long. We're still learning things about each other. What if we move in together and realise we can't stand each other outside of the bedroom? What if our working relationship suffers because we rushed our personal one?"

She had a point, a very sharp and valid point. Which Toby chose to ignore. "What if I admit I'm scared shitless of the exact same things, but told you I want to live with you anyway? What if I told you you're worth taking a risk on?" When she started shaking her head he fisted her hair at her nape and made her look at him. "I've never known anyone like you, Lucy. When I'm with you I feel... comfortable."

Lucy pursed her lips and raised one brow. "As compliments go, 'comfortable' isn't a great one."

Toby grinned. "When you're as big as me, and into the kink I am, feeling comfortable in my own skin and knowing I can be myself around someone is just about the best compliment I can think of, but if you don't like it, then how about this? I adore you. I adore everything about you. You are clever and sassy and sexy and beautiful and barely a second goes by when I'm not thinking about you in one way or another.

"I adore fucking you until your voice runs dry, and waking up beside you knowing I get to fuck you all over again. I adore reading books under trees together. I adore how you scowl at Charlie for being a dick when he puts the salt mill back in the wrong place. I even adore listening to you sing off-key when you cook."

Her spine straightened. "Hey! My singing isn't that bad," she spluttered indignantly.

"Baby, it really is, and I don't care because, fuck it, I—" He swallowed hard, the words "I love you" on the tip of his tongue and ready to fly at a moment's notice. But he knew this woman, knew she wasn't ready to hear a declaration of love.

She was afraid to trust him, to trust their connection as anything more than sex. And he wasn't willing to do anything that would jeopardise that connection. He didn't want her running scared.

Lucy trusted Toby with her body but not her heart, so before he told her he loved her, he had to show her, had to prove to her that he was worthy of that very special gift.

"You what?"

"I want you to meet my family," he said, a plan forming in his mind. "This weekend, I'm taking you to The Forge and you'll meet my sister and her fiancé, my dad, a few of my brothers, Charlie's girls. It'll be great."

Lucy's gaze narrowed. "That wasn't what you were going to say, was it?"

He grinned. "Maybe."

She stared at him a moment longer then mirrored his grin. "Fine. Don't tell me." Then she stroked her fingertips across his brow. "You feeling better now?"

"Yes."

That impertinent eyebrow went up again. "And do you still want me to move in with you?"

Toby didn't hesitate. "Yes."

She rolled her eyes and shook her head. "Eat your muffin," she said. "I have work to do." Then she struggled out of his lap.

As soon as she found her footing, Toby grabbed her hips

and pulled her backwards so she stood between his knees. "How's your arse?" he said, running one hand over her plush backside, gently kneading her flesh through the soft denim of her knee-length skirt. "Did the message sink in this time?"

Lucy's sharp inhale of breath followed by a quiet whimper was like music to Toby's ears, and he'd bet anything her panties were wet. He checked the time. It was just after one. Four more hours and that wet pussy was all his. *Soon, baby.*

"I really do have to get back to work," Lucy protested, wriggling her hips as she attempted to escape his grip. Because, yeah, that wasn't helping.

His cock twitched to life.

"Answer my question first."

"Are you asking as my boyfriend or my boss?"

He grinned. "Which one makes it sound more dirty?"

She half turned around at that and he saw she was trying not to laugh. "You're incorrigible, and this is against the rules." She swatted at his hands. "I'm not answering any more personal questions until after five o'clock," she said, her voice taking on that prim tone that made him want to put her over his knee and spank her until her voice turned sultry again.

"Fine," he said, letting her go and reaching for a muffin. "Go back to work. I'll just sit here and eat something else delicious. Speaking of which, what would you like for dinner? It's my turn to cook. And by cook I mean order in because I haven't been grocery shopping yet."

Lucy unlocked the door and stood poised to open it. "Who says I'm having dinner with you?"

Even though he detected her teasing lilt, Toby didn't like what Lucy was saying and let his displeasure show on his face, in his voice. "Why wouldn't you be eating dinner with me?"

"Because it's Tuesday." Toby stared at her until she explained why the day of the week made a difference to their dinner plans. "I go to the rock climbing gym on Tuesday. Or did you think this arse you're so fond of just happened by magic?" she said, lightly slapping her butt with both hands.

"Cheeky girl," Toby laughed, conceding defeat. He did that a lot with Lucy. Both the laughing and the concessions. "What time do you go to the gym?"

"Straight after work. I'll only be an hour or two."

"Two hours to climb a wall? What the hell takes you so long?"

"It doesn't usually take me that long but I'm doing a catch-up session to cover the one I missed over the weekend. Besides," she said, shooting him a look that dared him to contradict her, "the exercise is good stress relief."

Toby growled. "So is bending you over the dining table and making you orgasm so hard you black out."

Ducking her head to hide her expression, Lucy dropped her hand from the door knob and stalked towards him.

"Are you ordering me to not go to the gym," she said.

When she raised her face again Toby couldn't miss the thin slash of her mouth or the narrowing of her amber gaze.

Ah, crap. If he said yes, he was a controlling douchebag, and while he loved controlling her, he didn't want to do it like that. He wanted to control her body, her orgasms, her pleasure, sometimes even her breathing, but not her life.

He'd watched his sister go through two relationships like that and they hadn't ended well. He wouldn't make the same mistake with Lucy.

She was a grown woman, more than capable of making

her own decisions and if Toby wanted to earn her trust, her heart, then she didn't need him monopolising every second of her day.

She needed her own space, to do her own thing.

"No, baby," he said, staying seated, allowing her the position of power. Showing her she could trust him. "I wouldn't dare."

Her expression softened, her gaze dipped. "You could always come with me," she said, reaching out to steal a piece of his muffin.

To avoid answering her, Toby grabbed a coffee off the table and gulped it down, thankful it wasn't overly hot. But as her wide-eyed amusement at his non-answer became more apparent, he said, "Thank you for the offer, but, no. Rock climbing isn't my thing."

Her grin broadened. "Not afraid of heights, are you?"

His silence spoke for itself.

Dangerously close to earning another spanking of the not-fun variety, Lucy laughed at him. "Seriously? You're afraid of heights? But you're a giant!"

"Oh, like you're not afraid of anything?"

She scoffed then polished her fingernails on her shirt. "Of course not. I'm invincible." But Toby saw something akin to fear flit over her expression, and she didn't hide the shudder rolling through her shoulders as well as she thought.

Oh yeah. His girl was scared of something. He just had to figure out what.

Then crush it.

Chapter Twenty-Three

Jane's awake. She's coming home Friday. Family barbeque Saturday. Bring your lady friend. Gotta go. Love you. Bye.

The text message from Toby's sister seemed to be the catalyst that sent the rest of the week into overdrive. And Lucy didn't help. She had so many people coming and going from the garden centre, Toby couldn't keep track.

On top of the massive landscaping job he and his crew were undertaking, new software was installed on the office computers, every single fire alarm was replaced with the latest models available, and the number of fire extinguishers around the garden centre almost doubled.

Professional cleaners were called in to give the café a thorough going over, as was the administration building. His office manager had also informed him the conference room was being repainted the following week, and told him to choose a colour from a palette of nine different shades of grey.

Toby didn't know the first thing about decorating, and he told her so. "Give me a bare patch of earth, a shovel and a truckload of plants and I'm your man, but if you want to know what colour to paint the walls, call my brother Crispin. He decorated my house, he may as well do my office too."

And then Friday afternoon rolled around. Toby had been looking forward to clocking off and spending a relaxing evening at home before taking Lucy to meet his family on the weekend.

He'd planned to tie her up, drip hot wax all over her beautiful body then fuck her into oblivion. And he would have done exactly that if a team of people hadn't shown up at closing time, ready to install the new security system Lucy had ordered.

Instead of introducing his woman to the wax play he knew she craved, he'd spent three hours completing paperwork and staring at Lucy's sketch of his soon-to-be updated conference room, complete with chic grey walls and indoor palms.

He dreaded reading the mounting stack of bills his lover was racking up, but Lucy had assured him they could afford everything she had planned, and he found he trusted her judgement and experience. Plus he'd almost kissed her when she'd said "they" in the meeting where she'd laid out those plans for him, asking for his approval. "They" meant them. A unit. A team. A couple.

A future.

"They" had made his dick hard and gotten him in trouble for being inappropriate in the workplace during office hours.

"I never used to have this problem," he'd grumbled.

"Because you had rules and you followed them," Lucy reminded him. "And if you'd follow my rules now you still wouldn't have this problem." Then the cheeky minx had cupped his aching cock through his cargo shorts and leaned up to whisper in his ear, "I promise I'll make it up to you at home, Master."

That was the other word she kept using. "Home."

She still hadn't agreed to move in with him but when she stayed over, which she had almost every night that week, she'd referred to his house as "home". He didn't know if she was even conscious of it, but he sure as hell was.

Now it was Saturday morning and he was taking her to see his other home. The Forge. The Bennett family home was in Melville's Cross, a tiny town hidden away in the Sunshine Coast hinterland, and the weather was perfect for a weekend away.

Lucy had been quiet for most of the drive, which normally Toby would appreciate, but there was something off about her. Her silence was that of a busy mind, not a relaxed one.

He reached for her hand and gently squeezed. "What are you thinking about?"

Lucy took a deep breath and turned to face him. "I need to talk to you about something."

Her tone made his lips flatten into a stern line. "Is it work related?"

"Yes, Sir."

Toby shook his head. "No shop talk on the weekends, baby. Work stays at work."

"This is important," she said, standing her ground.

"So is a healthy work/life bal—"

"It's about Ashley," she said in a rush, cutting him off.

Toby put both hands back on the steering wheel, his grip tightening until his knuckles blanched. "Lucy—"

"I think she's skimming."

Blinking slowly, Toby said, "You wanna repeat that?"

Lucy rubbed her forehead as if she had a sudden headache. "I think Ashley is skimming the till in the café," she said, sounding tired, resigned.

Anger pulsed under Toby's skin and he gritted his teeth. *God-fucking-dammit.* "Do you have evidence?"

"Yes, I've spent most of this week going through your financials and while the rest of the business adds up, the café is woefully over budget. If she's not skimming then she's grossly mismanaging the place."

"But you think she's skimming," he said, more to confirm what he was hearing than ask her opinion. "Why?"

Lucy shrugged. "Because she's smart. Smart enough to make it look like mismanagement in the event she ever got caught." She pushed her fingertips against her forehead again. "Everything I've found so far is highly suspicious, but circumstantial."

"Like what?"

"Invoices for goods and services that don't seem to have ever existed. Everyday items used in the café invoiced at far greater prices than the industry standard. But without catching her in the act, I don't know that any of it would stand up in court."

Toby swore. "That's why you installed the new security system after hours. So she wouldn't know about it."

"Yes."

He swore again. "I'm not sure if I should be impressed or pissed off."

"Which way are you leaning?" she asked hopefully.

"Right now, pissed off."

Lucy turned to look out the window. "Would you have preferred I didn't tell you?" she asked quietly.

Fuck. He reached for her hand again. "No. You're right.

I needed to know. But why didn't you tell me this at work? Why wait until now?"

"You've been on site at the McMillan job for most of this week and rarely in the office, and honestly, I think she's on to me. She keeps making excuses to come into the office and hovers around my desk like she's trying to see what I'm working on.

"And when I spoke to the postman the other day about why he left the post at the café instead of the office, he said Ashley asked him to, told him she was helping out. And when I've tried to talk to you around the garden centre, she always seems to just pop up out of nowhere and interrupts us."

Toby frowned. She was right. Ashley had appeared around every corner lately. But why? "Why would she do this? And how long has she been doing it?"

"Best guess, since your last office manager left."

"It doesn't make any sense."

"How well do you really know her?" Lucy asked, genuine curiosity colouring her tone.

"I've know her since she was a kid. I worked for her parents. They owned the garden centre before me," he said. "They were the only ones willing to give me a chance after—"

Turning her body towards his again, Lucy said, "After what?"

Toby took a fortifying breath and slowly let it out again. "After I did something stupid." He almost laughed when she used his own trick against him and just stared at him, silent, until he filled in the blanks.

"It was my first job in the industry and I was working for a woman whose nursery specialised in Australian natives. It was a busy place and she hired a lot of people." He grimaced. "A lot of men. Young, naïve, horny men."

"I think I get the picture," Lucy said, her brows raised. "How old were you?"

"Nineteen."

"And the woman?"

"Thirty-four," he said, remembering. "Her name was Christine. She made me feel special." He huffed a sardonic laugh. "She made me feel a lot of things."

"Love?"

"I thought so at the time, so when I discovered I wasn't the only bloke she was screwing, I didn't handle it well."

"What did you do?"

"I made an absolute arse of myself," he said, grimacing at the memory. "I got shit-face drunk and serenaded her from outside her apartment building at two in the morning. By the time the cops showed up to tell me off I'd already broken out in the worst case of hives I've ever had in my life and had to be taken to hospital." When he glanced at Lucy she had both hands clamped over her mouth and her eyes were as big as saucers. Toby chuckled and shook his head. "It's okay. You can laugh."

Loud peels of laughter erupted out her, filling the cab of his truck, and she clutched her sides as though trying to stop them from splitting open. It would have been demoralising if she hadn't sounded so free and easy and open.

And if he didn't have eight siblings who took great delight in reminding him of his folly from time to time. He hoped introducing them to Lucy would put those times to rest for good, but knowing his luck it would all blow up in his face.

"I'm glad you're enjoying yourself."

"Well, I guess that explains where your rule about

sleeping with your employees comes from," she said, her laughter dying down to little more than a giggle.

Which reminded him... "And what about your rule about sleeping with the boss? You never did say why you left your old job."

Her giggle died and she made a weird face—half disgusted, half bemused—and Toby had a hunch he wasn't going to like whatever she had to tell him.

"Sure I did," Lucy said, shifting uncomfortably in her seat, avoiding his gaze. "In the interview."

Toby narrowed his eyes but kept them on the road. "No, you spun me a line of bullshit about wanting a change of pace and a new challenge. Out of all the questions I asked, that was the only one you dodged."

He heard her sigh and when he glanced at her, she was staring at him, her gaze shrewd. "If you knew I was lying, why did you hire me?"

"Because you were the best person for the job." A fact he was even more certain of now he'd seen what she could achieve in just one week. "I figured you'd tell me in your own time, and even if you didn't... well, your references all checked out so I wasn't overly concerned. Everyone has secrets, Lucy."

She was quiet for a long moment, then shook her head and said, "I don't want to keep secrets from you."

Warmth flooded through him, settled comfortably in his chest. "I'd kiss you for that but I can't without taking my eyes off the road for an unhealthy period of time." The sound of her seat belt unbuckling made his adrenaline spike. "What the hell are you doing?"

But then she slid across the bench seat to the middle and fastened the seat belt she found there—right beside him

—and rested her head on his shoulder, her hand on his thigh.

Lucy poked at the small rip in Toby's jeans, and even though her voice was soft it was underscored with the strength of steel. "I left because my boss—a man I'd considered my friend, and not just the kind with benefits—used me in the worst way possible."

A quick glance down revealed a deep frown cutting grooves across Lucy's forehead, and Toby was damned if he could tell what she was feeling. Perhaps she didn't want to talk about it, perhaps she wasn't ready. And that was okay. He wasn't going anywhere.

"You don't have to tell me right now if you don't want to," he said. "We have all the time in the world to learn about each other."

But Lucy shook her head. "No, I want to tell you. I think we need to be open with each other from the start, otherwise, what's the point? I'm just not sure how to put it in words without wanting to hit something. Or someone."

Toby wasn't sure how to respond to that so he reverted to his default setting and said nothing at all.

Thankfully, Lucy filled the void. "My boss was a man named Steven Rossi. I'd worked for the company for almost ten years when Steven bought it out and renamed it VIP Solutions. He was energetic and clever and sexy. Not in the ripped-for-her-pleasure cover model way, but there was just something about him, even if it wasn't obvious at first." She snorted. "He was over fifty, a little soft around the middle and shaved his head because he was balding, but,"—she sighed—"he was so tall."

Toby chuckled. "And you do like tall men."

"I *love* tall men." When Toby laughed again, she grinned up at him. "Hey, you try being an almost six foot tall woman. I'm as tall as if not taller than most men, and I've been told that makes me 'intimidating' and 'aggressive' and 'scary as fuck'."

"And yet you wore five inch stilettos to speed dating last Friday night," Toby said, one brow raised.

Lucy shrugged and flashed an impish grin. "Sometimes being intimidating works in my favour." She dragged her fingernail over Toby's bicep and sighed appreciatively, so of course he had to flex the muscle and show off for his woman. He smirked when her eyes glazed over and she pinched her bottom lip between her teeth. "Helps weed out the weak from the strong," she said.

"I see. And was Steven intimidated by you?"

"Not even remotely," she said. "Which made for a pleasant change. He was ex-army and could be a larrikin, but for the most part he behaved like a gentleman, always polite, always professional, and even though I found him attractive, I figured it was one-sided and didn't pursue it. Until he asked me to stay late one night and help him go over the office budget. One thing led to another and before I knew it we were seeing each other on a regular basis. Although, we never went out in public, and we never told anyone about us, but at the time I didn't really care. For the first time in a long time, I wasn't alone."

"So what went wrong? How did he use you?" *And what am I going to do to him for hurting you?*

Lucy went still. "Just before I quit, the company courted a new client—a movie mogul from the US who makes more money in a week than most people make in a lifetime. Suffice to say the man is used to getting his own way. For a week Steven did the whole wine and dine thing, hoping to land this creep as an exclusive client for any business undertaken in Australia, and apparently, during their final round of drunken negotiations, my preference for kinky sex came up. Mr Mogul decided he wanted a taste... and Steven agreed."

Toby clenched his jaw so hard it ached, and his lip curled in disgust at the thought of other men discussing his Lucy, talking about her like she was nothing more than something to be ordered off a menu. Men like that didn't deserve the gift of submission. "Arseholes."

"The day after their final... hell, let's be generous and call it a meeting, Steven asked me to stay late and speak with our potential client. I had no clue why he wanted to meet me, the office manager, but I'd trusted Steven and went along with it."

She paused for a moment, her silence almost as telling as what she said next. "But when Steven introduced me, when the client shook my hand, every hair on the back of my neck stood on end and I knew something was off. The way he looked at me, the way his eyes slid over me and lingered on my scars.... I was fully dressed and I'd never felt so exposed in my life. And then he propositioned me and I felt sick and... ashamed."

Rage tore through Toby's chest and flew out of his mouth on a curse. In an instant he'd pulled off to the side of the road and slammed on the brakes, jolting them both forwards in their seats. Lucy braced her hands on the dash and shot him a bemused glare but Toby was too incensed to take heed. He killed the engine. "Was this the guy who wanted you to prostitute yourself so he could film you?"

"Yes."

"Mother*fucker*." He slammed the heel of his palm against the steering wheel, immediately regretting the action. It hurt like a sonofabitch. Lucy laid her hand over his and turned her slim body to face him, then she brought his hand to her face and pressed a kiss to his aching palm. She blinked slowly and shuttered her gaze, but not before he recognised the darkness in her eyes.

He knew what it was because he'd seen it reflected back at him often enough in Charlie's eyes, and in his own when he looked in the mirror.

Bad memories.

"After the initial shock wore off, I was furious. I told him exactly where he could stick his proposal then stormed out of there and found Steven. And that fuck-knuckle actually had the nerve to ask me how it went. He'd known exactly what was going to happen and he sent me in there anyway. He betrayed me completely, as a lover and a friend." She drew in a shaky breath. "It still makes me sick, thinking about what might have happened if that guy hadn't taken 'no' for an answer."

Lucy let go of Toby's hand and tried to turn away, but he cupped her cheek and refused to let her. He wouldn't allow her to get lost inside her own head, not with that darkness still overshadowing her eyes. He would help excise her wound, even if all he could do was listen to her and hold her hand.

"I'm so sorry you had to go through that," he said, keeping his voice gentle as he held her gaze. "What happened when you confronted Steven?"

"I told him I wanted to file a complaint with HR, and he then proceeded to tell me exactly why that was a very bad idea—namely that it didn't look good for *me*, especially since I already had a reputation for sleeping with the boss. He said if I knew what was good for me I'd just forget it ever happened."

Lucy drew in a deep breath then slowly let it out, and Toby hated the sound of defeat in her voice, hated seeing her eyes glaze with tears. "The shitty thing is, I knew he was right. If the client was looking to hire VIP exclusively then he had deep pockets, and there was no way I was going to win a lawsuit against someone with that kind of money. Not without chewing through every last cent of my savings and then some. So I quit."

A frown tugged at Toby's brow. "How long ago was this?"

Lucy shrugged. "Back in March."

Almost six months ago.

"And how have you been living since then, paying your bills?"

His question made her smile, and while he didn't understand her reaction, he was glad to see the shadows fade from her eyes. "I inherited Nan's house when she passed so I don't pay rent and I don't have a mortgage. And you've seen the place. I live a fairly Spartan life. And I'm good with my money." Her smile became a grin and she looked up at him from under her lashes, as though about to impart another secret. Toby's curiosity piqued. "The only reason I started looking for work again was because I was so damn bored. I was going crazy sitting at home doing nothing. In all honesty I need a job for financial reasons about as much as you do."

Toby's heart stopped momentarily, then slammed into overdrive. *Clever girl.* He'd known it wouldn't take Lucy long to figure out he could buy and sell half of Bayside, but bragging wasn't his style. So he schooled his features, and said, "What do you mean 'as much as you do'...?"

Lucy cocked one brow and threw him a look that said he was insulting her intelligence, and he bit back a grin. "You know *exactly* what I mean," she said, then changed the subject. "Now, what are we going to do about Ashley?"

Toby started the truck and got back on the road. "Let me have a think and I'll get back to you," you said, knowing exactly what he should do—trust Lucy and fire Ashley—but he still had trouble reconciling the sweet little girl he knew with the woman willing to betray him. "I don't suppose you want to tell me Steven's address?" he added with undisguised menace.

Lucy glanced up at him, amusement dancing across her features. "Why?"

"No reason in particular," he hedged, thinking of ways he could repurpose the additional truckload of manure delivered to the McMillan job site.

If a steaming pile of shit in Steven's driveway didn't send a strong enough message, Toby figured rounding up his seven equally large brothers, paying the wankstain a visit and making him piss his pants might also satisfy his urge to avenge Lucy's honour.

"You're thinking about that truckload of manure, aren't you?"

Toby said nothing, but his shoulders bounced as he laughed, which said more than enough.

Lucy chuckled quietly then rested her head on his shoulder again, poked at the rip in his jeans. "Thanks, Toby. Let me have a think and I'll get back to you."

Chapter Twenty-Four

The closer they got to Toby's family home, the more Lucy seemed to sweat, and by the time they arrived, she felt like she needed a shower to rinse off the evidence of her anxiety.

Had it really only been two hours since she'd leapt into Toby's truck with a smile and a can-do attitude? Ha! She was more nervous than a first-time climber tackling an overhang.

"What if they don't like me?" she murmured, letting her gaze drift towards the house as Toby parked his truck.

It was a beautiful house built from hand-cut stone with an aged timber veranda running along the front of it. A low wall, also made of stone, hemmed the property and helped contain a gorgeous garden overflowing with roses and agapanthus and a bunch of other plants she couldn't name if her life depended on it. She made a mental note to learn more about gardening.

"Impossible," Toby said with a smile. He squeezed her knee. "They'll adore you."

But his assurance did nothing to settle Lucy's nerves. She chewed her bottom lip. "You don't know that."

"I do know that."

"Because *you* adore me?" Her words sounded snippy in her distress.

Toby's heavy sigh was all the warning she got before his hand fisted in her hair and she was forced to look at him.

Pain flared across her scalp and sent tingles down her spine. "Master," she gasped.

"What have I told you about belittling yourself?" he asked, his voice dropping a full octave as his free hand closed around her throat.

Lucy swallowed hard against his hand, leaned into its controlling warmth and let the dominant action calm her. "That you'll punish me," she breathed.

"Yes. I'll punish you. But I think what you really need right now is a reminder of who you belong to." His steely gaze flicked over her, where she sat with her seat belt still buckled like a safety line anchoring her in place. "Unbuckle that belt," he demanded. "And spread your thighs."

Not daring to disobey him in case he withheld her punishment—something she needed to ease her mind— Lucy did as she was told.

Toby dropped the hand from her throat, slid it under her skirt and along her inner thigh, gently brushed his rough palm over her soft flesh again and again, back and forth until she was so on edge waiting for the slap or the pinch or whatever he was going to do to her, that she didn't antici- pate him nudging her panties aside and spearing two fingers inside her.

A surprised whimper escaped her lips followed immedi- ately by a wanton moan. "Yes."

Toby leaned his forehead against her temple and she

felt his breath brush against her jaw, shivered with wanting. "Who's going to take care of you, baby?" he half whispered, half growled, as though he too were having trouble controlling himself.

"You are, Master," she said, clamping down on his fingers.

"And who will you turn to when you're afraid or unsure?"

He pushed his thumb against her clit and she gulped down a lungful of air, felt the burn of her desire heat her blood and scald her from the inside out. "You. I'll turn to you," she said on the exhale.

"Good girl," Toby cooed, languidly stroking his fingers in and out of her wet heat, winding her higher, tighter. "You're not alone, Lucy. You never need to be alone again. Say it."

"I'm not alone," she whispered, her breath stuttering in and out of her. "I never need to be alone again."

Toby pressed his forehead harder against her temple and his mouth moulded to her ear. "Tell me why," he whispered, his breathing as uneven as hers.

His fingers quickened their pace, made it difficult to concentrate.

"Because you're here with me." Her fingers curled into the leather of the seat beneath her, stopping her from sliding to the floor of the truck. "Because you promised me."

"What did I promise?"

Lucy thought back to Monday night when she'd flipped out before their date and answered the door in her underwear. She remembered his hands on her body as he'd pinned her to the wall of her bedroom, then again as she'd sat in his lap on the bed.

His touch had been gentle, sensual, grounding. His

voice a soothing caress for her soul, his words filled with more understanding than she'd ever heard from anyone before.

"I promise I'll be there for you. I'll support you, shield you or just stand back and watch you kick arse."

"Everything. You promised me everything."

She felt his lips curl against her ear. "Who do you belong to, baby?" he purred.

"You. Tobias. My Master."

A third finger joined the others invading Lucy's body, pistoned in and out of her greedy pussy until she cried out. Close. She was so close. Her back bowed, her toes curled and her head thrashed from side to side. She knew what she looked liked. A woman possessed. Absently she wondered if that made Toby her sexorcist.

Or maybe he was the demon.

Because the next thing she felt was empty. Frustrated, unfulfilled emptiness consumed her as Toby withdrew his hand from her panties and sucked his pussy slicked fingers into his mouth one at a time.

"I fucking love the taste of your cunt."

Confusion pulled at Lucy's brow as she stared at the giant man sitting beside her—the giant, *smirking* man—and before she could think better of it, she hiked her skirt up and swung herself over Toby's lap, straddled his legs. It was a tight fit but she was slim enough to make it work.

Gripping the headrest behind her lover, Lucy used it as leverage and ground her body against his. Mashed her clit against the enormous bulge tenting his jeans. When Toby rolled his hips, encouraging her to continue, a sultry moan slipped from her lips and vibrated against his throat.

He tilted his head, giving her better access to his skin. "You want my cock, baby?"

"I always want your cock," she whispered against his neck. "Toby, I'm so horny."

"I know," he said, then he chuckled, the cocky sound vibrating through his big body and into hers. They hadn't been together long, but Lucy knew that sound.

And it was never in her favour.

"Oh no," she groaned. Pulling back enough to look her man in the eye, she saw the devilry twinkling in his pale blue gaze.

This was her punishment.

Because what better way to punish her than make her horny as fuck, then deny her satisfaction? And then introduce her to his family knowing full well she was gagging for his dick.

Arsehole, she thought, though the word lacked any real rancour. He'd said he needed a better way of punishing her, and he'd obviously found it.

Orgasm denial.

He didn't even have to say it. She just knew. The one raised brow, the impish grin, his hands clamping around her wrists preventing her from releasing his magnificent erection. "You're so mean."

"I know." He laughed again. "Now get out of the truck." Then he playfully swatted her arse as she popped open the driver-side door and crawled off his lap.

As Toby grabbed their bags from the back, Lucy bit the inside of her cheek, stopping herself from begging for one little orgasm. Just one. Was that so much to ask?

But she knew her quiet giant would deny her until he saw fit to give her what she wanted, just like she knew he'd edge her towards that blissful endgame over and over again should she try to force the issue. He was nothing if not consistent.

What she needed was a change in subject, something to distract her from the delicious ache between her thighs, which she realised, as they walked hand in hand towards the house, had done its job by distracting her from her nervousness.

Chancing a quick glance up at the walking monolith beside her, she caught sight of that cocky smirk still gracing his handsome face, and when he caught her looking at him, another chuckle shook his big body.

"Oh, shut up," she muttered, conceding defeat, making him laugh louder. But as they passed through the wrought-iron gate and entered the garden, as they got closer and closer to the house and all those people she didn't know, her nerves returned and her mind went completely blank. What was Toby's father's name again? And Charlie's daughters were... Jessie and....

Fuck.

Lucy was usually more prepared than this. If this had been for a job interview she would have taken notes and studied them and quizzed herself, but it just seemed weird to do that while your boyfriend was talking about his family, so she hadn't. She hadn't done any of that and now her mind was blank.

"You getting nervous again?"

Looking up at Toby from under her lashes, Lucy nodded. "I know you told me last night," she said, holding Toby's hand as they walked along the path, "but for the sake of me not making an absolute arse of myself in front of your family, can we go over it again?"

"Sure thing." Toby smiled down at her then leaned in conspiratorially. "Okay, here goes. My sister Abby lives and works here as a blacksmith—"

"Which is insanely cool, by the way."

"And her fiancé, Wolf, is a novelist and also her Dom." Lucy nodded both in acknowledgment of the information and at the thought of meeting someone else like her. Maybe Toby was right and this wouldn't be as scary as she imagined?

Toby continued, "My youngest brother, Oliver, is hard to miss. He's almost as big as me but he looks like a Viking. He's also a blacksmith and currently in residence at The Forge, much to Abby's irritation. Expect bickering. He's also the only blond in the family. If he flirts with you—which he will—do not engage." His lips twisted. "Little shit will use any means to get under my skin. My father, Ulysses, is also in residence. He's an incorrigible man-whore who will definitely flirt with you. Don't pay him any attention."

"But he's your father and I'm his guest," Lucy teased, a modicum of satisfaction swirling through her at her lover's look of instant irritation.

"And I'm his son and you're *mine*," Toby growled. "I don't share. Not anymore."

Lucy's heart fluttered against her ribcage and she almost forgave him for the orgasm denial. "Yes, Master."

"My older brother, Crispin, is here, too. He's also easy to spot." A sly grin played around Toby's sensual mouth causing Lucy to narrow her eyes. He was definitely up to something, but she simply nodded and followed Toby up the steps to the veranda.

"You already know Charlie but today you'll meet Josie and Diana, his twin girls. Just think of them as very tall, very excitable puppies. And then there's Rafe and Jane, now officially—fucking *finally*—engaged, and already expecting their first babies. Rafe is a lawyer. He's usually pretty reserved. Jane, on the other hand, is a chef who rarely has a thought she doesn't immediately give voice to. I love her like a sister but she's exhausting."

Lucy laughed at the pained expression on Toby's face. He looked tired already and she guessed being an introvert wasn't something he could turn off just because he was dealing with his family, and she realised he needed her to get through this weekend as much as she needed him.

"Jane's mum is also here. Mary." He smiled in a way that filled his whole face with peace, and said, "She's just about the closest thing to a real mother most of us ever had."

"What about Isobel?" Lucy asked. Toby had avoided talking about the woman all week and Lucy's curiosity was beyond piqued. Mostly because she wondered how anyone could possibly be a worse mother than her own.

But she realised she should have left well enough alone when the warmth in Toby's expression instantly faded, replaced with a hatred that was frightening to see. He closed his eyes for a moment and Lucy watched his chest rise and fall as he took a deep breath, and when he stared down at her next he was back to his usual stoic self.

"Are you ready?" he asked quietly, turning her to face him as they stood in the open doorway. Isobel, or any mention of the woman, was seemingly forgotten.

Lucy took the hint. Casting one last nervous glance inside, she straightened her shoulders and gave Toby a quick, sure nod. "Let's do this."

Toby chuckled and swept her hair away from her face. She'd left it down, the way he liked it. "It's going to be fine, baby. Trust me."

"I do trust you," Lucy said, the words slipping from her mouth without hesitation. For the first time in a very long time there was no forethought or second guessing or any doubt at all. She felt it down to her bones, deeper even than that.

Lucy trusted Toby.

And her heart beat more stridently at the thought because if she trusted him then there could be no further doubt.

Lucy *loved* Toby.

And it was on the tip of her tongue to say so when they were interrupted by a tall blond Viking. Oliver. "Oi!" he called out from the other end of the hallway. "Are you pair coming inside or what?"

A surprised laugh escaped Lucy, and Toby rolled his eyes. He lifted a hand in greeting. "We'll be there in a minute."

"Well hurry up or you'll miss out," Oliver continued. Toby wasn't wrong about his brother's size. He practically filled the doorway, especially as he stood there with his hands on his hips. "Jane's already demolished the potato salad, and the way she's eyeing the barbeque doesn't bode well for the rest of us." Then he raised his voice slightly and called over his shoulder, "Anyone would think she's pregnant with an entire horde of kids, not just twins."

A distant, yet shrill "I heard that" echoed through the house.

Oliver shook his head. "Welcome to the madhouse, Lucy." Then turned around and walked in the direction of the shrieking woman.

Lucy tilted her head to one side. "Did he have flowers in his beard?"

Toby's grin reappeared. "Yes he did. Come on. Let's dump our gear and get something to eat while we still can."

Toby handed his twin brother one of their home-brewed ginger beers, then took a seat beside him on the ancient daybed nestled against the back of the house. Lunch had long since finished and the rest of their family had scarpered off to do their own thing.

Rafe and Jane were taking a nap, Cris had taken the twins to the patisserie for milkshakes, Ulysses had disappeared into his studio, Wolf was working on his next bestseller, and the soft tinkle of piano keys echoing through the back door informed them of Oliver's whereabouts. And Abby was giving Lucy a lesson in blacksmithing.

With the big oak doors of the forge thrown wide open, Toby had a clear view of his lover—and the huge smile stretched across her face—as he watched her bring the hammer down on the anvil in strong, controlled movements.

She looked like she'd been born with a hammer in her hand, and as he listened to the rhythmic *clang, clang, clang* of metal on metal followed by the *hiss* of steam as hot iron was thrust into the water barrel, he took a moment to admire his woman. She'd changed into jeans and one of Abby's old T-shirts and wore a heavy leather apron over her clothes, and the long blonde hair she'd left loose for his benefit, had been piled on top of her head in a messy bun.

The forge was too far away for Toby to hear any of Lucy's conversation, but she appeared to be chatting freely with his sister. She was relaxed and having fun, and Toby was loving the ease with which she'd blended into his family.

Like she was meant to be there.

It'd felt right, bringing her home and introducing her as his girlfriend, and Ulysses had finally seen for himself what Toby had known all along: no one took advantage of Lucy unless she wanted them to.

And as much as she'd worried they wouldn't like her or that she'd make a fool of herself, she'd taken their uniqueness in her stride as easily as they'd accepted hers. Even when he'd deliberately withheld information that would have made those strides far easier to take, such as not telling Lucy that Crispin was part Japanese, or that Wolf wasn't just a novelist, but one of her all-time favourite novelists, Adam Wolfe.

Did not telling her these things make him a dick? Perhaps. But as much as he cared for Lucy and wanted to protect her from all the bad things in the world, his instinct to do the same for his family would always be there too, and seeing Lucy's true and unrehearsed reactions had only cemented the knowledge that she was a perfect fit for him. And his family.

She hadn't even blinked at Crispin, just shaken his hand and shyly thanked him for his design acumen in bedroom furniture.

"She's particularly fond of our bed," Toby had said, making her blush three shades of pink.

"I'm rather fond of that design myself." His older brother had then winked at Lucy, and added, "If you ever get tired of dating the Sasquatch, give me a call."

"Back off short-stack," Toby had snarled, then tightened his grip on his woman. "She's mine."

His possessiveness had made his brother laugh. And made Lucy curl against his side like a pet wanting attention. Attention he was yet to give her. As liberal as his family was, even they drew the line at going down on your submissive at a family barbeque.

"It was mean of you not to tell Lucy about Wolf," Charlie said, dragging Toby from his thoughts. "Don't get me wrong, the look on her face when she realised who she was talking to was hilarious, but it was still mean."

Toby's grin was broad and unrepentant. "Probably. To be honest, I'm still impressed by her reaction to Cris."

"What reaction?"

"Exactly." Toby knew he'd pay for his deceptions when he and Lucy were alone. And he couldn't wait. Sometimes her displeasure with him was just as enticing as her submission. He jerked his chin at the forge and the two women shooting furtive glances in his direction. "Anyway, if Abby's teaching her to make what I think she is, I'm pretty sure she's already plotting her revenge."

Charlie sighed heavily. "Speaking of which...."

Toby knew what was coming. He'd been avoiding the topic all week but knew he couldn't dodge the issue forever. Hell, the fact he'd almost snapped Lucy's head off just for mentioning his mother's name was all the evidence he needed to realise they had to get this sorted, and soon.

"We need to deal with Isobel," he said, registering Charlie's shock that he'd brought up the subject with little prompting. But screw it. It was time to do something about her. Toby was in love with an amazing woman and he wanted to move on to the next chapter of his life. He wanted to start a family, wanted to turn his house into a home. Wanted Lucy by his side for better or worse. And he wanted to do all of that without the threat of Isobel Bennett dangling overhead, waiting to drop like the fucking sword of Damocles. "As much as I'd like to tell her to go fuck herself, that's not going to solve our problem, is it?"

"No, it isn't." Charlie took a sip of his drink. "I told Dad, just so you know."

"And?"

"And he said if we wanted him to deal with her, he would."

Toby's lips jerked up in a half smile. They were grown men who owned and ran their own businesses, but their father never hesitated to step in and protect his children. He never had and Toby doubted he ever would.

His love for his family was too strong.

Toby's gaze flicked to Lucy. From what she'd told him, the only people who'd cared that deeply for her were her brother, Michael, and her Nan. And they were both long gone.

She should have been able to rely on her parents, just as he, Charlie and Rafe should have been able to rely on their mum, but some people didn't deserve the children they had. Some people lost that privilege a long time ago.

Toby grunted. "That just means he'll pay her off again. No. We need to do this." He stared at Charlie, lifted his chin. "We need to end this."

His brother pulled him into a hug so tight Toby felt his bones pop, then Charlie butted their foreheads together and whispered, "Then let's do it. Let's put this shit to bed once and for all."

Chapter Twenty-Five

After nearly an hour of brainstorming about the best way to rid themselves of the destructive force they reluctantly called their mother, Charlie went back inside.

Toby quickly took advantage of having the entire daybed to himself and lay down, giving himself a better view of the forge—and in turn Lucy—in the process. Propping his bare feet on one end, he crossed them at the ankles, then knitted his fingers together and rested them on his chest.

He enjoyed watching Lucy. He didn't even particularly care what she was doing either—reading a book, flipping pancakes, typing at her computer at an inhuman pace—he just found her infinitely fascinating. And it wasn't just her body either, although he doubted he'd ever get enough of her long, lean, muscled figure or the feminine way she moved.

Lucy had a gracefulness he rarely saw in people anymore, like a cat winding its way around its Master's legs. She was all strength and stealth. Sexy. But he also loved watching her thought processes play out across her face as she put plans into action. Toby doubted she was even aware of it, but Lucy had a habit of chewing on the left side of her bottom lip as she worked. That and drumming her fingernails on her desk, which was admittedly annoying, but still endearing as it afforded him an excuse to drag her over his knee and spank her, watch her go limp, feel her body melt into his....

"Toby."

Lucy's voice tickled his senses.

"Toby?"

Now she was giggling. Last thing he remembered he'd been spanking her so why was she giggling? Cracking one eye open, Toby stared at Lucy smiling down at him and slowly came to the realisation he'd dozed off.

"What time is it?" he said, the words spilling out on a yawn. The sun was lower than before but it wasn't getting dark just yet, but night time wasn't too far off either if the chill in the air was any indication.

"Time for you to wake up. Jane put together some platters of leftovers and nibbles in the kitchen if you're interested. An early dinner."

"Cool." He stretched his arms above his head. "How long have I—"

"Been snoring like a drunken bear? Not long."

Toby scowled. "I do not snore."

Lucy's grin was swift and brazen. "If you say so."

"I say so." When her grin broadened, Toby dragged her down on top of him and banded his arms around her middle, then flipped them over and pinned her beneath him. Giggling turned to shrieks of laughter as he tickled her, merciless in his task.

"Stop! I give, I give," she cried out.

Toby stopped tickling her and playfully nipped at her lips instead, teased her with a sharp pinch from his teeth. Thrust his hips and his hardening cock into the cradle of her thighs. "What will you give me?"

Lucy's hand, small and warm and gentle, cupped his cheek, but her gaze turned heated and she locked her ankles beneath his arse. "Anything my Master wants."

"Anything?" he asked, rocking against her.

Gently smoothing her hair away from her face, Toby studied Lucy's scars, whispered his lips over her shortened eyebrow, the tiny sneer at the corner of her mouth, then licked one long line along the sensitive skin of her neck until she closed her eyes and moaned, "Anything."

"Move in with me."

This time when she stared up at him, her eyes weren't bugging out of her head in shock. Quite the opposite, and Toby took the time to memorise every golden striation hidden in the depths of her intoxicating eyes. Eyes that called to him, eyes that had seen things even more fucked up than his had, and he realised that's why he felt so comfortable around her, why she was so easy to love.

It wasn't just their shared experiences of being screwed over by their mothers, or their need to control their environments. Somehow her inner damage had called out to his and together they'd started to heal each other, had begun to fill in and fix the cracks inside them, not just plaster over the top and hope for the best.

"You are persistent, I'll give you that," she said softly, her lips lightly brushing against his.

Toby grinned, hoping Lucy could feel it. She had no idea how persistent he could be when he really wanted something, and he really wanted her. Lucy Barton. His perfectly imperfect woman. His baby. His fuck toy.

His everything.

Then Toby realised something else. While he'd kept up his reputation for uncompromised stoicism, Lucy had bared her all. She'd shared her damage with him, shown him where to find the cracks she hid from the rest of the world behind her mask of efficiency and to-do lists.

She'd risked everything to be with him, and he was ashamed to say he hadn't done the same. When Lucy had tried reaching out to him, when she'd asked about Isobel, tried to take a glimpse at that most detestable portion of his past, he'd shut her down.

His mood sobered. It was time he let her all the way in. It was time he told her everything.

He just wasn't sure he could.

Not without losing her.

Later that night when Lucy slid into bed beside him, Toby reached for her, needing desperately to feel her soft skin, her firm body, her beating heart. Wishing he could melt into her and stay there, safe and warm and protected.

Except he was supposed to be the protector, not her.

Toby stood at six feet and eight inches in height and could bench press his own body weight without breaking a sweat, and all he wanted to do was hide from his mummy. Hide from the memories he'd pushed so far down inside him he was afraid of what would happen should he let them see the light of day.

After so much time, it felt strange to be so unsure of himself, to feel like he didn't have control.

"Toby, are you all right? You've been quiet all evening. More quiet than usual." Lucy's voice was soft but strong and Toby clung to that strength, hoping she was strong enough for both of them. Because he wasn't sure he could go through with Charlie's plan if she wasn't.

Rolling to face her, he swallowed hard and blew out a calming breath. "I need to talk to you about something, someone." He took another breath. "About Isobel."

His lover's gaze snapped to his, alert and focussed. He'd been avoiding the topic ever since she'd seen that bloody text message from Charlie, but she needed to know. He couldn't keep her in the dark and keep her safe. And now he knew he had her trust he was going to do whatever it took to keep it.

That meant telling her everything. It meant shining a light on all his darkest memories and asking her to understand why he was the way he was.

Why he needed to be in control.

Lucy's small hand slid along his side then over his bicep, his shoulder, his neck. She touched him in a way that calmed his mind, soothed his soul. She explored his body with such wonder, as though she couldn't believe he was real, and when her hand came to rest over his heart, he felt the same about her. She couldn't possibly be real. He wasn't that lucky.

After tonight, he'd know for sure. The conversation they were about to have could only end one of two ways: either Lucy accepted him and his darkness, or she didn't. And for the first time in a long time, he wasn't confident of the outcome.

"I'm listening," she whispered.

Here goes. "Isobel Bennett is an evil human being." He barked a short, sharp laugh. "And that's not even her real name. Dad never married her but she insists on using it anyway." Toby clamped his hand on Lucy's hip and dug his fingers in, needing to feel her flesh, needing to hear her quiet gasp of surrender. Needing an anchor, something to hold him in the present so he didn't get lost in the past.

"Master," Lucy whimpered, then pressed herself closer. *Good girl.*

Breathing easier, Toby continued. "Isobel is a manipulative, deceitful gambling addict with no moral compass. Over the four years they were together, Uly estimates she stole at least a hundred grand from him, probably more, and she lost every cent of it."

"Jesus."

"Dad tried kicking her out when Charlie and I were toddlers, but she fell pregnant with Raffy so he let her stay. But things didn't improve. I was only four when Dad finally succeeded in kicking her out but I remember the screaming matches they had. He wouldn't let her take us, threatened to take her to court if she didn't leave, told her no judge would ever award custody to a gambling addict. Isobel told him he had no right, that we weren't even his kids, but she was lying, and thankfully Dad knew it."

"How?"

"After he'd caught her stealing from him, he'd had paternity tests done on me and Charlie. He had one done when Raffy was born too, just to be sure. So he knew we were his and he told her so." Toby paused and took a breath, let it out slowly, calmly. He needed to be calm for what was coming. "Then she said she'd leave, she would go and he could have us... for a price. One hundred thousand."

"Holy shit," Lucy gasped.

"For each of us," Toby said, his tone disdainful. "Uly wrote her a cheque for a flat half million then told her to fuck off. Told her to stay the hell away from his kids. He never wanted to see her again. And we didn't, not until we were twelve."

Lucy's voice was strained, as though she didn't want to ask her question but her curiosity compelled her to. "What happened when you were twelve?"

Acid boiled in Toby's gut at just the thought of what happened then, and the scalding burn of tears built behind his eyes. "She tried to sell us," he said, spitting out each word like it was poison. "Her own children."

With the curtains open and the moonlight shining in, Toby could see just enough of Lucy's face to know she was close to tears herself. Her eyes were wide and her mouth opened and closed uselessly as her words dissolved into nothingness.

She had so much heart, his woman. A soft heart. A kind heart. He'd seen the way she watched people at the garden centre, the way her lips would form a pensive smile when she saw a baby cradled in their mother's arms.

He'd seen her help people with all manner of things, even when they were wary of her and her scarred face. And he'd watched with a wistful smile of his own as she'd crouched down to let curious children touch her cheek, let them see she wasn't the monster others thought she was.

Lucy would never hurt her own child the way his mother, her mother, had hurt them. It simply wasn't in her.

"Why would she do that?"

"She'd gotten in deep with some very bad people and ran out of money." Toby hugged her closer, comforted them both. "She'd contacted Dad and demanded he bail her out, but he refused." He shook his head. "He had no idea what he'd set in motion with that one little word. No."

"What did Isobel do? How did she get to you?"

"Charlie and I were at boarding school in Brisbane. It

was our first year there and we stuck to our own company for the most part. Charlie may be show-off now, but when we were twelve, he was just as reserved as me. So when Isobel showed up at school demanding to see her sons, we didn't protest. We should have. We should have shouted the buildings down, but we were scared. Two skinny, gangly kids with the shared confidence of a skittish stray."

Confusion furrowed her brow. "If she was estranged, why did the school let her see you?"

"Dad never told them she was estranged. As far as he was concerned, she was out of our lives and that was that. And the admins at school only asked us if she really was our mother, and with no note in our files to say we couldn't go out with her, they allowed it."

Toby swallowed against the thick lump forming in his throat. "She told them she'd have us back by dinner time. She lied. Isobel drove us to the Gold Coast, to some warehouse in an abandoned industrial complex. The people she owed money to had made her a deal. If she couldn't pay them in cash, she could pay them in kids. If they liked what they saw, they'd cancel her debt."

Lucy sniffed and Toby knew she was trying not to cry, his brave girl. Her words came out strangled and wet. "Did you—" She tried again. "Were you—"

"No, baby," he cooed, tucking her under his chin and holding her close. "We were lucky. We were terrified, but we were very lucky. The men making the deal were just middle men. They had no interest in young boys in private school uniforms, and one of them, the one who shoved us in the back of a van and told us to keep quiet, was an undercover cop. He saved us that day."

Lucy burst into tears and wrapped her arms around him

so tightly, pressed her body so close he could feel her heart thudding against his own.

"The next thing we knew there were cops everywhere, swarming the place, and Isobel was arrested along with everyone else. Dad arrived about three hours later and I don't think he's ever hugged us as tightly as he did that day." And then another memory swirled to the surface and Toby smiled, slow and wicked.

"In the middle of the police station, surrounded by cops, Uly told Isobel if she ever came near his kids again, he'd kill her, and no one, not a single cop blinked." He shook his head, the disbelief still raw and fresh. "It's the only time I can remember my mother looking scared."

Then Toby sighed and got to the point. "She shows up every few years looking for money, but this time feels different. Desperate. Like she was back then. But we've decided, Charlie and me, we're not giving her any more money. It's time to end this once and for all. It's time to say no."

Lucy was quiet for a long time, then said, "How old are Charlie's girls?"

He knew she'd get it, knew she'd read between the lines and understand. "Thirteen. Only a year older than we were."

"They don't look thirteen."

"We didn't look twelve. Apparently that's part of the appeal for these sick fucks."

"No." Lucy clung to Toby's shoulders, her grip strong and sure. "Fuck no. And fuck Isobel," she snarled. Then she pinned him with a determined stare. "What do you need me to do?"

Toby ground his erection against the apex of Lucy's thighs and she moaned so loud she'd feared the rest of the house would hear her, then she remembered this crazy rabbit-warren of a house had seven bedrooms and in all likelihood she could scream until her throat was sore and no one would be any the wiser.

"Right now I just need to be in you, baby," Toby said, his voice a low rumble, thick with desire. "This is going to get rough but I need it. I need you hard and fast and dirty."

And then to prove his point, he shoved two fingers in her pussy and made her gasp, "Yes, Master."

Rolling so he was on top of her, he took her mouth in a long, deep, life affirming kiss. The type of kiss that waged war and slow danced and made love all at once as their tongues teased and their lips plucked and their teeth clashed and they breathed the same breath.

Lucy drowned in her Master's passion, came alive in it. He possessed her totally and she surrendered completely, she gave him everything, her body, her mind and yes, her heart.

Her heart was his. Toby's. Utterly his. And she no longer cared if it was too soon to say it. Two weeks or two years, it made no difference to how she felt. The moment he broke the kiss, she whispered, "I love you."

Toby stilled above her and her breathing stalled as she waited for him to speak. The dark seemed to close in on her and time slowed to a standstill, then his deep voice rumbled through the darkness, so bogged down in doubt it made her heart ache to hear him speak. "Say it again."

Threading her fingers through his hair, she tugged him closer, close enough her lips brushed his once more. "I love you," she said again, louder this time so there could be no confusion. No doubt.

He traced the tip of his nose along her scarred cheek, making her shiver with need. "I don't deserve you," he said quietly. "You know that, right?"

Lucy tried to sound serious but failed miserably. "Oh, absolutely," she said, giggling softly.

And for the first time all night, Toby relaxed and chuckled too, his big body bouncing against hers. "Good, because I love you too, baby. I've loved you from the moment we met." Then he flipped her over on her hands and knees and took her, slid his cock deep in her pussy, his fingers deep in her arse. "Play with yourself," he demanded. "Let me feel you fingering that juicy little clit."

Lucy reached between her legs and touched herself, circled the tip of her finger around the sensitive tiny nub of flesh and gasped at the feeling of total abandon.

"Yes," she hissed, her pussy contracting around Toby's thick cock.

He was in so deep and pushing deeper. It hurt, burned. She wanted more. She wanted all of it. She felt all of it. Toby's body was so big, his skin so hot. His fingers curled around one hip and dug into her flesh, just like he had before, and Lucy welcomed the bite of pain.

"More," she cried, the warped receptors in her brain switching her pain to pleasure. "Please, Master. More."

Toby slowed his pace, tortured her with measured thrusts of his hips instead of the furious fucking he'd promised, knowing it would irritate her. Then he laughed when she snarled at him, when she swore and slammed her fist against the mattress where it bounced ineffectually and made a mockery of her frustration.

"What's in it for me?" her lover said, and she could hear the smirk in his voice. "What do I get if I give you what you want?"

Her irritation forgotten, her shoulders bounced in time with her own laughter as she conceded defeat. "You get me," she said, huffing out a breath to blow her hair out of her face.

"But I already have you," he said, and slapped his palm against her arse, the loud *crack* of flesh on flesh drowning out her startled gasp. "You'll have to do better than that."

"What if you had me 24/7...? Would that whet your appetite?"

Toby stilled completely and gripped both her hips in his steely grasp. "You'll move in with me?"

"Yes."

Suddenly his hand was fisted in her hair, her head was yanked backwards and his breath tickled her cheek. "Yes, what?" he snarled, and her pussy clenched around his cock in response.

"Yes, Master," Lucy whispered, her whole body quivering, excited. Alive.

Toby's lips brushed over the shell of her ear. "Good girl."

He straightened, taking her with him until his chest was pressed to her back, his hands were clamped over her breasts and his cock was buried so deep inside her she might never get him out again.

And then he fucked her.

Deliciously hard.

Insanely fast.

And very, very dirty.

Chapter Twenty-Six

For what felt like the millionth time that day, Lucy checked her watch. It was a little after three o'clock on Monday afternoon and besides the occasional text message asking for updates—of which she had none— she hadn't heard from Toby all afternoon.

Charlie had picked up Toby around lunch time, their intention being to see their mother and tell her in no uncertain terms they wouldn't give her any more money, nor would they bail her out of any more trouble.

They were cutting her off, for good, knowing bad people would do bad things to their mother if she couldn't pay what she owed. Knowing it would make Isobel desperate, possibly desperate enough to try something stupid, which was why the twins absolutely would not let the woman within barking distance of Charlie's girls.

Josie and Diana would be at the garden centre soon, but Lucy had expected the older Bennett twins to be back by the time the girls arrived. So far they were nowhere to be seen. And she was beginning to panic.

Nervous tension had Lucy out of her chair and pacing

the floor as she weighed her options. Should she lock up early and take the girls home as soon as they arrived? Or did she wait for the men as planned?

The girls knew what was going on, knew their psycho grandmother might try something stupid, which was why they were staying with Charlie until the situation had been dealt with. Until it was certain the girls were safe.

The security at Toby and Charlie's property was better than their mothers' house, and with the new security network Lucy had installed at the garden centre, if anyone tried anything to hurt the twins, it would all be captured on high definition cameras and stored as evidence on a private server.

Still, she'd feel a lot better if Toby was there when the girls arrived. She hardly knew them, and them her. They had no reason to trust her, no reason to believe she could keep them safe from harm. What if something happened? Would they obey her instructions, or would they, in typical teenage form, argue with her until they were blue in the face?

Lucy really hoped she never found out.

In light of the Isobel-possibly-wanting-to-kidnap-Charlie's-daughters drama, the Ashley-is-a-light-fingered-thieving-bitch drama had been shelved for now, but Lucy had still spent most of the morning installing additional measures on all computers the café manager had access to, including keystroke spyware.

As far as Lucy could tell, Ashley had spent half the afternoon shopping online for cheap cosmetics and trashy lingerie no man in his right mind would ever find appealing. But then, Lucy enjoyed being tied up and punished during sex, so who was she to judge? She just hoped it wasn't being paid for with the money stolen from Toby. *What a waste.*

A taxi soon pulled into the carpark and Josie and Diana climbed out. Lucy met them at the front gate with a smile then ushered the pair inside the administration building.

"How was school?" she asked.

"Boring," came the duel reply, and Lucy smothered a grin. She'd probably thought the same thing when she was their age.

"Do you have any homework?"

"I have to finish reading Romeo and Juliet for English," Diana groaned. "It's so dumb. Someone should have told Juliet no guy is ever worth killing yourself over."

Josie dumped her school bag on the conference table and flopped into the chair beside her sister. "And I have to design a science experiment to test rates of corrosion in various metals. You don't know anything about that, do you?" She looked up at Lucy with such an imploring look in her eyes that Lucy really wished she knew the answer, but she didn't.

"No, sorry. But if you ever want to learn how to make rainbow fire, I'm your girl."

Diana's face lit up and her smile was as evil as her father's. "Rainbow fire?"

"Don't encourage her," Josie said, rolling her eyes. "She almost got suspended last year for trying to make explosives in chem lab."

"Fireworks. I was trying to make fireworks."

Lucy grinned. "Okay, well, I'll leave you to it. I need to finish up out here and hopefully your dad and uncle will be back soon. If you're hungry, there's fruit and water in the mini fridge, and I think Toby said we're getting pizza for dinner."

Both twins pumped their fists in the air. "Score!"

Chuckling, Lucy turned to leave, but the girls stopped her in her tracks.

"We're glad you're dating Toby," Josie said.

"I beg your pardon?" Lucy turned back again.

"Yeah," Diana added. "We discussed it and we think you're good for him. He smiles a lot more now. I never realised he had so many teeth."

Lucy burst out laughing. "Do your homework," she said, then quickly turned away before she let it slip that she knew exactly how many teeth Toby Bennett had because he'd spent half the previous night biting her breasts and tugging on her pierced nipples.

They were still deliciously sore.

She sighed. She really needed girlfriends, people she could talk to about grown up things, like bragging about the size of her boyfriend's dick or... nope, that was pretty much it. She just wanted to tell someone about the size of the cock she was getting on a daily basis. Someone other than Maisie.

As she settled back into her chair, Lucy pulled up the security camera app and selected the cameras around the café. She'd been playing with the system on and off throughout the day, learning the motions and the range of vision possible, and Ashley made for a convenient target, but as she zoomed in on the barista and the woman she was serving, Lucy froze.

Grabbing her phone, she pulled up her photo app and looked at the picture Toby had given her that morning, the last known likeness of Isobel Bennett.

It was her. It was Isobel. But if she was there, where were they? And... fuck. Did she just smile at the camera?

"Holy shit," she muttered, hitting the speed-dial. "Shit, shit, shit."

"Hey baby—"

"She's here."

"What?"

"Isobel. She's here. She's fucking here and you're not. Where are you?"

Muffled voices bled through the phone as Toby relayed the information to his brother. "Stall her, Lucy. We're on our way."

Lucy put her phone down without ending the call so Toby could listen in, then she rounded up the girls. "Quickly and quietly grab your gear and lock yourselves in Toby's office," she said, keeping one eye on the door. When they looked like they were about to argue she held up one hand, and added, "She's here."

The girls exchanged a look so similar to the silent conversations of Charlie and Toby that Lucy almost laughed, then they grabbed their books and bags and ran into their uncle's office, but before they could shut the door, Lucy handed them her keys too.

"So I can't get in either," she said. "Now lock the door and call the police, and whatever you do, whatever you hear, do *not* open this door for anyone except your father. Do you understand me?"

They both nodded and Lucy hated the fear she saw in their crystalline eyes. Eyes exactly like their father's. Exactly like Toby's. "We understand," they said, the slight shake in their sweet voices breaking her heart.

Lucy quickly squeezed their hands. "Good girls." Then she shut the door and waited to hear the lock engage, only taking her next breath when she heard the familiar click. A moment later she smiled as she heard the sound of Toby's desk being dragged across the floor and banged against the door.

"Good girls," she murmured again, and not a moment too soon.

Turning just in time, Lucy watched Isobel enter the reception area like she belonged there, and if she hadn't known exactly who and what the woman was, she'd have been fooled too.

Dressed in jeans and a T-shirt with the girl's school logo and the words "Proud Grandma" printed on it, the woman certainly looked the part, but when Lucy looked into the other woman's eyes, she didn't see a doting grandma. She saw shrewd calculation, determination, desperation and yes, she saw evil.

"Oh, hello," Isobel said, smiling easily and half lifting the take away coffee cup in her hand in some sort of half-arsed non-threatening greeting. "I think I have the right building now. My name is Isobel Bennett. I'm here to collect my granddaughters."

The lie fell so easily from her lips that Lucy almost believed it herself. But one didn't grow up with an alcoholic parent without learning a thing or two about telling lies.

Repressing the urge to vomit, Lucy smiled at the horrible woman like she was just another customer. "I'm sorry, but I don't think you do have the right building. As you can see," she said, waving her hand to indicate the empty reception and conference areas, "I'm the only person here."

And that's when fate decided to kick Lucy in the face and one of the twins sneezed. Loudly.

Isobel's smile sharpened. "You were saying?"

Lucy mirrored the older woman's expression but kept her voice saccharine. "I'm terribly sorry, but without Mr Bennett's approval, I'm afraid I can't let the girls leave. You understand, I'm sure. It's a matter of safety."

"But I'm their grandmother. Exactly how unsafe do you think they're going to be?"

Does she want an honest answer to that?

Lucy pretended to think about it, frowned slightly and chewed on her lip for effect. "Well...." Isobel's eyes brightened with victory. *Sucker.* "Maybe if you could show me some photo ID?"

Sighing impatiently, Isobel rested her coffee on top of the thick privacy wall that hemmed Lucy's desk and made a show of searching through her handbag for her purse, but before she could produce anything to satisfy Lucy's request, a tall, bulky man entered reception.

A dangerous looking man with a shaved head, a goatee and more tattoos than she could count.

"What the fuck is taking so long?" he barked, and Lucy saw a flicker of real fear in Isobel's eyes.

"It's all right," Isobel called over her shoulder, smiling again as she held Lucy's gaze. "This helpful young lady is just making sure I am who I say I am. We don't want anyone trying to kidnap my grandbabies, now do we?"

The scary dude scoffed. "Whatever." But he didn't leave, just stood there blocking the door with his arms folded over his chest and a scowl on his pudgy face.

"So," Isobel said, trying to sound chipper, "are we good to go?"

"I'm still waiting to see some ID," Lucy said, causing her enemy's eyes to narrow ever so slightly. Then she spoke to Scary Dude. "Perhaps you'd like to take seat while you wait, sir? I think you'll find it more comfortable on the couch than blocking the only fire exit."

She held his gaze until he grunted and sat down. She made a mental note to get the couch professionally cleaned. Or use it to teach the girls the rainbow fire experiment.

"Here." Isobel thrust her driver's licence at Lucy, which she took and read as slowly as possible.

Come on, Toby. Where are you?

"This says your name is Isobel Peters, not Bennett."

Isobel shrugged. "Yes, well, I reverted to using my maiden name after Ulysses and I broke up. I don't see—"

"Enough!" Scary Dude lumbered to his feet. "Open that fucking door and give me those girls. Now."

Drawing on every ounce of strength she owned, Lucy moved to block the office door, to add another layer between the world and Charlie's daughters. "Over her dead body," she snarled, nodding at Isobel.

Scary Dude barked a laugh. "I like you, girlie. You've got guts." His grin dropped. "But that mouth of yours is gunna get you in trouble." And he took two menacing steps forwards.

Lucy levelled her best glare at the man. "Wouldn't be the first time."

"Just do as he says. Please," Isobel said, her hands twisting together in a show of anxiety, but there was no actual concern in her tone or expression, not for her grand-daughters anyway.

She wanted the same thing her creepy friend did, to get the girls and get out of there before the cops arrived. Before Toby and Charlie arrived.

But Lucy had no intention of helping these fuckwits do anything of the sort.

She would protect Josie and Diana, she would keep her promise and keep them safe. With her dying breath if necessary. For the first time in a long time, Lucy had a family. Toby's family.

The Bennett's and the Melville's had welcomed her with open arms and given her brothers and sisters and nieces, a father and mother who hugged her and smiled at her and treated her with respect and kindness, and she had a boyfriend who loved her, who told her she was perfect just as she was, scars and all.

And she loved him, Toby Bennett. Her gentle giant, her Master. Her heart.

Lucy was not tossing that aside to save her own skin, and certainly not to save the likes of a manipulative bitch like Isobel. She just had to stall them a little longer, keep them there until the police arrived and arrested them.

She could do that for her family.

"It's not in my nature to abandon children," she snarled at them, her hands curling into fists, ready to fight.

"But they're not even your children," Isobel snapped, throwing her hands in the air.

"Yes. They. Are. And you can take them when I'm dead."

"Works for me." Scary Dude stepped around the desk and grabbed Lucy's throat, squeezed hard.

"Is that all you've got," she taunted through gritted teeth, staring him down. He looked less scary when he was right in her face, when her temper reared its head and her knee flew upwards of its own volition. Twice, in sharp succession.

Dude crumpled to the floor in a heap, groaning and cupping his balls. "Fucking bitch."

Isobel pinched the bridge of her nose and any concern, pretend or otherwise, disappeared. "I told them sending a man would be useless. They never listen."

"They never listen? How many times have you done this?" Lucy demanded. "How many times have you lured innocent children away from their families to get yourself out of debt? Because that's what this is all about, isn't it? Saving your arse at the expense of theirs."

Again real fear flickered across Isobel's face but was gone in an instant, replaced with an uptilted chin and a tight smile. "I owe them," she said, her haughty expression failing to disguise the tremor in her voice. "If I don't do this they'll kill me."

"Better you than them," Lucy snarled, holding her ground. "I'm not giving you what you want, you entitled bitch. I'm not letting you do to those girls what you did to your own sons." Then she shook her head and scowled, unable to contain her disgust. "You're their mother. You were supposed to protect them, not offer them up as sacrificial lambs." Angry tears wet her cheeks. "What the fuck is wrong with you?"

The sound of distant sirens rent the air and Isobel's desperation came roaring to the fore, chased away all remnants of her fear. Grabbing the coffee cup, she popped the lid and threw the contents in Lucy's face.

Coffee went everywhere and Lucy screamed as it burned, scalding her arm and neck as she tried to block the hot liquid and prevent it from getting in her eyes.

Using the distraction to her advantage, Isobel shoved her out of the way in one last ditch attempt to open the door. Stumbling sideways, Lucy came face to face with Scary Dude as he levered himself off the floor.

His greasy smile was the last thing she saw before he backhanded her hard enough to knock her down.

Hard enough to knock her out.

When Lucy came to she was still lying on the floor, but

now an ambo—Andy, according to his name badge—was looming over her, applying something cold to her cheek, and the police were marching her assailants out in handcuffs.

Isobel was kicking and screaming, hurling threats at anyone within spitting distance, and Scary Dude had blood all over his swollen face and down the front of his shirt, like someone had broken his nose and possibly his jaw.

Lucy blinked slowly. "What did I miss?" she asked, then sucked air through her teeth, the pain in her jaw from Scary Dude's backhand and the sting on her arm where the coffee had scalded her skin beginning to register in her consciousness.

"Lucy." Toby suddenly appeared behind Andy and smiled down at her, a look of relief blanketing his handsome face. "My brave girl."

"What happened? How long was I out?"

"Watch my finger," Andy said and slowly moved the digit in front of her face. Lucy tracked the movement easily. "Good. You're not showing signs of concussion." He looked up at Toby. "Keep an eye on her just in case. If she has any nausea, light sensitivity, persistent headaches—"

"My head aches now," Lucy said.

"You hit the chair on your way down," Toby said, crouching beside her. He smoothed her hair away from her face, the touch gentle and reassuring. "You were out of it for a couple of minutes. You gave me the fright of my life. And you'll probably have a few new bruises tomorrow."

Andy's gaze sharpened with concern. "New bruises?"

Lucy blushed even as she offered the poor medic a sly grin. "I'm fine," she said softly. "I promise." Then her gaze shifted to Toby's and she smiled up at him, let her love show for all to see. "My Master takes very good care of me."

Awareness dawned on the ambo's face. "Ah. I see. Well, if you start exhibiting any other symptoms—"

"I'll take care of her," Toby said, helping her to her feet.

Lifting the arm she'd shielded herself with, Lucy inspected the bandage lightly wrapped around it. Andy nodded at the limb. "It's a superficial burn but I put some cooling gel on it to ease the sting. It should heal fully in a week or so. The bandage is just to keep the dirt out of the gel. You can take it off when you get home."

"Can I take her home now?"

"Sure," Andy said, packing away his kit. "Give her paracetamol for the pain and, uh,"—he cleared his throat —"maybe go easy on her for a couple of days."

Toby thanked the ambo then lifted Lucy in his arms as if she weighed nothing, and cradled her to his chest, careful of her sore head and arm. From the corner of her eye she saw Toby's office door was open and Charlie was hugging his girls, tears streaming down their cheeks.

"Are the girls okay?"

"Thanks to you they are. I heard everything you said over the phone, baby. You were amazing."

She snuggled closer, clung to the security he was offering her and let out a steadying breath. "I was terrified."

"Terrified?" he teased softly as he walked them through the garden centre, ignoring the people gawking at them as they passed. "I thought you weren't afraid of anything."

"Except losing you," she admitted quietly. "And the girls and Charlie." She sniffed back her tears even as she began to shake. Shock was setting in. "You gave me a family. You all did. And every day I wake up scared that it was all a dream, that it will all be gone. That you'll be gone." His thick arms tightened around her, crushing her. "I love you, Toby. I love you and I want to spend my life with you."

"I love you too, baby. And I'm so sorry you had to go through this alone," he said, gently fingering the bruise she could feel swelling her cheek. "I'm sorry we didn't get here sooner."

Lucy swiped the back of her hand over her eyes in a vain attempt to dry her tears. She really hated crying. "What took you so long?"

"Isobel sent us on a wild goose chase, then Charlie got pulled over for speeding, then the cops took their time verifying our story. But when they got the go ahead, they gave us a police escort all the way here."

"Schmancy," Lucy said, hiccoughing a laugh. Toby helped her into his truck as they watched his mother and Scary Dude being loaded into the back of a paddy wagon. "What happened to his face?"

Toby grunted. "My fist happened. Repeatedly." At Lucy's wide-eyed stare, he added, "No one hurts my woman." Then his expression turned sheepish. "There may be an assault charge heading my way."

Lucy grinned. Toby's brother, Rafe, could probably get the assault charge dropped in five minutes flat for extenuating circumstances. "Okay, so what happens now?" she asked as Toby climbed into the driver's seat. He'd put her in the middle seat again, and she leaned her head on his shoulder, took comfort from his big body being so close to hers, so warm and strong and protective.

Her lover took her hand in his and threaded their fingers together. "I take you home, wash what I'm hoping is just coffee out of your hair and put you to bed."

"Is that all," she asked, pouting slightly with disappointment. She'd expected a better reward than an early bedtime.

Hooking a knuckle under her chin, Toby lifted her face

to his. "How about I make you scream my name first," he whispered, his deep, sensual voice liquefying her insides into pure molten lust.

Lust she saw reflected in his stormy gaze. "How many times?"

She felt his smile against her mouth before he kissed her, slow and long and deep. "As many times as you want, baby."

The Forge, Christmas morning

"You go first," Lucy said, thrusting the small, delicately wrapped present into Toby's hands. He felt like the giant he was, sitting on the bed and staring down at the thing his lover had placed in the middle of his palm. It was about the size of a pen box.

He curled his fingers around it and shook his head. "You go first," Toby said, proud of the fact he'd kept the nervous shake out of his voice as he settled her gift in her lap. "I insist."

He actually had three presents for Lucy and all of them had only been wrapped the night before. Not because they were last minute gifts—he'd put his gift-giving game plan into action months ago—but because it had taken that long to get them.

He maybe also kinda asked Abby and Jane to wrap them for him.

He'd tried, he really had, but as he'd sat at the kitchen table and nervously fumbled with the wrapping paper for the sixth time, he'd conceded defeat and begged his sisters for help. Thankfully they adored Lucy and agreed she shouldn't be given gifts that looked like they'd been wrapped by a toddler on a sugar high.

"Okay." One corner of her mouth twitched up as she lifted the present and ripped off the brightly coloured paper. The picture frame was upside down. "What's this?" she asked, turning it over so she could see the photo. And then she almost dropped it. "Michael."

Toby's gaze was glued to Lucy's face, watching her every flicker of emotion as her eyes devoured the long lost photograph of her and her brother standing in front of their old fire station. Dressed in yellow reflective pants, navy shirts and red braces, the siblings stood with their arms around each other, looking happy and relaxed and free.

Silent tears streamed down Lucy's cheeks as she brushed her fingertips over her brother's image. "Where did you find this?"

"Our local RFS chief owed me a favour. He's been hunting for it since our first weekend here at The Forge, at the end of winter. Someone finally got back to him last week. An old friend of your brother's, Max something, still had this tucked away somewhere."

Lifting her face to his, Lucy opened her mouth to speak but no words came out, then she launched herself into his arms and hugged him so tightly he thought she'd never let go. "Thank you," she whispered, and he held her until her tears subsided.

"I have something else for you," he said.

Lucy sat back on her heels and clutched the picture frame to her chest. "You just gave me the world," she said, shaking her head. "You gave me my brother back. I don't need anything else."

"But I need you to have it," he said, pressing her second gift into her hand. Especially since Crispin was visiting and still thought it was hilarious to flirt with Toby's woman.

Lucy carefully placed her brother's photo aside and ripped the paper off the smaller gift, revealing the black velvet jewellery box bearing Avery Bennett's logo. Toby's brother had custom-made the piece especially for this occasion. That and the other gift Toby planned on giving her—if she said yes.

Lucy's hand fluttered to her chest when she opened the box and her mouth fell open on a gasp.

Exactly the reaction he'd been hoping for.

"It's beautiful." Lifting the silver necklace from the box, Lucy examined the small heart-shaped pendant then laughed happily. "Baby," she said, reading the inscription.

"Turn it over."

She did, then laughed again. "Property of Tobias." Lucy shook her head and swiped at the fresh tears tracking down her cheeks. "Thank you, Master," she said, and held out the necklace for him to fasten around her neck.

"Now," she said, pointing at the gift he'd put aside. "Open yours."

Picking up the present, Toby did as Lucy had done and ripped the paper off, revealing a small non-descript rectangular box. Frowning he plucked the lid off and dropped it beside him, then lifted out the thing wrapped in layers of black tissue paper. It didn't feel like a pen.

"Remember when I moved in with you," Lucy said,

grinning slyly, "and you took me to the doctor to have my implant removed...?"

Toby's heart stopped for a split second, then slammed into warp speed as he shredded the tissue paper and revealed the thing inside.

"Seriously?" he demanded, staring at the two little lines on the plastic stick, his heart beating at a million beats per second and his mind spinning out of control. "We're having a baby?"

Lucy nodded, her bottom lip clamped between her teeth and her eyes wide in amusement, until Toby scooped her up and spun her around, making her shriek with laughter.

"We're having a baby!" he boomed, making sure he was loud enough that the whole damn house would hear him. He didn't care if it was only six o'clock on Christmas morning.

This shit was worth waking people up for.

"I love you, Lucy Barton," Toby said, letting her slide down his chest until her feet almost touched the floor. He wasn't ready to put her down just yet. "You are the best thing that has ever happened to me, baby, and I want to spend the rest of my life with you." He leaned his forehead against hers. "Will you marry me?"

Tilting her head so her lips brushed over his, Lucy whispered, "Yes, I will." Then she threaded her fingers through his hair and yanked his head backwards, stared into his eyes with her fire-whisky gaze until his blood was on fire and his cock was like iron. "Because I'm yours. And you are all mine."

The End

I hope you enjoyed Lucy and Toby in

His Own Heaven

Please consider sharing the love by leaving a review for other readers to find. It doesn't need to be very long, and every review is greatly appreciated.

Want something sexy yet sweet?
Check out Jennie Kew's steamy romance series,
The Brisbane Bachelors Series.

Want something short and not-so-sweet?
Check out Jennie Kew's short erotic stories,
The Q Collection.

For more information about
The Bennett's Bastards Series visit
www.jenniekew.com

More from Jennie Kew

The Bennett's Bastards Series

Third Time Lucky

This Time Around

His Own Heaven

The Viking Blues (coming 2021)

Size Doesn't Matter (TBA)

The Brisbane Bachelors Series

Revenge and Redemption

Sacrifice and Seduction

Torment and Temptation (TBA)

Audiobooks

Revenge and Redemption

The Q Collection

No Rest For The Wicked

I Saw, I Conquered, I Came

Pushing Rope

Dirty Laundry

Santa Claus Is Coming

Between A Rock And A Hard Place

Tying The Knot (TBA)

The Q Collected

Dirty: 3 Short Contemporary Stories

Grind: 3 Short Paranormal Stories

The Whole Shebang (TBA)

Acknowledgements

To my family for all their encouragement, their love and understanding, thank you for being you and for putting up with me being me, especially when deadlines are involved.

A special thank you to my crit partners, my cheer squad, my sisters-in-arms, Bec McMaster and Kylie Griffin. You always challenge me to be a better writer and I really couldn't do this without you. Thank you for keeping me sane...*ish*.

To my editor, Kristin Scearce, who accepts my weird writing style and quirky humour as canon and is still willing to work with me, you rock!

And finally to my readers, thank you for taking this journey with me, and for allowing me to share with you all the people and places who occupy my head and my heart. I hope you enjoy reading about them as much as I enjoy writing about them.

Meet the Author

Jennie has always enjoyed reading but is a relative late-comer to writing. She never had aspirations of becoming a published author until a dance with death made her ask herself what she really wanted out of life, and she's been writing ever since.

When not sitting in front of her computer, Jennie can usually be found reading a book, watching a movie or building stuff out of Lego.

She lives in regional New South Wales, a stone's throw from Australia's capital, Canberra, with her husband, her husband's magnificent beard, a teenage giant and their feline overlords, Max and Tallulah.

www.jenniekew.com

Glossary

As all of my books are set in Australia and use a lot of Australian terms and slang, I've created this guide for my readers to keep you on track when you come across any Aussie-isms in my books.

A bit of all right: If someone is 'a bit of all right' they're considered to be very attractive.

Ambo: Short for ambulance, the term has come to mean anyone associated with any of the public or private ambulance services, their drivers and paramedics.

Arse: Aussie spelling of ass, aka buttocks, bottom, booty and bum.

Arvo and *Sarvo*: Afternoon and 'this afternoon'.

Copper: On occasion, Australians will actually lengthen words or use them in their original format. Cops (i.e. The police) was originally 'copper'.

Fashion Rag/Local Rag: Fashion magazine, any locally produced magazines or newspapers.

Fierie/s: Firefighter/s.

Fuck-knuckle: An idiot.

G'day: Pronounced 'gidday', this official Australian (and Kiwi) greeting is a contraction of the words 'good' and 'day'.

Kiwi: Pronounced 'kee-wee', A person from Middle Earth (New Zealand).

Larrikin: An unruly, boisterous but generally good natured person, usually male.

Mate: Unlike paranormal or sci-fi erotic romances where your 'mate' is the person you're fated to be with for the rest of your life, in Australian culture 'mate' could mean anyone from your best friend to some random bloke you just met.

Pav: Pavlova, a dessert made from baked meringue, topped with cream and fresh fruit, particularly popular around Christmas. We nicked it from the Kiwis.

Phwoar: An estimation of the sound one makes when a bit of all right enters your vicinity. See also, 'panting' and 'drooling'.

RFS: Rural Fire Service.

Sanga: Sandwich.

She'll be right, mate: Usually given as a response when someone is offering aid of some kind, it means 'Everything will be fine but thanks for asking'.

Togs: A swimsuit.

Tradie: Any tradesman.

Uni: Pronounced 'you-nee', University aka College.

Yeah, nah and *Nah, yeah*: Another instance where Australians have made something sound more complicated than it needs to be, is 'Yeah, nah' and 'Nah, yeah'. Whichever word the phrase ends on, is the affirmative answer, therefore 'Yeah, nah' means 'No' and 'Nah, yeah' means 'Yes'.